Ms Middleton

MELISSA TEREZE

GPC
PUBLISHING

First Edition March 2021
Published by GPC Publishing

ISBN: 978-1-915242-02-0

Cover Design: May Dawney
Editor: Charlie Knight

Find out more at: www.melissaterezeauthor.com
Follow me on Twitter: @MelissaTereze
Follow me on Instagram: @melissatereze_author

ALSO BY MELISSA TEREZE

Another Love Series

The Arrangement (Book One)

The Call (Book Two)

The Ashforth Series

Playing For Her Heart (Book One)

Holding Her Heart (Book Two)

Other Novels

Breaking Routine

In Her Arms

Before You Go

Forever Yours

The Heat of Summer

Forget Me Not

More Than A Feeling

Where We Belong: Love Returns

Naked

Co-writes

Teach Me

Titles under L.M Croft (Erotica)

Pieces of Me

"To burn with desire and keep quiet about it is the greatest punishment we can bring on ourselves."

- Federico Garcia Lora

CHAPTER ONE

Well, this was it. The moment Emma had been dreading for months.

It was one thing to be back in the UK after living a life of simplicity in another country, teaching kids' sports, but to have to share a home with her best friend…it was going to be painful. Lauren Middleton was everything Emma had ever wanted in a friend, but a lot had changed since Emma left the UK eighteen months ago. Oh, not with their friendship, that could never be broken, but with…something else.

As friends, it shouldn't have worked. When they met back at university, Emma was twenty-one, while Lauren was only eighteen. But from the moment they'd met at freshers, they'd hit it off. Lauren wasn't an average eighteen-year-old, and it showed. She had her head firmly screwed on. Within months of starting their degree together, Emma and Lauren had become the best of friends, some might even have said sisters.

Emma had spent the nine-hour flight home from Ghana thinking, yet nothing seemed any clearer than the day she first left home. She couldn't wait to see her best friend. She was excited to spend some cherished time with Lauren before she jetted off to Australia on her own three-month adventure. It was the idea of staying in Lauren's parents' home that had her so on edge.

Because Mrs Middleton would be there.

Emma braced herself as she walked through the double doors at the airport, the temperature quite pleasant considering she'd expected it to be colder. After eighteen months, she'd gotten used to the African heat. Now, to be here in this less intense heat, Emma didn't know how to feel about it…or anything else for that matter.

Life was about to become interesting.

Vanessa Middleton was Lauren's mum. With huge crystal blue eyes and a smile that lit up the entire world, Emma had foolishly fallen in love with her over the years since meeting Lauren at university. And then the family dinners started whenever they both went home to visit their parents. Except Emma rarely visited hers. Instead, she was joined at the hip with Lauren at the Middleton's. Emma was *always* invited over by Vanessa.

Then came the summer holidays, more occasions for which Emma was present. She'd had a love-hate relationship with her own mother since she was a teen, and, though she wasn't looking for another mother, Emma would admit that the Middleton's felt like family to her.

But it wasn't what Emma wanted from their relationship with one another. From the day she'd met Vanessa, Emma's feelings for her had spiralled. Almost out of control. She'd managed to keep those feelings at bay for over ten years, but the night before leaving for Africa, Emma had called Vanessa in a drunken haze and confessed everything to the older woman. Mrs Middleton had been a sweetheart, but it had only made everything worse. A part of Emma wished Vanessa had told her not to come home again, and if she did, not to show up at her door. That would have been much easier to deal with. But Vanessa hadn't said any of those things. She told Emma she was flattered and that she was very fond of her before wishing her well on her travels.

Eighteen months of long-distance pining had only sent Emma's head into a spin as she stepped onto the plane this morning. And now here she was. Unable to comprehend the moment she would lay eyes on Vanessa again. In Emma's ideal world, Vanessa would have aged dramatically and turned into a cold-hearted bitch. But this wasn't an ideal world, and when Emma's flight landed forty minutes ago, she checked her social media. Searching Vanessa Middleton hadn't been a wise decision. That woman had only gotten better with age. Her vivid blue eyes shone back at Emma through her profile picture, her once long blonde hair now cut into a stylish shoulder length bob.

Emma was in a lot of trouble.

But she would manage. So long as she didn't make Vanessa uncomfortable, everything would be perfectly fine. It had to be. And if she blotted out the fact Vanessa was going through divorce proceedings from her mind, Emma wouldn't crave to comfort her. *She's your best friend's mother. That should be enough to deter you!*

A flash of dark blonde hair caught Emma's attention. She picked up her pace, almost bumping into someone in front of the taxi rank. "Oi."

Lauren spun, grinning. "You're actually here."

"Unfortunately, yes."

"Well, that fills me with joy," Lauren said, rolling her eyes. "And why do you have shorts on? It's not exactly hot."

"I needed everyone to see my tan as I walked through the airport." Emma's teeth chattered. "You're just jealous. But you needn't be; you'll have your own tan soon enough."

"It's like...winter in Australia." Lauren laughed, throwing her arms around her best friend. "It's so good to see you."

"It's good to see you too. But I'm freezing my arse off, so can we head to the car?"

"We can. I had yours serviced last week for you. Running like a little cracker again."

"Mrs Middleton hasn't minded it being on the drive all this time, has she?"

Emma hadn't been given a rollicking by her best friend, so as far as she was aware, Lauren knew nothing about her outpouring before she left. Vanessa didn't seem like the type to tell everyone about the thirty-something with a crush, thankfully.

Lauren shook her head, linking her arm through Emma's. "You know she doesn't. And if she hears you calling her that, she'll kill you. Call her Vanessa and save me from having to listen to her harp on about how old it makes her seem."

"It's…respectful." *And to save me from feeling the intimacy of being on a first name basis.* Emma cleared her throat. "And she's a teacher, so she's used to it."

"She hates it."

"How is she?"

"Better now. Things have been hard for her this year, but she's getting back to herself. And I'm hoping if you're free now and then, you could swing by and say hi to her when you find a place. No rush, by the way, but with me going away, I hate the thought of her being alone."

Emma bristled. She shouldn't agree to Lauren's ask. "I don't think she'll want me around, but a cuppa and a chat are something I can manage."

"You know what she's like. She'll say she's fine, but I know she gets lonely. When I'm at Rob's, I hate knowing she's home alone."

"She's a grown woman; I'm sure she does just fine."

"Still." Lauren sighed, shrugging. "I feel bad for buggering off to the other side of the world for three months. And I know she wants me to go, I do too, but since Dad left…she's not been the same person."

"I still can't believe he was sleeping with another woman."

Truly, she couldn't. In some ways, at least. Mrs Middleton was the most attractive woman Emma had ever laid eyes on. Perhaps it was the smouldering eyes and the power suit, maybe it was the elegance she carried, but whatever it was...Emma had been smitten at one time. *You still are, you complete fool!* "Was he having some kind of midlife crisis?"

"They just grew apart."

"And that's fine. But you don't shag the secretary. You explain and then leave on good terms. I mean, when you called me to tell me...I was floored. Your mum is so lovely, and I can't believe he did that to her," Emma lied. She'd known for a long time how much of an arsehole Richard was, his eyes always straying towards other women. She suspected Vanessa knew too, but it wasn't Emma's business to get involved.

"I haven't spoken to him."

Emma couldn't blame Lauren for making that decision. "I'm sure you're still angry with him."

"It's not even anger anymore. It's disgust. How dare he sleep with another woman when he's been married to Mum for thirty years."

God, that had to hurt. Emma felt awful for not being there when her best friend needed her. To be in another country while she was going through divorce proceedings with her parents... "I'm sorry I wasn't here for you."

"Don't apologise. You've always dreamed of Africa. I'm so happy you took the opportunity. You didn't know my dad was going to do what he did."

If only that were the truth.

"Still, I didn't like knowing I could only be on the phone when the reception allowed."

"You're here now. And I can't wait to spend the entire week with you before I have to take a ridiculous flight to Australia."

"Honestly, I hate flying."

Relieved when she spied Lauren's car, Emma grinned as the lights flashed, climbing inside the second her luggage was safely in the boot. Lauren joined her, firing up the engine and backing out of the space. "Fancy a takeout and catch up tonight?"

Emma relaxed her shoulders. She'd been tense all day. "I can't wait."

CHAPTER TWO

If she received one more call this week from her lawyer, Vanessa was going to book a flight to the farthest country possible and never return. Richard was playing hardball, she had the end of year exams coming up, and her bout of migraines hadn't lessened at all this week. It was Friday; she was supposed to be relieved. Instead, she found herself slowly climbing from her car, dragging her handbag from the passenger seat.

But then Vanessa stopped mid-stride, glancing at the car which had been on her drive for the last eighteen months. Emma...was home. *I don't know if I can face her.* Vanessa's stomach lurched, the idea of coming face-to-face with a woman who had confessed her undying love for her over the phone now a reality. Emma Bradley was stunning, astonishing even, but Vanessa hadn't expected a call late one December night while Richard was away. Honestly, she hadn't known what to do with any of the information.

Emma...loved her?

How? And why? Her own bloody husband didn't even love her, so how could a thirty-something possibly feel the way she did towards her?

But now, standing outside her home, Vanessa ached to see Emma. While she had initially been shocked, Vanessa secretly shared many of the feelings Emma did. The problem was, she'd been a married woman at the time. Okay, things hadn't been great within her marriage for a while, but Vanessa couldn't throw her family away for a potential fling. Because that's all it would have been. A fling. Emma Bradley couldn't have been looking for a serious relationship with a woman seventeen years her senior. Life didn't produce those happy endings.

At the thought of seeing her luscious black hair, those grey colour changing eyes, Vanessa felt her heart begin to pound. Emma had no idea how Vanessa had felt about her over the years, but it didn't matter. It was far too late for them to sit down and talk. Emma had spent eighteen months in another country; there wasn't a chance she still felt that way about Vanessa. The nights Vanessa had lay in bed thinking about her daughter's best friend, how her laughter always brightened the house...God, this was a lot to take in right now. But then she reminded herself that Emma was Lauren's best friend, and her heart settled. It couldn't possibly work. To think otherwise would only add issues to Vanessa's life that she didn't need.

She steeled herself. She should be spending this time with Lauren, not worrying about something she had no control over. Her daughter hadn't stopped preparing for her best friend's arrival for over a fortnight, wanting to be sure Emma could be as comfortable as possible. Vanessa had made up the spare room, the en-suite attached had been fully stocked, and now the day had arrived. The day when she would see her daughter smile for the first time since Rob left for Australia.

She never had understood why Lauren chose to fall in love with someone who often worked so far away, but her happiness mattered, and Lauren was elated to finally find a man she felt complete with. She'd told Vanessa as much several weeks ago when they shared too many bottles of wine. A lot of crying had been on the agenda for that night. From Richard and his adultery to Rob and his beautiful smile.

Vanessa scoffed, rummaging for her keys in her handbag. *I hope he doesn't do to Lauren what Richard did to me.* The anger and bitterness were beginning to eat Vanessa up inside. She didn't want to always feel this way. Rob had done nothing to warrant Vanessa's incessant worries; this was all down to her own experience. And in all honesty, Rob was a lovely guy. He held down a steady, well paid job, and he still lived at home with his parents. If Vanessa could hope for Lauren to fall for anyone, Rob was the one.

The sound of laughter made Vanessa smile as she opened the front door. She couldn't recall the last time Lauren had been so carefree. Vanessa knew what it had done to her daughter when Richard packed his bags and left. She felt resentment towards him more so for that than anything else. She could deal with him cheating on her, but to hurt Lauren too…it tore at Vanessa's heart every night as she climbed into bed.

They'd gotten pregnant and married when Vanessa was twenty. From the moment, they looked into Lauren's little blue eyes, Richard had fallen hopelessly for his daughter. She'd always been a daddy's girl. Nothing was too much. Everything Lauren wanted, she got. But it hadn't resulted in Lauren being a spoilt child, no. Lauren was caring and supportive; she was respectable and worked for her own living. Richard may have provided her with everything she would ever need, Vanessa too in some respects, but Lauren had taken the divorce all in her stride.

She cleared her throat and stepped into the living room. "I have to say, I much prefer the sound of laughter on a Friday night."

"Mum. You're home. Where the hell have you been?"

"Meeting overran," Vanessa lied, eyeing Emma on the opposite end of the couch. Her heart thrummed. Emma looked even better than the last time they'd seen one another. "Well, Africa has certainly been kind to you, Emma. You look truly wonderful."

"Thank you, Mrs Middleton." A blush settled on Emma's cheeks immediately, but Vanessa batted the past away. She had to for the sake of her relationship with her daughter.

Vanessa quirked an eyebrow at the name, though. Emma knew better. "Excuse me?"

"Sorry. Hard habit to break. How are you?"

"Pour me a glass of red, and I'll feel much better." *That's right. Just pretend it never happened.*

Emma scrambled from the couch, hurrying into the kitchen. Vanessa shook her head and smiled. "I was actually talking to you." Vanessa stared at her daughter. "Emma is our guest. I hope you didn't make her cook her own dinner."

"We've ordered in. You joining us?"

"Oh, I don't know." Vanessa turned her watch towards herself, her handbag dropping to the floor. "I'm sure you two want to catch up without me around." *And it's probably best if I'm not around.*

"No, we'd love it if you joined us."

Emma returned, holding out a glass of wine. Her tanned hands were soft as Vanessa took the glass, her fingers brushing Emma's. "Thank you. Really."

"You've been working all day. It's the least I can do since you've given me a roof for a few days."

Vanessa's brows rose with surprise. "You've found a place to rent already?"

"Well, no." Emma smiled weakly. "But Lauren leaves next week, so I have to start house hunting."

Vanessa offered a single nod, hiding her disappointment. Even if they couldn't be together, Vanessa could still admire Emma around the house. And Emma would be good company since Lauren was leaving. *You know it's not possible.* "Let me change and then I'll be down to catch up, okay?"

Emma grinned. "Okay."

As Vanessa placed one foot on the stairs, her phone vibrated in her pocket. She removed it, staring down at the screen.

D: Wonderful evening with you. Sad to see it end. Maybe next time we could go back to my place and carry on the conversation...

Vanessa sighed, looking up briefly at her daughter. Lauren was watching her with a frown. She simply smiled and made her way up the stairs, locking her bedroom door as she kicked off her heels.

Vanessa had recently wandered into old territory. This evening, she'd been on a date with a woman from work. Vanessa dated several women many years ago before she met Richard, so once she knew their divorce was going through, she'd chosen to broaden her horizons again. She loved women, appreciated everything about them, so why not see what was on offer some thirty years after she married Richard?

The issue was, she didn't feel any kind of connection to Dani. She'd left their third date feeling less than inclined to meet with her again. She had initially wondered if she wasn't ready, but Vanessa knew that wasn't the truth. Dani...wasn't her type. She wanted a woman who would make her feel alive. *Emma always made you feel alive.* Someone who looked at her as though they never wanted to be without her. *You know exactly how Emma used to look at you.*

Vanessa clenched her jaw. *Stop!* Maybe in time Dani could do those things she desired, but Vanessa didn't have the time or the patience to wait around for the possibility. No, she wanted to grab life right here and right now. And she wanted the sex to be incredible.

Now, she just needed to find the right person...

"Okay, I want to know all about Africa." Vanessa lounged along one velvet couch while Emma and Lauren huddled up on the other. "It must have been an experience."

"God, it was." Emma crossed her legs beneath her, a bottle of beer resting on her knee. "I lived in the middle of nowhere. The nearest city was twenty miles away."

Vanessa tipped her wine glass towards Emma. "It sounds like exactly what I need right now."

"If you're someone who likes to be on the go, you know…in the city, then it's not the place for you. But if you want to be out in the wild with nature, I couldn't recommend it highly enough."

"And now you're back here. How depressing."

Emma shrugged. "I had been thinking the same thing while I was on the plane, but I knew it was coming. They couldn't fund me forever. But I'd love to go back some day when I can fund myself."

"What will you do now you're home?" Lauren asked.

"I'm looking at a few teaching positions. As much as I loved being away, I think it's time to settle down."

"Settle down?" Vanessa took an immediate interest. Whenever someone brought up potential love or something similar these days, she had to prepare herself to lay out the repercussions. But Emma had her head firmly screwed on. Vanessa didn't imagine she could fall into the trap of being fucked over.

"Yeah. I'd like to find a girlfriend. It wasn't possible while I was away, I simply didn't have time, but I'd like to find someone I can commit to."

"And if you find someone but they don't share your enthusiasm for going back to Africa some day?"

Emma's face fell, frowning as she stared at her beer. "I hadn't thought that far ahead."

"Jesus, Mum. Could you be any more miserable?" Lauren laughed. "Let the girl dream, will you?"

Vanessa winced internally. She hadn't meant to sound so

harsh. She also hadn't intended to pull the plug on Emma's hopes for the future. At least she *had* a future. The same couldn't be said for Vanessa. "I'm sorry."

Emma looked up at her, smiling. Those grey eyes always appeared soft in Vanessa's company. Kind and honest. "If I found the right person, I'd give up Africa for them."

Wow. That was a bold statement. Honestly, Vanessa was impressed.

"It was my dream, and I fulfilled it. If I now find the woman of my dreams," Emma continued to stare directly at Vanessa, her gaze pinning her to the couch as her heart raced, "I'd do everything I could to make her happy. To make her smile and feel good about herself."

Vanessa, suddenly feeling flustered, lowered her eyes to her wine glass. "Sounds lovely."

"It would be lovely. Because I'm the kind of person who is in it for the long haul. I'm not the type who plays with one thing until something different comes along."

Vanessa knew Emma's remark was aimed at Richard. But it didn't change anything. Vanessa was far too old for someone so young and free like Emma. And whether she'd considered the potential or not—and she had—it all still came back to the fact Emma was her daughter's best friend.

"What do you consider a long haul?" Vanessa asked, scoffing. Emma was young, she surely couldn't know what she wanted yet. *You married Richard at twenty.* Vanessa realised she was being irrational. Emma had her head screwed on more than Vanessa ever did. *She's thirty-three for God sake, not fifteen.*

"For life."

"Mm." No longer willing to sit here and put Emma off the idea of dating, Vanessa got to her feet and drained her glass. "Well, it's been lovely. I'm going to refill and climb into bed."

As Vanessa moved towards the mantelpiece, taking the watch

she'd placed there earlier, Lauren's phone started to ring in the kitchen. "Sorry, I'll just get that."

Vanessa turned to find Emma watching her. She blushed as she dipped her head, picking at the label on her beer bottle. *Oh, honey. Don't even consider it.*

"You can stay as long as you need to, Emma. Whether Lauren is here or not." Those words fell so effortlessly, Vanessa wondered if she'd been desperate to say them sooner.

"Thanks, but I should start looking tomorrow. Get out of your hair. I'm sure you have a lot to be getting on with."

"Oh, just a bitter divorce and work. Nothing too taxing."

Emma lifted her head and smiled. "I am sorry for what you're going through. I know I'm Lauren's friend, but if you ever need someone to talk to, especially while she's not here, I'm only on the end of the phone."

"That's sweet. Thank you."

"I can sit and drink wine. I can also be a sounding board. If you ever need someone, please call me. Lauren is already worried about leaving you. So, if I have to step in, I can."

"I'll take you up on your offer at some point." Vanessa fixed her watch to her wrist and motioned towards the kitchen. "I'll let you two be. She's missed you a lot."

"I've missed her too," Emma said, her voice low. Those eyes bored into Vanessa, leaving her slightly breathless. "And you."

"I've missed having you around the place." It was true. But what did Emma think of her admission?

"I'm sure you haven't." Emma gave Vanessa a knowing look. "And while I appreciate your offer of a spare room for a while, I don't think it's a good idea. Do you?"

Vanessa knew it wasn't a good idea. But she would never see Lauren's best friend living somewhere less than acceptable.

"It's just a room. It doesn't mean anything." *Liar!*

Emma focused on the coffee table, her shoulders sagging. "No, I know."

CHAPTER THREE

Emma woke to the sound of a light knocking on the door. She'd slept like a baby last night, and if her dead arm was anything to go by, she hadn't moved since she climbed into bed. A bed that was a million miles from what she was used to. It was soft and warm, comfortable, and it smelled like Mrs Middleton.

That thought sent Emma's eyes wide as another knock sounded. She covered herself up and cleared her throat. "Come in."

The door opened, and Mrs Middleton poked her head into the room. "Good morning, sleepyhead. I didn't want to wake you, but Lauren said I should. Would you like some breakfast?"

"Oh, don't worry. I can make myself something when I come down. You two do your thing."

"Nonsense. When you're ready, let me know, and I'll prepare it."

"Mrs Middleton..."

"Vanessa," she said, her voice dripping with honey.

"S-sorry." Emma cringed. "I really am trying."

"I know. I'll see you downstairs, okay?"

Emma nodded, sinking back down into the bed as the door closed. God, Mrs – *Vanessa* was stunning. Even on a Saturday morning with no makeup. Her skin was immaculate. Emma knew she had to use some kind of expensive moisturiser, but Vanessa had always looked the same. Pristine, but not overbearing. The gentleness in her voice and the crinkles around her eyes when she smiled helped to relax anyone in her company.

But Emma had to remember not to get too comfortable here. Doing so would only bring back the feelings she used to have. Feelings which had encouraged her to leave for Africa a year and a half ago. Emma had changed, she'd grown in the time she spent on her own in another country, but seeing Vanessa, smelling her sweet perfume…she could quickly spiral into another mess. One she didn't need. How she felt would *always* be there, but Emma had learned not to dwell on it.

She blew out a breath, grabbing her hoodie from the floor. Vanessa always had a warm house, the heat turned up to a perfect temperature, so she climbed from the bed and kept to the shorts she was wearing. She was yet to acclimatise to the weather back home, but before too long, Emma knew it would feel like she'd never left.

A knock on the door followed by her best friend's voice had Emma laughing. "You awake, lazy arse?"

"Of course I'm awake. I'm used to waking at 5 a.m."

"Ooh, look at you." Lauren barrelled through the door, rugby tackling Emma to the bed with a thud. "Surprise!"

"Jesus Christ. That's some wake up call. Are you okay or have you always been like this and I've just never noticed?"

"Eh. You forgot how much fun I was."

Lauren was right. Emma couldn't recall the last time she'd had fun. Not Lauren's kind of fun, anyway. "I forgot. My bad."

Once Lauren had punched her in the arm—her signature go-to move—she dragged Emma from the bed and pulled her out of the bedroom. "Mum has a full English on the go. I know how much you love her breakfasts."

"A full English?" Emma's stomach growled. She was also certain she would throw up after it. Emma hadn't eaten those kinds of food in the time she was away; it simply wasn't available. "I'm not sure how much I can stomach, but I'll give it a good go."

"I'm sure you'll manage." Lauren winked.

"Hey, so I have something to ask you..." Emma gripped Lauren's wrist as they reached the bottom of the stairs. "Why are you still living at home?"

"Rob suggested we have a look for a place of our own not long after you left for Ghana. But then everything happened with Mum and Dad, and I figured I needed to be here with her. And with Rob heading to Australia before me, I thought it wouldn't be a big deal if we waited until we were both back in the UK."

"Fair enough."

"Do you think I still want to be living at home at 30?"

Emma blew out a breath, lifting a shoulder. "No idea. I'm 33 with no place to go...technically." God, what a depressing thought. Shouldn't she be married with kids by now?

"This is your home until you find something. I know Mum will be here, but she won't bother you. She's pretty cool like that. Do your thing and have a brew with her when you can. That'll satisfy her."

"I'd need to discuss rent and stuff with her. She has bills to pay, and I'd like to contribute." As much as Emma knew she should get the ball rolling with a new place, she had to admit that having somewhere to stay in the meantime was more than some people had. Instead of rushing to find something, she would take up the offer of a spare room. Now, she just had to convince the Middleton's to take rent from her.

"You know she won't let you," Lauren whispered. "Clean up after yourself, and there will be no issues."

Emma chewed her lip, glancing into the kitchen. Vanessa had her back to the door. "I don't know. This all feels wrong. I can't expect your mum to let me stay here when her own daughter isn't."

"It'll be fine. She offered."

And then it hit Emma. What if she met someone and wanted to bring them home after a date? She couldn't exactly rock up to Mrs Middleton's home with another woman. "I'll…figure something out. Come on, let's eat."

Vanessa dropped a stack of papers onto the kitchen island, getting comfortable on a stool for an afternoon of marking. She could think of a million things she wanted to do on a Saturday afternoon, and marking student papers was at the bottom of the list. Still, she had nothing else to entertain her, and by finishing this today, it would give her Sunday to herself.

But from the moment Vanessa had woken this morning, her mind had constantly flitted towards Emma Bradley, just sleeping down the hall. The call. *The declaration.* And the months which had followed. Vanessa's life had never felt so up in the air, but from the moment Richard walked out, everything had been a whirlwind. Emma being back home didn't make any difference at all. It was simply one more thing to add to Vanessa's never-ending issues.

But, really, Emma wasn't an issue.

Vanessa sat back in her seat, her eyes closing as she remembered that night in December eighteen months ago. The night that cemented Vanessa's desires once and for all.

The sparkling lights on the Christmas tree had Vanessa mesmerised, her stare not wavering even though her eyes burned. She loved Christmas, always would, but this year felt…off. Richard hadn't been available to decorate with them. For twenty-eight years, Richard hadn't missed a tree decorating evening; he always insisted he leave his work at the office for the night, and traditions would begin the moment he stepped into the family home. Mince pies, eggnog, a glass of Baileys with ice once the tree was set up and looking beautiful. Then he would sit down with Vanessa and Lauren while they put on a festive film to get them fully into the holiday spirit. But this year, he hadn't managed it.

Vanessa knew they were growing apart. She couldn't say she was surprised; she knew exactly what Richard was up to this evening. A work event...with his personal assistant. Until around six months ago, Vanessa would have been the one to attend a work event with him. She had always been the woman on his arm while he mingled with potential clients and donors. But suddenly, she was no longer flavour of the month. Or his life. This wasn't the first affair, but it was certainly the longest.

She couldn't bring herself to confront him, though. And if her suspicions were correct, it would break Lauren's heart. How could she possibly ask Richard to leave the family home when they had a daughter together? Okay, Lauren wasn't a child, but it would still be a devastating blow for them all. Vanessa simply couldn't do it.

Lauren wasn't home tonight. With a new boyfriend in her life, her best friend about to leave the country for two years, and nothing going on at home, Lauren had decided to meet with Rob so he could console her. Lauren and Emma had become inseparable since they met at university, and now that the eve of Emma leaving had finally arrived, Vanessa knew her daughter was struggling with it all. And if Vanessa was being honest with herself...so was she.

Emma Bradley had become a breath of fresh air around the Middleton household. Just watching her decorate the tree three nights ago—the final gathering before she packed her belongings—Vanessa had tears in her eyes. Because Emma wasn't only Lauren's best friend. No, she was Vanessa's secret guilty pleasure. It was wrong, Vanessa was fully aware, but since Emma had become more of a permanent fixture around the house, Vanessa found herself looking and wishing for things she shouldn't. Emma's silky raven hair flowed down her back, and those silvery eyes always had the ability to leave Vanessa weak at the knees. But it was the smile above all else which had drawn Vanessa in. How her eyes lit up when she spoke about something that meant a lot to her. Emma was...stunning.

And she was a lesbian. It was no secret. But it hadn't helped Vanessa when it came to her own past relationships. She'd ultimately fallen in love and started a family with Richard, but women had been her thing during college. Women just...yeah. It was always women.

Without Emma ever knowing, Vanessa had spent many nights, many family holidays, watching her. She may have caught Emma doing the very same thing on more than one occasion over the years, but Vanessa had chosen Richard, and Richard it would remain.

She knew she was out of her mind to sit here night after night while he was away with his much younger assistant. But this was all for Lauren. She wouldn't be one of those women who the world laughed at because her husband had fallen for the attractive blonde thirty years his junior. "I used to be the attractive blonde."

Vanessa lifted her wine glass from the coffee table, sinking back into the comforting couch. This was her life now. The odd text message from Richard, the apologies for having to stay a few more days because something had come up with a client or whatever other excuse he could think of, the perfume on his suit which didn't belong to his wife but some other young thing he'd spent the night with. This...was her life.

She sipped her wine, swallowing down her emotions along with the Malbec she'd chosen this evening, when her phone started to ring on the arm of the couch. Her eyes strayed towards the handset—it would be Richard putting on his charm before he went to dinner with her*—but then Vanessa frowned. It wasn't her husband.*

"Emma, hi."

"Hi, Mrs Middleton." Emma cleared her throat, thumping music drowned out as she closed a door, Vanessa assumed. "How are you?"

"Very well. You know me, sitting in a darkened room with a glass of wine." Vanessa hated being addressed so formally, but when Emma did it, it was kind of sexy.

"Lauren not home? Or Richard?"

Vanessa made herself comfortable. She could listen to Emma's soft voice all night. "Lauren is with Rob. I think she's drowning her sorrows."

"Why?"

"Because you leave in..." Vanessa paused, eyeing the clock. "Seven hours."

"Yeah."

"But I'm sure she'll be okay without you. She'll just be counting down the days until you return." Vanessa wasn't talking about her daughter. No, it was purely how she, herself, felt. "And this is a once in a lifetime opportunity for you."

"Yeah. I'm still going to miss all of you, though."

"We'll miss you, too." Vanessa closed her eyes, the sound of Emma sniffling painful to hear. "Are you okay, Emma?"

"Y-yeah. Just..." Emma paused, and then she sighed. "I have a lot of stuff on my mind."

"Well, if you ever need to talk, you know you can tell me." Vanessa didn't like knowing Emma was upset and alone. She never wanted to hear her cry.

"I have all these feelings, Vanessa. And I don't know what to do with any of it."

Vanessa frowned, reaching forward to set her wine glass down. If Emma was upset, she had to be there for her. If Vanessa took her own feelings out of the equation, all of this would be fine. Because tonight, Vanessa could do with Emma's company. And it wouldn't be via a phone line if she had her way. "Okay, well I'm alone right now and not busy. So, what's going on?"

Emma exhaled a shaky breath. "I...it's...you."

"What's me?" Vanessa's forehead creased further. Emma wasn't making much sense this evening. "Have you been drinking?"

"Sometimes it's the only way to help with how I'm feeling."

"Emma, if you're in trouble, I need you to talk to me." Vanessa's concern grew. Emma was always so put together and full of life, but on the eve of what was supposed to be her dream job, Vanessa felt as though Emma was seriously struggling with something.

"M-Mrs Middleton?"

Vanessa calmed her nerves. Something in Emma's voice seemed... intimate. "Yes?"

"You're way too good for him." Emma said, her voice barely audible. "And you're so beautiful."

"I, uh...thank you." Vanessa felt her cheeks heat. Emma was awfully forward tonight.

"But it's not just how gorgeous you are. It's the little things, too. Like how you chew your lip when you're concentrating, or the way you fiddle with your necklace when you're nervous. And when you smile...God, those little crinkles around your eyes. They're just you." Emma sighed. "Then there is your voice. It's incredibly sexy. But it's your kindness and genuine nature I'm most attracted to."

Emma took a breath, but before Vanessa could respond, Emma spoke again.

"I wish I'd watched you smile more. I wish I could whisk you away and show you how happy you could be, but I know I'm completely out of my mind. Still, it's all true. And it hurts so much, deep down in my stomach. But I wanted you to know, b-before I left, that I'm so in love with you."

Vanessa's lips parted, her entire body thrumming with an energy she hadn't experienced in many years. Emma Bradley was breaking her heart with every breath she took. Her voice, how she sounded a little breathless as she spoke...Vanessa wanted to scoop Emma up into her arms and hold her.

"And I know I'm crazy for even calling you tonight, but I had to tell you. I didn't want to leave without saying the words. It means nothing to you, I understand, but you mean the world and more to me. You mean everything, Vanessa. And if I could take back how I feel, how I've

felt for the best part of ten years, then I would. Because even though I have the most incredible memories with you...loving you is wrong."

"Oh, Emma..." Why did that realisation hurt so much?

"No. Please don't say anything. I feel dreadful already."

Vanessa swallowed down the lump in her throat. If things could be different, she would insist on meeting Emma right this very second. While Richard was off cheating on her left, right and centre, Vanessa couldn't do it. Not only had she spoken vows the day she married Lauren's father, but Emma was like a part of the family. It wouldn't be right.

"I'm very flattered," Vanessa lied. It was all she could do to stop this before it started. "You're wonderful...and I'm very fond of you, but—"

"Please, don't finish that sentence. I'm not looking for any kind of mutual attraction. I know there is none. But still, I needed you to know. Just...please don't tell Lauren."

Oh, if only Emma knew the truth. But Vanessa couldn't even contemplate it. "I-I wouldn't."

Emma sniffled as she cleared her throat. "So, I'm going to end the call now. Because I've made a complete idiot out of myself. So, take care, Mrs Middleton."

"Emma?"

"Y-yeah?" Emma's voice changed. She sounded more hopeful. But it only broke Vanessa further. "Vanessa, you there?"

Vanessa closed her eyes, savouring the sound of Emma's soft breath as it filtered down the line. "Have a safe trip, okay?"

"I will. Goodbye."

As the call cut out, Vanessa allowed every emotion she felt to spill out of her. Whatever she was feeling...Emma was too? How could it be? How on earth was it possible to feel yourself falling for your daughter's best friend? Someone you'd never touched? None of this made any sense...and nothing about it could be considered healthy.

Though Vanessa would miss Emma terribly, it was just as well she was leaving in a few hours. Because right now, Vanessa's hands itched to touch the younger woman she'd spent too long admiring from afar.

Vanessa bit back a sob, curling into a ball on the couch. "Fuck you, Richard."

Suddenly brought from the most heartbreaking night of her life, bare feet padded across the tiles in the kitchen behind Vanessa, a gentle perfume wafting past her. A small smile tugged at her lips; she was more than aware of Emma's presence. "Coffee is in the pot if you'd like some…"

"Sorry to interrupt you," Emma said, her voice tired. "I was hoping to sneak in without disturbing you."

"You're doing me a favour. This is hell." Vanessa eyed the red scribblings she'd already added to one paper, blowing out a breath. She lowered her glasses from her face. "Lauren will be home soon. She had to pop out for some last-minute toiletries."

"Oh, no worries. I could sleep for a month; I'm shattered."

"Can I get you anything?" Vanessa asked, turning on her stool to find Emma standing in a vest top and the world's shortest shorts. *Oh, my...*

"Would you mind if I make a sandwich? Once I've gotten my bearings, I'll head out and replenish the cupboards."

Vanessa climbed from her stool, stepping towards Emma and placing a gentle hand on her shoulder. "Sit down. Let me get it for you."

Emma spun around, looking startled. "Oh, I-I can do it."

"You can make dinner one night. When you've gotten back into your sleeping pattern. Now please, have a seat, and I'll make you some lunch."

"Thanks."

Vanessa noted the blush on Emma's cheeks; it was hard not to when she was standing so close. *Why am I standing so close?* And then Emma stepped away, her body heat missed immensely.

"I'll sit on one condition," Emma said, sipping her coffee as she eased into a seat at the dining table. "You tell me how you're doing."

"I'm…okay." It was all Vanessa could offer. People didn't often ask her how she was, but then again, she wasn't quite sure how she felt. Her husband had run off with another woman. It would *always* damage a person. "Things are different. Sometimes I forget I'm going through a divorce, but then I realise I should have seen it coming. Or, maybe I did see it coming and chose to ignore it for the sake of my family." Vanessa winced. Emma didn't need to hear this. "Lauren doesn't know, and I'd appreciate it if you kept that to yourself."

Emma held up a hand, watching Vanessa intently. "Nothing goes further than here. You kept my secret, so..."

Vanessa chose to ignore the end of Emma's comment. She was still flattered that someone like Emma could be attracted to her. But it could *only* be attraction. Vanessa could live with that, regardless of how long she'd lay awake last night knowing Emma was in the next room. "Thank you."

"So, have you thought about how you're going to tackle all of this? The single life?"

Vanessa chewed her lip. How honest could she be with Emma without Lauren getting wind of it all? She'd thought about confiding in her daughter, but Lauren had enough going on with her temporary move to Australia. "I've had a date or two."

"Yeah? That's great."

"It would be if we were even remotely compatible." Vanessa added some salad to Emma's ham sandwich, then sliced it and moved towards her. "But it's been a long time since I dated, so perhaps it's too late to start over with someone else." Emma always had a way of bringing out conversation in Vanessa. "And I'm going to shut up now."

"No way. You're gorgeous. You won't have a hard job finding someone, trust me."

Vanessa flushed. Okay, she wasn't all bad, but for Emma to tell her she was gorgeous meant a lot. Too much...maybe. "Thank you."

"So, why have these dates been so bad? Because they're not

Richard?" Emma closed her eyes. "I'm so sorry. I shouldn't have said that."

"Not at all. Richard…kind of did me a favour. I miss him, at times, but I knew we were falling out of love."

"Doesn't give him the right to do what he did, Mrs Middleton."

Vanessa cocked her head as those familiar feelings resurfaced. When Emma called her Mrs Middleton…*oh, Lord!* But she wouldn't be a Middleton for much longer.

"Sorry."

"Thank you. But I agree," Vanessa said. "He hurt me, he hurt Lauren, but we weren't happy."

"Does Lauren know that things were rocky before he left?"

Vanessa sighed. This was a conversation she should be having with her daughter. But Emma was so easy to talk to. She felt safe in her company. "She doesn't. I've considered talking to her, but she's far too busy to listen to me talk about my miserable life."

"She loves you."

"I know. But I need time to find myself. I was married to Richard for thirty years. I don't know who I am anymore."

"And that's why you've been on a few dates? Surely they weren't all bad." Emma sat forward, her chin resting in her hand. When Emma looked at Vanessa the way she was right now, explosions rocked Vanessa's insides. They had done so for quite a number of years.

"It's more like three dates with the same person. But I don't know, Dani doesn't spark life inside of me."

"And do you have a picture of this Danny bloke?"

Vanessa hesitated. This was about to throw Emma into a spin if any of those old feelings remained. "I…it's…Dani with an i, not a y."

Emma frowned, her brain evidently not quite catching up with what Vanessa was saying. And then her eyes widened. "Mrs

Middleton are you saying…" Emma shook her head, lowering her eyes as she exhaled a shaky breath.

Okay, I didn't expect her to be so shocked.

"You've been dating a woman?"

Vanessa swallowed. "Yes. But please, keep that to yourself, too. I won't see her again outside of work."

"But, Lauren?" Emma's brow furrowed. "You should tell her."

"It's…better if she doesn't know."

"Why? Because you're *suddenly* dating a woman? If it gets serious, it's kinda going to be hard to hide."

"I'm not *suddenly* dating a woman. I'm bisexual, and I always have been. But no, Lauren doesn't know. And I'm fifty, Emma. What's the point in telling her now? She'll think I've hidden it from her all her life."

"D-does Richard know?"

Vanessa nodded. Thankfully, Richard had never been concerned by the fact that Vanessa dated women before she met him. And some of them, over the years, had become friends. "He does, and he's fine with it. It was never a problem."

"I had no idea that you were into the ladies."

And that was just as well really. Because Vanessa knew *exactly* what the consequences could have been.

A key in the front door had Emma sitting upright while Vanessa got up from the table. She busied herself at the sink, plastering on a nervous smile as Lauren forced herself through the door with bags from her shopping trip. She needed Emma to do this one thing for her and keep quiet.

"Hi, Mum." Lauren stepped up to Vanessa, kissing her cheek.

"Get everything you need, love?"

"No idea. But if I don't have it, I'm not taking it."

"Well," Emma chirped in, "you're definitely not like me. One suitcase and a hut in the middle of nowhere. You'll rock up in Sydney with an entourage."

Lauren grinned, shaking her head. "I wish you were coming with me. This week isn't long enough to catch up."

"When you get back, I'm going to throw you a party. And if Rob behaves, he's invited, too." Emma got to her feet, pulling Lauren into a hug. Vanessa watched it play out in front of her; those strong arms of Emma's looked incredibly gentle. Maybe one day Emma would hug Vanessa, too.

Yeah. Get real.

CHAPTER FOUR

Emma repeatedly tugged at the cuff of her hoodie, her eyes focused on the TV while she wore a frown. She sat alone since Lauren was showering, but it only gave her too much time to think about the conversation she'd had with Vanessa earlier. Honestly, she had no words.

Vanessa Middleton…was bisexual. No, no way. It simply couldn't be.

But then, Emma's heart wanted it to be true. It made her life much more difficult, but at the same time, it kinda made sense. Vanessa had always been flirtatious when she was around, batting her eyelashes and offering slight touches of her hand. More so as they got to know one another over the years. But she'd always put it down to Vanessa's personality.

If Vanessa had been flirtatious over the years, did that mean she found Emma attractive? Or again, was it just her personality? Her mind instantly wandered to a night she would never forget. The night which had kept Emma going for the entire time she was out of the country.

Emma sat as still as she possibly could, her right arm resting over the back of the couch. Lauren had taken herself to bed over an hour ago, mid-movie, but Vanessa had chosen to remain on the couch with Emma until it finished. She knew Vanessa would drift off to sleep, she always did, and tonight had been no different. Emma had no idea how they'd ended up in the position they were in, but she didn't have the heart to wake Vanessa. That, and her own selfish needs took precedence tonight.

She looked down. Vanessa's head of soft blonde hair rested against her chest. If Emma dipped her head half an inch, she could smell Vanessa's sweet shampoo. Her light breathing as she slept lulled Emma into a different world, but it was the arm wrapped around Emma's midsection that thrilled her. It shouldn't, it was wrong, but Vanessa was doing the one thing Emma had always dreamed about. She was cuddling her.

Emma lowered her head as carefully as she could, her eyes closing as she breathed in deeply through her nose. Emotion exploded inside of her. The slightest touch from Vanessa's hand had a million thoughts roaring through Emma's mind.

This woman...was her life. But she would never know. She couldn't.

Instead of allowing this to continue a moment longer, Emma placed her hand on Vanessa's back and nudged her awake. "Vanessa?" she whispered, half hoping Vanessa would wake and half hoping she wouldn't yet.

But Vanessa tightened her grip around Emma, nuzzling her face further into her hoodie.

"M-Mrs Middleton." Emma shook Vanessa ever so slightly.

Vanessa suddenly lifted her head, her arm remaining around Emma. They stared at one another, Emma giving her a second to get her bearings. "I fell asleep? I'm so sorry."

"Don't be. It's fine." They didn't need to make a big deal out of this. "I was almost asleep, too."

Vanessa frowned as she released Emma from her grip. "You should have woken me up."

"Why? It's almost midnight."

"No, I know." Vanessa ran a hand through her hair, a blush settling on her cheeks. "But I was sleeping on you. I'm so sorry."

Emma put down the cup she'd been holding against the arm of the couch for an hour and sat forward. "I should head off. I'll see you soon, okay?"

"Come for dinner tomorrow?"

As much as Emma wanted to, she had to think about it first. This was the only time she'd ever been this close to Vanessa. Her head was ready to explode. "I'll see what plans I have."

"I'm making your favourite. Chicken parmigiana."

It was Emma's favourite, Vanessa was right. She couldn't turn down the invitation, even though she knew she should. "I'll be here."

"Perfect," Vanessa said, smiling fully. And then she leaned in, pressing her lips to Emma's cheek. "Goodnight. I'll see you tomorrow."

Emma remained in her seat as Vanessa stood and stretched her body. The moment she left the living room, Emma's mouth finally fell open, her eyes wide. "Holy fuck," she murmured. "She's going to drive me insane one of these days."

"Did you want wine with dinner?" Vanessa popped her head into the living room. "And if so, red or white?"

Emma heard her talking and willed her own lips to move, to speak. But nothing came. She'd never quite been in her own headspace like this before. This was a whole new ball game now. *Shit!*

"Emma?" Vanessa took a seat beside her, placing a gentle hand on her knee. "Is everything okay?"

Emma snapped out of her thoughts, quickly shifting on the couch until Vanessa's hand fell away. "Of course. Yeah. Sorry. I'll have water, thanks."

"About before..." Vanessa sighed.

"No. Not now. Lauren is upstairs, and I don't want her to come down to find us discussing something she has no idea about."

"Okay. I'll leave it be." Vanessa got to her feet, her warmth disappearing.

God, that hand felt good. "Sure. Yeah."

"Dinner will be ten minutes. Come through when you're ready."

Emma offered a nod, her hands clammy as Vanessa stared back at her. She hadn't aged at all in the time Emma had been away. The very definition of a fine wine was what sprang to mind.

But then Emma found her feet moving as she got up from the couch, following Vanessa into the kitchen. She had one question, and then she would forget the ridiculous idea of her and Vanessa together. "Hey, do you need a hand?"

"I...yes, thank you." Vanessa placed a bowl of salad in the middle of the table, her fitted black slacks hugging her ass as she leaned forward. "You're okay with chicken parmigiana tonight?"

Chicken parmigiana. Emma swooned, her mouth watering. She'd missed Vanessa's food. Amongst other things. "Absolutely."

"I have some fresh rolls ready to come out of the oven. If you could take care of them, that would be great."

"Sure." Emma took the oven mitt from the counter and removed the bread from the oven. Her stomach growled as it had been all day when she smelt food, but she needed to curb her cravings. She'd be the size of a house within the week otherwise.

Vanessa sidled up beside her, clearing her throat. "It's great to have you back. Lauren has been beside herself for months."

"I've missed her so much," Emma said, smiling. "Talking on the phone was nice, but it wasn't the same."

"No. And it's what I'm dreading when she leaves. But she'll be back before I know it. It doesn't feel like eighteen months since you left."

Emma swallowed, her eyes straying to Vanessa. God, this woman was devastating in every way possible. "I'm sorry about the call I made the night before I left."

"You were drunk. I wouldn't worry."

"That...doesn't mean it wasn't true." Emma's eyes lowered to the counter, her heart beating hard in her chest. She never thought she'd have this conversation with Vanessa, but here she was, honesty and all. "But I shouldn't have told you."

"Oh, I don't know." Vanessa grinned. "It certainly made me feel better about myself knowing some young beauty is attracted to me."

"Did, uh…" Emma shook her head. She couldn't possibly ask what she wanted to ask. But then she looked up at Vanessa, surprised to find her waiting for the end of her sentence, eyebrow quirked. "Did you ever think about me?"

"I was married." Vanessa spoke low, looking away and focusing on the chicken parmigiana in the glass dish.

"No, I know." Emma felt ridiculous. "And I'm sure even if things were different, I'm not the kind of person you'd look at. I mean, look at *me*…and look at *you*." A nervous laugh escaped Emma's lips, but Vanessa didn't find it amusing.

Vanessa turned, taking Emma's chin in her hand in one hell of a shock move. "I…was…married."

Emma's entire body lit up, but Vanessa's hand was steady. So sure. "Yeah."

"That's all I'm saying. It'll only complicate things further, and I don't want you to be uncomfortable while you're here. I'd never do anything to ruin your friendship with Lauren."

"How would you possibly ruin anything?" Emma was lost. Vanessa had nothing to worry about. She wasn't going to pin her against the counter and take her. But God…she wanted to. "Vanessa?"

"I was very flattered, okay? You're beautiful, I thought so before you called me that night, but you're Lauren's best friend. And I can't."

"Can't what?" Emma frowned.

"Allow anything to happen between us."

Emma's heart fell into her stomach. Had Vanessa actually insinuated she *wanted* to go there with Emma? Surely not. "You mean, it would have been a possibility?"

"I think it's only fair for me to be straightforward with you after you were so bravely honest with me. I know how hard it must have been. But to answer your question…yes. I did think about you. More than I should have."

"Fuck." Emma's eyes slammed shut as she willed her tears to remain where they belonged. Pushed deep down with everything else. "Shit."

"Hey, don't cry." Vanessa's thumb brushed her cheek, forcing a gasp to escape Emma's lips. "It wouldn't do either of us any good to allow our feelings to get the better of us. Please…understand that."

Vanessa was right. How could she ever explain to Lauren that she was in love with her mum? It sounded ridiculous in her own head, so Lauren would blow. But Vanessa had just told her everything she'd ever wanted to hear over the years. Of the twelve years she'd known Lauren and her family, Emma had been in love with Vanessa for most of them.

"I should finish dinner." Vanessa pulled away, but Emma gently gripped her wrist, holding her hand in place.

She turned her head, kissing Vanessa's palm. "Thank you. For being honest with me."

"It's the least you deserve."

Vanessa sat across the table from Emma while Lauren sat by her side. They spoke amongst themselves, but Vanessa could barely stomach her food let alone get involved. She'd made one hell of a mistake in admitting how she felt to Emma, because now she couldn't get the thought of it out of her mind. And as Emma looked at her across the table, her expressive eyes so very pleasing, Vanessa wanted to drag her across it and kiss her.

The last time they'd conversed with one another in this

kitchen was via video call, eleven months into Emma's placement. Vanessa remembered it like it was yesterday.

Vanessa dragged her bag from the boot of the car, rummaging through her pocket for her house keys. Everyone she came across today had gotten on her last nerve, but she was home, and now she could lock up and leave the world outside. As she'd wanted to since this morning when her second coffee hadn't budged the tiredness she felt.

She wasn't sleeping lately.

She'd bumped into Richard the night before when she was picking up some groceries. It shouldn't have irked her to see him with his girlfriend, Vanessa actually felt free for the first time in too many years, but the bitterness remained. He'd left her for a younger woman. Vanessa couldn't help but feel insignificant because of it.

As she pushed the key into the lock, her weary body stepping into the hallway, she smiled. Lauren was sitting on the couch, her laptop resting on her knees. "Hi, love. Good day at work?"

"Yeah." Lauren set her laptop down on the coffee table. "You didn't sleep last night, did you? I heard you creeping around at three, then five."

"Sorry I woke you up." Vanessa needed to sort her sleeping pattern out. It wasn't healthy to lie awake most nights. "I think I might speak to the doctor. Maybe he could prescribe me some sleeping tablets."

"No, Mum. You don't want to go down that road."

Vanessa agreed, she really didn't. But she wasn't sure what else she could do. It was torture lying awake thinking over everything. And by everything, she wasn't talking about Richard. It was all Emma. And it had been for the last eleven months since she left the country. "Maybe I'll try some meditation, I don't know."

"Could work." Lauren offered a gentle smile. And then she grinned when her laptop started chiming at her. "Oh, quick! Come here. It's Emma!"

Vanessa's heart sank deep into her belly. She couldn't see Emma. She'd avoided every video call her daughter had tried to drag her into. "I have stuff to do, love. But say hi for me."

She rushed into the kitchen, closing the door so she couldn't hear the soft voice she dreamt about most nights when she finally succumbed to sleep. It was too much for Vanessa right now. But it wasn't Emma's fault; this was all Vanessa and her ability to allow things to get the better of her.

Had she always been so weak when it came to love and emotions? Was it supposed to feel this way? Painful but beautiful all at the same time?

The kitchen door opened. "Yeah. Wait a minute. I'll get her."

Vanessa swallowed down the fear that had suddenly risen. She wasn't getting out of this one. Not tonight. "Lauren, I need to start dinner."

"Oh, hush. You look shattered. We'll order in." Lauren waved a hand, placing her laptop down on the kitchen island. "Someone is dying to say hi to you."

Vanessa was dying to say hi, too. Emma had been such a big character in this house; not having her here was difficult. And then Vanessa realised anything could happen at any given moment, and avoiding Emma wasn't what she wanted. Not deep down. She was across the world alone. The least Vanessa could do was be a friendly face.

"Give me a minute," Lauren said, peering at the screen. And then she approached Vanessa. "Mum, she wants to speak to you. I think she wants to know if you're okay with everything happening with Dad. So, I'm going to give you ten minutes. Maybe speaking to someone who isn't me will be good for you. I'll be upstairs if you need me."

"Lauren, no—"

"Just try, Mum." Lauren squeezed Vanessa's shoulder, leaving the kitchen via the door at the back of the house.

Exhaling a deep breath when Lauren's footsteps could be heard above her, Vanessa checked her hair in the mirrored microwave door, internally scoffing when she realised she was being ridiculous. Nobody cared what she looked like. She poured herself a coffee from the machine and rounded the island.

Oh, this wasn't good. Emma was staring back at her, her hand resting under her chin, the sweetest of smiles beaming through the screen. "Hi, Mrs Middleton."

Every memory they'd shared flashed through Vanessa's mind, her heart hammering against her ribs. "H-hi."

"Have a seat." Emma grinned, tipping her head forward. "I've been summoned by Lauren."

On weak legs, Vanessa perched herself on a kitchen stool, setting her coffee down. "Emma, it's wonderful to see you, but you don't need to do this. Lauren is worrying for nothing. I'm fine."

Emma studied Vanessa through the screen, frowning as she cocked her head. "You look tired. She said you're not sleeping."

"I have things on my mind," Vanessa confessed. "But it's to be expected. I need to find something to keep me busy."

And then Emma leaned in closer, lowering her voice. "Are you avoiding me?"

"N-no."

"I never wanted what I said to make you feel uncomfortable. But it's been almost a year since I've spoken to you, so I think maybe I've ruined everything back at home by opening my big mouth."

"You haven't ruined anything." Vanessa listened for any sign of Lauren. She heard her rummaging around upstairs. "Please, don't think that."

"I'm sorry about everything that's happening. I thought Lauren would be struggling since she was so close to him, but she seems okay."

"She's been a star. I don't know what I'd have done without her."

"Sorry I couldn't be there for you." Oh, it was just as well Emma wasn't here; Vanessa wouldn't be held responsible for her actions lately if they'd been in a room alone. "But I don't suppose you'd want me around anyway. Which is completely understandable."

"I told you you'd always be welcome here. I meant it."

Emma swept a hand through her hair. "You also said it before I made that stupid call to you."

Hadn't Emma meant anything she'd said? Vanessa wasn't sure how she felt about the potential of Emma only making that call because she was drunk. During all of this, her divorce and the fact her life was slowly falling apart, Emma had been the only thing keeping her going. "Look, we don't need to talk about it. Nothing has changed. You're still Lauren's best friend, and we both still miss you ridiculously."

"I miss you guys too."

"And you still have a while before you return. It's what? Thirteen months..."

Vanessa hadn't been counting, honestly.

"Actually, the two-year contract isn't going to work out for me. The agency has been struggling to keep the funding going. I'll be home by the middle of next year."

Vanessa's heart almost burst from her chest with that small piece of information.

"But don't worry, I won't call by. I'll hang out with Lauren when I find a place to live."

The sadness in Emma's voice as she said those words tore through Vanessa. It shouldn't be this way. Emma had been honest when she made the call, and though Vanessa couldn't act on anything or even tell Emma that she felt the same, they could learn to live with it, surely. "Please, don't avoid me when you come home, Emma. Everything is going to be perfectly fine."

"Still...I feel like a complete idiot."

"Why?"

"Oh, I don't know," Emma laughed. "Maybe because of the tiny fact I let slip while I was plastered outside a bar."

"Well, I was flattered," Vanessa said, saddened this was ending as she heard Lauren coming down the stairs. "Lauren's coming."

"So, yeah." Emma coughed, her demeanour changing in a split second. "It's so quiet here, you know?"

"Sounds it." Vanessa smiled, enthralled by Emma's voice, her smile... everything. But she couldn't sit here for much longer. With every breath Emma took, Vanessa wanted to crawl through the screen and kiss her. "Look, I should go."

"Okay. But if you ever need to talk, you have my number. I'm available in the evenings mostly."

"Thank you. I appreciate it."

Vanessa shook her head. She'd forgotten she had company for a moment. Realising Lauren was waving a hand in front of her face, Vanessa glanced down at her untouched dinner plate, then back up at her daughter.

"Don't you think, Mum?"

Vanessa frowned. "Sorry, what?"

"I was just saying it'll be nice to have Emma around while I'm away. She can be your adopted daughter."

"Oh, one daughter is plenty for me, thank you very much." Vanessa smiled weakly, pushing her food around her plate. "No offence, Emma."

"None taken, Mrs Middleton."

Vanessa didn't bother to correct Emma. The more she spoke, the harder it was to avoid eye contact. Vanessa had been raised to always look her company in the eye, but tonight she couldn't. As Emma had so gently kissed her palm before dinner, Vanessa felt a rush of everything she'd been missing over the years surge through her. Because while Richard was wonderful, an incredible father to Lauren, Vanessa had always been missing *something* in life. If she was being honest with herself, it was the touch of another woman. Soft lips, a tender touch, a delicate scent...*Stop it!*

"No, but it'll be nice to have the company. And since Emma isn't working at the minute, and you won't take anything for the bills, she can wait on you hand and foot when you get home from work."

Vanessa dropped her fork to her plate, standing abruptly. "Sorry, you've just reminded me I had something to take care of for work. Enjoy your dinner, both of you."

Without another word, Vanessa rushed up the stairs and slipped off into her bedroom. With the door closed and her back pressed firmly against it, Vanessa looked up to the ceiling, her eyes fluttering closed. She needed to breathe for a second. She needed to get all thoughts of Emma out of her head. If she didn't, things could get *very* complicated, *very* quickly.

All Vanessa wanted was someone who only saw her in their world. Someone, who, when things got tough, could turn to her and say "let's fix this. I can't lose you". Emma couldn't be her person, though. Vanessa wouldn't put herself or Emma in such a position.

She openly told you she loved you...

But it wasn't enough. It could never be enough. And even if Vanessa had thought Emma's feelings had lessened, the feeling in her kiss told her otherwise. This was one huge mistake waiting to unleash itself. If Lauren found out...Vanessa wouldn't have only lost her husband, she'd lose her daughter, too.

A light knock on her door dragged her from all thoughts of Emma. When she opened it, those silver eyes staring back at her, Vanessa's breath caught in her throat. "Do you need something?"

"Lauren is on the phone to Rob. I...do you think maybe I should leave? I can crash on a friend's couch for now. It's no big deal."

"You're not sleeping on someone's couch. No chance."

"I know, but..." Emma rested against the frame of the door, her hooded eyes looking up at Vanessa. "If I stay here, I'm afraid I'll do something that will ruin *everything*."

"I-I..." Vanessa tugged Emma's hand, pulling her into the bedroom. The door closed quietly as Vanessa backed Emma up against it. She needed a second alone with her. To realise the mistake she was making in being honest about her feelings. "I don't want you to leave. We can be adults."

"Vanessa..."

Vanessa shivered when Emma spoke her name. God, it was the only sound she wanted to hear for the rest of her life.

"I've been in love with you since I was twenty-three. Everything you told me before has only complicated it all. And while I can push down my feelings when I need to, it doesn't mean I want to. When Lauren leaves…when it's just you and I…I don't know."

The thought of coming home from work to find Emma in bed waiting for her had every nerve ending blazing. She was dreaming of something impossible, but one wrong move, and it *could* happen.

She pressed her body to Emma's, recognising a shudder as she did so. "I wish things could be different."

"But they're not."

"No," Vanessa whispered, their lips millimetres apart. "No, they're not."

"Then I need to leave. I'll wait until Lauren goes, and then I'm gone, too."

Vanessa closed her eyes and nodded as she stepped back. This was becoming a dangerous game, and Emma had only been here for twenty-four hours. Perhaps it was the right idea for her to leave, but Vanessa would be sad to see her go. "If it's what you want."

"It's not. What I want is to be here *with* you. But we can't."

"If things could be different…" Vanessa trailed off. She had no idea what would happen if things were different.

Emma took her hand, kissing her knuckles. "If things were different, I'd spend my life making up for how he treated you in the end. And while we can't be together, I want you to go out into the big wide world and find the right person for you. Because you deserve so much more than being alone."

"Being alone is best for me."

Emma frowned. "But why?"

"Because the person I want…I can't have."

CHAPTER FIVE

The ticking of the clock soothed Emma as she lay in bed, her eyes glued to the ceiling. She'd had better nights, she couldn't lie, but she was safe with a roof over her head. That had to count for something. It didn't matter if a couple of hours ago Vanessa had pressed her body against her, her breath washing over her lips. What mattered was the fact that they'd stopped themselves before anything could happen.

Lauren had called Emma's name while she was behind closed doors with her mother, but she hadn't suspected a thing. Why would she? Lauren had no reason to assume anything untoward was going on. But it still tugged in the pit of Emma's stomach. She couldn't lie to her best friend, so it was better if she left and got on with her life while Lauren was away.

If something happened, how would she explain? If Lauren called one night and Emma was in bed with Vanessa, it would kill Emma inside. Or if they were sharing dinner and it meant more than Lauren knew, how would she keep her voice level and not give anything away? She couldn't do it. It wasn't fair to anyone.

The mess Emma thought she'd left behind when she went to Ghana was slowly creeping back into her life, and in this moment, she didn't know how to deal with it. Vanessa was saying all the right things, but it still couldn't be. And honestly, Emma wasn't sure she had the strength for a forbidden romance. Even though they were two consenting adults doing nothing wrong, Lauren wouldn't see it the same way.

Oh, God. She'll think I'm only her friend to get into her mum's pants. That thought sent Emma's stomach sinking. Everything they'd shared over the years, the special bond they had, could all be obliterated in mere moments. One kiss, one touch, and it would all be over for Emma. She wouldn't only lose her friend, but a family, too.

This very room felt like home. The nights she'd lay here wishing for more, the times Emma wanted to comfort Vanessa when she knew she was alone. Just the reminder of using this room in the weeks before she left had Emma's heart aching for more.

God, she was going to miss this place. The warmth and comfort of Mrs Middleton's home, the beautiful home cooked food, Vanessa. But Africa was the right thing for Emma, and she knew it. Every extra day she remained here, it got harder and harder to keep her thoughts and feelings to herself.

She'd let the lease go on her flat last week, so here she was, cooped up in Lauren's parents' spare room until next Thursday. Then she would be crashing with a friend who would drive her to the airport the following morning. Lauren had insisted, but Emma didn't want her to take time off work, and she'd have to if she was planning on driving to the airport. She also couldn't bear saying goodbye to her best friend. The initial contract she had was two years, and Emma could only hope it lasted as long. If she couldn't get over Mrs Middleton within two years, she had serious issues.

Emma knew she was kidding herself if she thought for one second this would all blow over. It hadn't in all the years she'd craved Vanessa, so it wasn't about to now. Absence makes the heart grow fonder, and

Emma was certain that was exactly what would happen. This...it was a mess.

She sat upright in bed as she heard the floorboards creak on the landing. "Come to bed, Vanessa."

"Don't you dare, Richard!" Vanessa whisper yelled. "You've been gone for three days longer than you promised. And I want to know why!"

"You know what work is like. We get one thing dealt with and something else crops up."

"Oh, that's bullshit, and we both know it. Don't insult me."

"My love, relax. Come on, let's climb into bed. I'll make it up to you."

Emma's stomach lurched. The thought of him with his hands all over Vanessa left one hell of a nasty taste in Emma's mouth. Vanessa may not see it, but Emma did. Richard was up to something with other women. She'd watched him creep in late at night far too many times for it to be anything else.

"I don't want you to make it up to me. I want you to stop disappearing for weeks on end. Dealing with clients does not take that long."

"I'm going to bed. Either you're joining me, or you're not."

Vanessa snorted. "I'm not. Goodnight."

The sound of footsteps descending the stairs had Emma narrowing her eyes as she focused on the door. Perhaps Vanessa needed a shoulder this evening, someone to talk to since Richard didn't care about how she was feeling. "I'd never make her feel that way," she whispered into the huge, silent spare room. "You don't know how lucky you are."

Emma shot from the bed, opening the door quietly. She could hear Richard whistling down the hall, so it had to be Vanessa who'd gone back down the stairs a few moments ago. She crept out, taking the stairs and landing in the kitchen barefoot.

"Oh, Emma." Vanessa cleared her throat as she turned her back, her voice trembling. "Did you need something?"

Shit. How could Emma tell Vanessa she'd been eavesdropping? No, she couldn't possibly. "No. I thought I'd hang out down here for an hour. Can't sleep."

"Of course." Vanessa turned to face her, her cheeks damp. "Help yourself to anything you need. I'm opening a bottle of white if you'd like to join me for a glass?"

Emma frowned. "You're upset. Is everything okay?"

"Everything is fine." Vanessa's gentle smile played on her lips, the warmth in her blue eyes leaving Emma breathless. Next week couldn't come soon enough. "Go into the living room. I'll bring two glasses."

"Sure." Emma shoved her hands into the pockets of her shorts, mentally slapping herself for getting involved in something which wasn't her business. She shouldn't sit here with Vanessa, but as the warmth of her body behind Emma intensified, Emma found herself sitting down, willing to do anything Vanessa asked. "So, Lauren isn't home tonight?"

"No, she's gone to dinner with Rob."

"That's nice."

"My daughter has a much better love life than me. I don't seem to be able to encourage my own husband to come back to the family home unless it suits him." Vanessa slapped a hand over her mouth, her eyes widening. "I'm sorry. You don't need to hear this."

"I can talk, if it's what you need."

Vanessa poured two glasses of wine, relaxing back after she'd handed Emma hers. "I appreciate the offer, but everything is fine. It always is."

"Well, if it makes any difference, it's nice having your company for an hour." Too much? "I mean, I've been hanging around here for so long, and next week when I leave, I'll miss you all."

"I'll miss you, too." Vanessa placed a gentle hand on Emma's, her entire body igniting, fire dancing through her veins. "We all will."

"Everything you've done for me over the years hasn't gone unnoticed, Mrs Middleton. I know I'm Lauren's best friend, but you've always been so welcoming."

"You're wonderful. Lauren loves you like a sister. You know you're always welcome in my home." The sincerity in Vanessa's voice enveloped Emma like the warmest of hugs. And being alone with her,

well... They seemed to connect so well, but Emma knew it was all in her head. "Come here. Give me a hug."

Emma found herself leaning into Vanessa, her lips parting, a silent sigh escaping. The times she'd hugged Vanessa on a whim were too many to count, but this one felt different. Vanessa, her perfume, her soft breath against her neck...whoa. She had no words to describe just how her arms felt this evening.

"It's going to be miserable not having you around," Vanessa said, her voice low against Emma's ear. "But you'll have the most incredible time, and I know how much you're looking forward to it."

"I am." Emma reluctantly pulled out of Vanessa's embrace, her pulse racing. "And it's only two years. Maybe less if they struggle to keep hold of me."

"Well, you know you have a room here when you return. I don't suppose it'll be possible to look for a new place while you're away."

"If it'd be okay nearer the time, I may double check the offer is still there. I'm not expecting the best phone reception while I'm gone, so yeah, house hunting when I return would be much easier."

Vanessa tucked Emma's hair behind her ear, her eyes smiling and bright. "I'd love to have you back here."

If only every touch and word from Vanessa meant something more. Emma was out of her mind to imagine it for one second, but at times, it did feel different. Intimate. "Thank you."

"Now, tell me all about the plans you have while you're in Africa."

Emma grinned. "You'll be sorry you asked. I could talk about it for days."

Vanessa sat back, her long legs crossed and so very enticing. "Be my guest. I have no plans."

A knock brought Emma from her memories, a familiar feeling of what she wished she could have settling deep within.

She exhaled a breath. She had to gather herself once and for all.

"Psst! You awake?" Lauren's voice filtered through the crack in the door.

Emma sat up in bed, sighing. "Yep, I'm awake."

Lauren crept through the door and climbed into bed with Emma. "How am I supposed to sit on a flight to Australia on my own? I'm going to be bored to tears."

"But Rob will be waiting for you. What more do you need to keep you going?" It shouldn't be so easy for Emma to switch from Vanessa to Lauren, but she had mastered it over the years.

Lauren snuggled into Emma. "I can't wait to see him."

"It's going to be good for you. You're always working. Taking this break and then coming back fresh is going to be the start of your new life with Rob. I know you've been together for a while now, but being with him in Australia is going to be epic."

Emma couldn't wait for Lauren to finally settle down fully. Rob was a local lad, but his job in marketing had him positioned all over the world. This stint saw him spending five months in Sydney, but Lauren couldn't get out of work for the entire time. She was lucky they'd given her three months leave.

"I'm going to miss you. But we've done it before, and this time isn't so long."

Emma had to be honest with her best friend. "I'll always be there for you on the end of the phone, but we're beginning to drift apart for good reasons. When you come back, you shouldn't expect to see me as much as you want to. Rob is your person now, and I'm happy to be second in command."

Lauren frowned, lifting her head. "What do you mean… drifting apart?"

"Just, you know. You're getting married. I'm here…with no idea what I'm doing with my life."

"I fully expect you to be involved when I get back. And if you're not, I'm going to arrange a date for you myself."

Emma shrugged. "I always go for people who are unavailable. Whether it's emotionally or not. It's easier to get back into the swing of things here single."

"Why the change of heart?" Lauren frowned. "I thought you wanted to find someone?"

"I do. It's just...I have other things to sort out here before I consider tackling my love life. Being alone isn't the worst idea in the world, you know."

"But I don't want you to be alone. I want you to have a plus one to my wedding, and I want it to be the most beautiful woman in the world."

Oh, if only you had any idea... "All the most beautiful women in the world are off the table, kid. Story of my life."

"Well, failing that, you can keep Mum company on my big day. I doubt she'll find someone to fall in love with."

"Why not?" Emma asked, hoping her voice didn't betray her.

"She's not looking. And I wish she would. I want so much happiness for her after how their marriage ended, but I don't know how to open up to her. She's very closed off lately. I mean, she's been so strange tonight."

"You did say she wasn't herself. But I suppose it's to be expected."

"She can't be single for the rest of her life. Have you seen her? She's drop dead gorgeous. Dad was a fucking idiot to do what he did, and I'll never forgive him. I'm not even inviting him to my wedding."

"You may want to sleep on it for a while. Anything can change, and you may want him there."

"No, thanks." Lauren scoffed. "I'm going to ask Mum if she'll walk me down the aisle."

"I think she'd love to." Emma relaxed into the mattress, her arm wrapped around Lauren. "And I think you two will look amazing on the day."

"Ems," Lauren said, curling her body around Emma. "Please will you keep an eye on her while I'm away? I know you have friends to meet up with and family to see, but if you're here in the evening...I know she'd love some company."

"Lauren—"

"You're the *only* person I trust to be there for her. And she loves the bones of you. Please…for me?"

Emma looked down at her best friend, rolling her eyes as Lauren stuck her bottom lip out. "I'll swing by when I'm able to."

"Thanks. Maybe you two could go out to lunch or something. You're on the same wavelength as one another. I think she feels younger when she's around you."

What? Why would Lauren say something like that?

"Your mum has her own things going on. She doesn't need me hanging off her."

"Fine." Lauren huffed. "But when I come home and find her sitting here like Bridget Jones, I'm blaming you."

"Not likely. She has a successful job, and she's going to find someone who worships her."

"Hope so," Lauren said, yawning. "Now turn the light off; I'm shattered."

Emma laughed, flicking off the bedside light. "So, who's spooning who tonight?"

"You can spoon me. Make up for all the time you've been gone."

Vanessa perched on a kitchen stool, savouring her morning coffee before she had to leave for work. Monday was always a dreadful day, and with very little sleep, she could only pray her students didn't get on her last nerve today. She could feel herself prepared to blow at any moment.

Sighing, Vanessa flicked through the newspaper, the same old rubbish printed as it usually was. Was it just her or did they have more adverts than news in them these days? Dissatisfied, she flicked it closed again, relaxing back into her seat. Another ten minutes, and she would be perkier. One more coffee, and she would be ready to take on the world. *Get real.*

Last night had been difficult for Vanessa. She hadn't expected Emma to come knocking on her bedroom door, and she hadn't for one moment anticipated the look of devastation in her eyes. Vanessa should have kept quiet before dinner, but Emma deserved to know it wasn't totally one-sided. It may have taken Vanessa some time to come to terms with it and, in turn, be honest, but it had always been there at the back of her mind. Emma Bradley had always been a light in Vanessa's dark, miserable world.

The number of times she'd laid in bed thinking about Emma while lying next to Richard were too many to count. But it wasn't so intense back then. She was a married woman; she would never cheat. Some may say just thinking about someone else was cheating in one form or another, but Vanessa became less and less content as the years passed with Richard. He worked late, couldn't possibly miss a working dinner, and had to leave for clients at the drop of a hat. Vanessa wasn't stupid, she knew what was going on, but she didn't know how to get out of it. While she was being stepped all over, it seemed easier to stay and go through the motions for the sake of Lauren. But if Lauren knew, it wouldn't be pretty.

Her daughter was headstrong and independent. If Lauren knew for one moment that Vanessa had only stayed for her, she would be truly devastated. And Vanessa couldn't blame her daughter if she felt that way. But to come out and explain she used to date women too, with the potential of falling for Lauren's best friend, was a whole different ball game. One Vanessa didn't know the rules to and one she wasn't sure she could bring herself to play. It seemed too…difficult.

"Mornin'," a tired voice spoke behind her. "Mind if I grab some coffee before I leave?"

Vanessa spun on her stool, frowning. Emma was leaving already? "It's…barely 7 a.m."

Emma shrugged. "Busy day ahead. I'm meeting with my cousin."

"Will you be back in time for dinner?" Vanessa watched Emma move around her kitchen, the hood pulled up on her hoodie and covering her beautiful profile. "Emma?"

"Mm?" Emma turned.

"Will you be back in time for dinner?"

"Probably not," Emma said, turning back to the coffee machine. "Unless I'm coming to get my things together. But either way, don't expect me for dinner. You've done enough for me since I returned…*and* over the years. I think it's time I found my feet."

Those words saddened Vanessa. She never wanted Emma to feel this way. She'd been a huge part of this family for too long. "If I could take back what I said last night—"

"Unless you didn't mean it, you can't take it back. And if you said it for the sake of it…"

"I meant what I said. That doesn't mean you needed to hear it, though." Vanessa ran a hand through her hair. "But I don't know how to fix this, Emma." Vanessa moved towards Emma, stopping her from leaving the kitchen. "You're my daughter's best friend. Surely you see the issue here?"

"I do." Emma agreed, offering a weak smile. "But it doesn't change how I've always felt about you, Vanessa. It doesn't stop me from wanting you."

"I'm sorry."

Emma lowered her eyes to her cup of coffee. "Don't *ever* be sorry for being beautiful and capturing my heart." She leaned up, pressing a kiss to Vanessa's cheek. "I'm sorry for ever telling you. Nothing good has come from you knowing."

Vanessa's eyes closed as Emma's lips lingered around her ear.

If she could turn her head and kiss Emma, all of this could be different. But Lauren remained at the back of her mind.

"I promise to try to get over you. It's all I can do. Just…I need to keep my distance. I hope you can understand."

Vanessa nodded. "I understand."

"So, I'm going to shower and change. I have some things to put in place. But thanks for the bed the last few nights. I appreciate it even if I've not quite shown it."

"You have shown it. And the guest room is yours anytime you need it."

"Yeah. Thanks."

CHAPTER SIX

"And do you have your passport and some cash?" Vanessa asked, spooning dinner onto plates for Lauren and herself. "I have some upstairs. I picked some up for you, but it's Aussie dollars."

"Thanks, Mum. I have enough English money to see me over, so now I'll have some for when I land." Lauren set the table, placing various condiments in the middle. "It's a shame Emma couldn't join us tonight. She loves your lamb stew."

Vanessa's heart tightened. Emma would always be welcome around her table. It was the idea of having her in her bed that seemed to be the issue. "I think she had plans."

"Yeah. She's gone to see Sharon. I don't know why; it only gives her anxiety when she gets home."

"Anxiety?"

"She…doesn't get on with most of the family. They're a bit too rough and ready for Emma."

"Well, I'll keep her some food back in case she's hungry when she gets home." Vanessa knew Emma wouldn't return. She'd never felt so uncertain around Emma as she had this morning.

The atmosphere was usually much more pleasant and inviting. Still, she could hope Emma would show.

Lauren squeezed Vanessa's shoulder. "You're too good to us, you know. I don't know what we'd do without you."

"Seems the pair of you are managing perfectly fine." Vanessa choked back a sob, turning her back on her daughter. "I'm so proud of you, Lauren. You've taken everything in your stride and look at you now. You're flourishing."

"I wish I wasn't leaving, but I'm so happy I'm going to see Rob. I've been waiting since forever. But I worry about you."

"He's good for you," Vanessa confessed. "Don't pay any attention to my bitterness. I'm so happy for you. And I want you to go off and live your life, your dream. If Rob is the person for you, I'm thrilled."

Vanessa would never forget the moment Lauren discovered her dad was a cheat. It'd hurt, but Lauren was at Vanessa's side in seconds. No blame. Just love for Vanessa.

Vanessa sat across the table from Richard, the ticking of the kitchen clock occupying her mind. Richard was beginning to sweat, little beads forming on his forehead, but Vanessa knew exactly where this was going. He looked up at her, smiling weakly.

"Are we going to sit in silence all evening?" Vanessa had no intentions of doing so, but Richard had walked in from work and demanded they talk. Yet here they were, without a single word spoken. "Richard?"

He cleared his throat, the clink of metal on the glass dining table startling Vanessa. "I want a divorce."

"Okay." She stared down at his wedding band.

Richard furrowed his brow. "Okay? That's it?"

Vanessa pushed her chair back, shrugging as she stood up. "I'm not sure what you want me to say. I'm not going to ask you to stay if it's what you're waiting for. And I have no intentions of stroking your ego by telling you how wonderful a husband and father you are or how devastated I am to see you go. Because quite frankly, I'd be lying."

"Ness—"

"Don't, Richard. I knew this was coming. We both did. But, why now?"

He got to his feet, running a hand through his dark cropped hair. At least they weren't yelling at one another. "I've met someone else."

"Correction," Vanessa paused, holding up a hand. "You've been sleeping with someone else. Don't hold back. Be honest if you're going to walk away."

"Yes. I've been sleeping with someone else."

His admission shouldn't have hurt Vanessa; she'd known for the best part of a year Richard was with another woman. But it did hurt. Because although they didn't work anymore, she wanted to believe she could keep the family together. "I'm sure our daughter will be thrilled to know you've been putting your dick in another woman. You know, while her mother sits at home alone night after night."

"Do you have to be so crass?"

"Do you have to be so fucking disgusting?" Vanessa countered. "Because while I may say it how it is, I'm not the one who is sleeping with other people while I'm married."

"How long have you known?" Richard asked, leaning against the counter.

"Since the first time it happened. You're not very subtle when it comes to your love for other women. Perhaps it's something you need to work on."

"And you've never..." He cleared his throat, shaking his head. "You know."

"Cheated on you? No, Richard, I haven't." Vanessa was beginning to wish she had. All this time spent admiring Emma from afar, the nights she wished she could undress her daughter's best friend against the moonlight...it was beginning to eat away at her. But Vanessa would never do that to another person, whether they'd hurt her or not. It wasn't her style. "And I'm saddened you'd even ask. I've been loyal to you since the day we met."

"I'm sorry."

"No, you're not." Vanessa poured a glass of wine, setting the bottle back down.

"Could I maybe have a glass, too?"

Vanessa shook her head, scoffing. "I think it's time to pack your things and run along to your whore, don't you?"

"A little harsh."

"Perhaps. But I'm finding it hard to have any kind of sympathy for you or your twenty-two-year-old assistant. You do realise she's with you for your money, don't you?" Vanessa stalked towards Richard, disgust roaring through her. "And I know what your family thought of me when we met, but one thing I never needed was your cash or fancy clothes." She stepped painfully close to Richard, tilting her chin. "Get your things and get out of my house."

"Your house?" Richard laughed nervously.

"I've stuck around for the sake of you and our daughter. If you think I'm walking away from this with nothing, you're sadly mistaken." The truth was about to pour out of Vanessa like molten lava. "Do you honestly think for the last several years I've been satisfied with you? I have more fun with the toys in my nightstand." Vanessa snorted, watching as Richard's face paled. "The opportunities I've missed out on because I wanted to be faithful to you are too many to count. I could have been happy with someone else a long time ago."

"So you considered it?"

"No," Vanessa said. "But I'm wishing I had now. This could have all been over long before this moment." She shook her head, sighing. "And now you're the one walking out on me. I bet your friends will love this."

"Vanessa. Let's not end this with so much hostility. We have a daughter to think about."

Vanessa's brows rose with surprise. Had Richard genuinely said that? "You didn't think about Lauren while you were fucking Rosanna. Don't pretend you care now."

"Lauren is the reason I waited so long to tell you. And I thought

about not doing this; I was willing to stay and work something out between us, but Rosanna wants to be exclusive."

"Don't ever be willing to do anything for me. I don't need you, and I certainly don't need you to take pity on me. I'm an independent woman, and the last thing I need is someone like you to do what you think is best. Please, walk away. Do us both a favour."

"I...don't know how to tell Lauren." Richard swallowed. Vanessa had always hated how much his Adam's apple stuck out. He didn't have a sexy throat like Emma. "Can we do it together?"

"I'll give you two space to talk. I want no part in it. You're leaving, Richard. You can deal with it yourself. I'll pick up the pieces later."

And then the front door opened. It was Lauren.

"You two home on time for dinner?" Lauren grinned as she appeared in the doorway to the kitchen. "This doesn't happen often. Good to have you here, Dad."

"Could uh..." Richard exhaled a shaky breath. "Could you have a seat, love? There's something I wanted to talk to you about."

"Do we have to do this now? Rob will be here in an hour, and I want to get showered."

"Lauren, sit down." Vanessa offered a slight smile. "Your dad only needs five minutes with you. I'm sure you can manage."

Lauren looked between Vanessa and Richard, a frown on her face. "Okay. What's going on?"

"We're getting divorced," Richard said, his voice wavering. "I'm collecting some things, but I'll be back to spend some time with you in the next few days. Give me your work schedule, and I'll work it out around you."

"You're...getting divorced?"

"We are."

"Why?"

Vanessa braced herself for the impact. If Richard had an issue with divulging his secret life, Vanessa would step in and tell her daughter exactly the man her father was.

"It's not working for us anymore."

Vanessa snorted, almost choking on the sip of wine she'd just taken. "A little understated, wouldn't you agree?"

"Mum, what's going on?" Lauren's eyes filled with tears. "You've been married since forever. You can't have just decided you want a divorce."

"Oh, it's your father who wants the divorce, love. And I'd appreciate it if you both remembered that." Vanessa pulled out a dining chair, easing into it. But Lauren didn't join them as Richard sat down, too. She stood with her arms folded across her chest. "Richard, say what you have to say. I've had a long day at work, and I'd like to soak in the bath."

"Dad?" Lauren quirked an eyebrow. She'd learned that technique from the best. Vanessa smirked. "Are you just going to sit there or what?"

"I've met someone else."

Lauren's features changed, anger flaring in her beautiful blue eyes. Vanessa hadn't expected it, but she felt sad for Richard. Because if Vanessa knew her own daughter, Lauren was about to disown him. "You've met someone? What does that even mean?"

"I've met someone else. It means exactly what I've just said."

"So, you've met someone, and you expect to fall in love with them when you walk out of here tonight? Like, do you even know them?" Lauren paused, standing heavier on one leg. "Because I know my own father wouldn't dream of sleeping with another woman behind my mum's back. So, I fail to understand how you've met someone when you're married to Mum."

"I...it's...complicated."

Vanessa laughed. "Show her more respect, Richard. Lauren isn't stupid."

"And Lauren is also standing right here!"

"Lauren, sweetheart..." Richard got to his feet, approaching his daughter.

Vanessa didn't know if Lauren was going to hug him or punch him in the face. It could go either way right now. She steeled herself for both possibilities.

"You know how much I love you—"

Lauren looked her father up and down, disgusted. "Have you been sleeping with someone else?"

"I...yes."

"Then back the hell up because I don't want you anywhere near me. You make me sick."

"Lauren—"

Lauren cut Richard off, instead focusing on Vanessa. Her eyes pricked with tears. "Mum, are you okay?"

"I'm fine." Vanessa offered an appreciative smile, holding out her hand. "If you want to go and do your own thing tonight, it's okay. Maybe call Rob and tell him there's been a change of plans. Go out to dinner with him instead."

"No. I'm staying here with you."

"I...need time to myself." Vanessa wasn't upset, but she did need to gather her thoughts. Perhaps have a soak in the bath and wash away this evening's events before they festered. "Rob is welcome here, but I won't join you. I'm sorry."

"See what you've done?" Lauren bellowed in Richard's direction. "Get out. I don't want to see you again. You're no father of mine."

"Lauren," Richard warned.

"No. The dad I know wouldn't do something like this. He wouldn't cheat on the woman he loves. I hate you. Just...FUCK OFF!"

Sighing, Vanessa set the empty dish in the sink, wiping her hands on a tea towel. Lauren would *always* stand by her. They were too close for any other outcome.

"Mum?"

Vanessa turned. "Yes?"

"Will you...walk me down the aisle on my wedding day?" Lauren offered a slight smile, her eyes filled with tears. "I'd love it if you would."

"Isn't that your dad's job?"

Lauren shook her head. "He lost the right when he left. I want you to be by my side. The way you always have been."

Vanessa could barely speak. Between Lauren asking her such a huge question and her feelings for Emma, she didn't know which way was up. "I'd be honoured."

"Good. You're the one I want with me on my wedding day. Not dad or his whore girlfriend."

"Now, now. We don't complain about such things," Vanessa laughed. "And I've never told you this before, but your dad and I were close to breaking point anyway. He…discovered something new before I did."

Lauren frowned. "What?"

"Life wasn't as rosy as you thought it was. And maybe it was my way of protecting you, but I don't regret it. I wouldn't change a single thing about my life with your dad."

"You hated one another?"

Vanessa cocked her head, smiling. "Not at all. I've never *hated* him. Well, until recently. We…wanted different things, I suppose. It happens."

"He still shouldn't have done what he did. It was a shitty move, Mum. Like, the worst. If Rob cheated on me, I'd cut his balls off and feed them to him for dinner."

"And that is exactly the beautiful young woman I raised." Vanessa winked. "Maybe…less ball cutting, and we'll be fine."

"No ball cutting. Got it." Lauren grinned, and then they both frowned when the doorbell rang. "Who's that? It's dinnertime."

"I don't know, my love. I can't see through walls." Vanessa placed a towel down, moving towards the kitchen door. "I'll get it. You put dinner on the table."

With the kitchen door closed over, a habit over the years, Vanessa tugged the front door open to be met with a shivering Emma. "Oh, what the hell happened to you?"

"Decided to take a walk in the rain. I ended up back here. I should go back for my car, but I have nowhere to go when I get there."

Vanessa dragged her inside, shaking her head. "Are you out of your mind? The rain has been relentless for over an hour." She peeled Emma's coat from her, throwing it to the wood floor. "Go upstairs and take a hot bath in my en-suite."

"No, it's okay. I'll be fine. I need a cuppa." Emma looked up at Vanessa, tears in her eyes. "I'm sorry. I shouldn't be here. I-I said I wouldn't, but it was the only place I knew I wouldn't be turned away."

Vanessa offered a sympathetic smile, gently cupping Emma's cheek. "I'd never turn you away. I wish you would stay here until you find what you're looking for."

Emma's bottom lip trembled. "I can't."

Vanessa took a step away from Emma when Lauren called her name. "You need to warm up. Please, take a bath. Everything you need is in there."

Emma simply nodded, trudging up the stairs. And then Lauren appeared. "What's going on?"

"It's Emma. She...got caught in the rain. She looks dreadful."

Lauren threw up her hands, scoffing. "I knew this would happen. She goes to visit family and comes home on a downer. Let me make sure she's okay, and then I'll be back down for dinner."

"I don't understand." Vanessa stopped herself from wringing her hands by retrieving Emma's sodden coat from the floor.

"Emma's family has nothing. Especially the side she keeps in touch with. Her cousin will have guilted her into lending cash, and now she's panicking about when they'll eat next."

"How awful." Vanessa felt a sadness move through her. "What can I do?"

"You can plate up another lot for Emma. She's going to need it. I'll be back down in a few, okay?"

"Go on. Do whatever you need to do. I'll be down here if you need me." Vanessa watched her daughter take the stairs two at a time. She wanted to be the one consoling Emma; she wanted to wrap her arms around her and never let her go. But she couldn't. And she wouldn't.

Just stay out of the way.

CHAPTER SEVEN

Sitting in her classroom, Vanessa rubbed at her temples. Another day over and done with. The end of the school year was approaching, the room was growing more humid as the days passed, and the kids were beginning to get rowdy. It was only natural considering the year she taught was about to leave high school, but she didn't quite appreciate their enthusiasm when they still had such important exams to sit.

She gathered the papers from her final class of the day, slipping them into her oversized messenger bag. If Vanessa could get home without sitting in a mile-long traffic queue, she would consider this day partially successful. Now she just had to manage being in the same house as one Emma Bradley.

Three days had gone by since Emma showed up soaked on her doorstep, and in that time, they hadn't seen much of one another. Vanessa could only be thankful for the fact that Lauren had convinced her best friend to stay with them. She didn't know what had been said, but she wasn't involving herself in it all.

Emma was avoiding Vanessa at all costs, and if it made life easier for her, Vanessa would step back and keep to herself. After all, it wasn't as though they could be in the same room without longing for one another. But Vanessa had come to discover that space in the house wasn't helping matters. For the last three nights, she had lay awake in bed thinking of Emma. She was close to sneaking into her room, truth be told.

She'd tried to pinpoint the exact moment she realised how much she wanted her daughter's best friend, but her mind swam with every memory they'd shared instead. Innocent memories, but a picture reel in Vanessa's head, nonetheless. And it was a beautiful place to be. If she closed her eyes, everything felt in place. Where it had always been.

But Vanessa still took full responsibility for what had emerged lately. If she hadn't opened her mouth, none of this would have happened. Poor Emma would be none the wiser. Basically, life would be better. *For her, but not you!*

"Penny for your thoughts..."

Vanessa's eyes flew open, her hand gripping the edge of the desk as her heart hammered. "Do you have to creep around, Dani?"

Dani Baldwin was a beauty. There was no doubt about that. From her tall, slim frame to her dirty blonde hair, she had the build and stance of a supermodel at London Fashion Week. A tad intimidating to Vanessa but incredibly beautiful still. Those green eyes pierced Vanessa as Dani grinned. Unfortunately, it didn't do anything for her. Now Emma's eyes...that was a different matter entirely.

"Fancy a drink when you're finished here?"

Vanessa shook her head, closing her bag. "No can do. Lauren is leaving for Australia tomorrow night."

"So?" Dani draped herself against the doorframe, her white, high-waisted pants pulling her middle in. "Lauren is a big girl."

"And my daughter...who I won't see for the next three months."

Dani rolled her eyes. "It's only one at the local. If we leave now, you'll be home in no time at all."

Vanessa considered it, but she still came back to the same conclusion. “No. But thanks for the invite.”

As she got to her feet, pushing her chair under her desk, Vanessa slung her bag over her shoulder. She wouldn’t miss carrying it around for six weeks once the summer holidays arrived. A day which was fast approaching, but one that couldn’t come soon enough.

“I’ll walk out with you,” Dani said, her soft smile inviting to anyone who wasn’t Vanessa. Which was a shame, because Vanessa was very fond of her colleague. But not in the way Dani wanted her to be. “Maybe we could arrange something for next week?” Dani chanced.

“I…yes, okay.” It would be company if nothing else. “Send me some dates, and I’ll let you know when I’m free.”

“Your daughter is buggering off to Australia tomorrow. You’re going to have plenty of time on your hands, Vee.”

Vee? Really? No, that wouldn’t work for Vanessa. “Believe it or not, I actually have a life, and it doesn’t include only being at the family home.”

“Oh, yeah?”

“Mmhmm.” Vanessa breathed a sigh of relief when she spotted her car in the distance. “Okay, well I’m up there, so I’ll see you around through the week, okay?”

Dani appeared deflated, simply nodding. “Sure.”

It hurt Vanessa to see Dani this way, but she couldn’t commit to something which didn’t feel right to her. Of course, they *could* have a no strings relationship—she guessed that was Dani’s plan—but Vanessa needed and wanted more. She was fifty; it wasn’t the time to sleep around with whoever she felt like. What she wanted…was love. “Bye, Dani.”

Emma set the table in the kitchen, smiling when an engine rumbled onto the drive. It had to be Vanessa; Lauren had been picked up this afternoon for her final few hours in work. It was nothing too heavy, collecting some belongings, but Lauren had insisted she walk home from work. Apparently, she needed the exercise. *I'm not sure how a physical education teacher needs exercise...*

She went about checking they would have everything they needed, setting wine glasses next to the cutlery. Lauren's last night here would be a positive experience, as Emma had repeatedly told herself all day. She could sit in the guest room twiddling her thumbs, or she could be down here, enjoying time with her best friend. If Vanessa happened to be around too, then so be it. Emma had mastered keeping her feelings in check. Now didn't need to be any different.

A key in the door had Emma's back straight, exhaling a shaky breath as she heard heels on the tiled hallway floor. The thud of the door closing made Emma jump ever so slightly, and she almost dropped the bottle of wine she was holding. She'd made an effort tonight, not only with dinner—neither Lauren nor Vanessa knew about it—but with her appearance too.

Lauren didn't want to go out to dinner, so this would have to be the next best thing. And spending so long away meant Emma hadn't had the chance to dress up in far too long. She wore a white wrap blouse, her tanned chest more exposed than it should be, with tight black jeans holding it in place. Emma quickly slid her heels on, clearing her throat as the kitchen door opened.

Vanessa stopped in the doorway, eyeing the dining table. "What's this?"

"I've made dinner. For Lauren's last night here."

"It smells divine," Vanessa said, not yet looking in Emma's direction. But it was a good thing. The less eye contact they made, the less likely Emma was to mentally fuck her best friend's mother. "And the table looks great—"

But then Vanessa looked directly at Emma, hesitating before she took a step closer.

Emma could only guess what Vanessa was thinking, and it would be something along the lines of *get out of my kitchen. I don't want you here.* Had this been a monumental mistake? How could Emma suddenly decide to show her face after being holed up in the spare room for days?

"Sorry." Emma cast her eyes on the floor, shaking her head. It had been foolish to think she could take over the kitchen while nobody was here. This was Vanessa's home, and Emma was merely a guest. "I wanted to do something for the two of you since you've been working."

The silence from Vanessa told Emma it was time to leave. It wasn't the reaction Emma hoped for, but what else would she have been given? A pat on the back? Perhaps a round of applause?

"I'll just..." She threw a thumb over her shoulder. "I'll let you and Lauren spend the evening together. Dinner is in the oven and will be ready in," Emma paused, squinting in the direction of the timer, "about thirty minutes. You have plenty of time to change, or whatever. Night, Mrs Middleton."

Emma cast one last glance at Vanessa. Her black pencil skirt and cream, silk blouse looked incredible on her. And the exposed collarbones...well, they hit *all* the right spots. Vanessa's ash blonde hair was styled in an immaculate beach wave, shining as the sun caught it through the front kitchen window. Emma smiled, backing up against the door at the opposite end of the kitchen. It led to the garage and the back set of stairs which stopped directly in front of the guest bedroom. "I-I'm sorry if I overstepped."

Vanessa strode across the kitchen, gripping Emma's face and pushing her against the door. Her lips claimed Emma's with a heated passion that raged through her body, her knees almost giving out as Vanessa pushed her tongue past Emma's lips. Those soft lips had an urgency Emma hadn't anticipated, but instead of remaining stunned, Emma wrapped her hands through Vanessa's hair, reciprocating every desperate swipe of the tongue, every press of Vanessa's lips.

The intensity of her grip told Emma everything; this woman wanted her. It was a moment to savour, and as one hand fell away from Emma's face, now braced against the door, Vanessa pressed her body to Emma, their breasts straining against one another. Her breath hot and heavy, Vanessa pushed her thigh between Emma's legs, whimpers falling from both their mouths. This moment was unravelling everything Emma had tried so hard to keep a hold of, but fuck, it was worth unravelling for.

"I'm home," Lauren yelled in a sing-song voice as the front door slammed shut.

They tore apart, the air thick with desire. All Emma could do was turn and leave the kitchen before Lauren caught the look in her eyes. It *would* be a giveaway. "G-great. I just need to pop upstairs. Won't be a minute." As she landed in the back hallway, Emma rested against the wall, breathing deeply. She had to regulate her heartbeat before she even considered going back into the kitchen. And then it hit her. As exhilarating as their kiss was, it couldn't happen *ever* again.

Emma swallowed. The one moment she'd dreamed about had happened...and now it was gone. Mrs Middleton had left a path of destruction in her wake, but Emma would willingly set herself up for trouble with Vanessa time and time again. She didn't possess the self-control required for this, and she didn't believe Vanessa did, either. However hard she tried, Emma would allow that moment to take place over and over again. Because it was Vanessa...and it made sense.

Well, Vanessa had made *everything* difficult. It didn't matter how good it felt, how incredible Emma's lips were, she'd destroyed everything they'd ever shared. Emma, in all of her breathtaking glory, was hard to refuse. But it wasn't Emma who had instigated anything in the kitchen. That was *all* Vanessa. Because while they couldn't be together, Vanessa couldn't wait one more second to taste the lips she'd dreamed about. She couldn't imagine a world where she never touched Emma. Vanessa wished, *prayed,* that Emma felt exactly what she had as she braced herself against the kitchen door earlier, but that knowledge would only make this harder. The passion in Emma's lips, her laboured breath…yeah, Vanessa had made things so much more difficult than they needed to be. *Fuck!*

Why couldn't life be simpler? Why couldn't Emma be someone she'd met in a bar and shared an instant connection with? Why, *for the love of God,* did Vanessa have to be attracted to her daughter's best friend?

"How's the food?" Emma asked, her eyes firmly on her plate. "I followed a recipe I found online for an Italian chicken bake with vegetables."

Lauren sighed. "It's amazing. I didn't know you could cook this well."

"Never gotten around to it. But I wanted to do something nice before you left."

Vanessa was yet to speak during dinner. Not only did she find herself speechless when she walked through the door to discover Emma dressed up, she was having a hard time forming simple words to pass the time by. But she had to do something, or Lauren would start to ask questions.

"Have you made this before?" Vanessa asked, her voice not quite there.

"No. This is my first time." Emma smiled in her direction, a light blush on her cheeks. *Oh, please don't.* Vanessa was struggling. Her body ached to press against Emma. She desperately needed more.

"Incredible."

"It's nothing. But I've been sitting around for a week since I got back, so I figured I could do something to show my appreciation. It really means a lot, you having me here."

"You know this is your home, too." Lauren placed a hand on Emma's forearm. "And when I go, you can take my bedroom. I'm hoping I won't need it when I return. I spoke to Rob earlier, and he's got a list of houses he wants us to sit down and look through together."

Emma beamed. "That's amazing. I'm so happy for you."

"I wouldn't get too excited yet. Rob and I have totally opposite tastes."

"But the fact you're even considering it together is huge," Vanessa cut in, thrilled her daughter was on the road to her happily ever after. If only the same could be said for Vanessa. "A marriage, potential house…it'll be kids next."

"You always tell me you're too young to be a grandmother." Lauren rolled her eyes playfully. "Has that suddenly changed?"

"I think it's beginning to. I'm not getting any younger, and if I don't find something to occupy my time once work is over for the summer, I'm only going to grow old here alone." Her admission devastated Vanessa. The only woman she could have dreamed of…was off the table.

"Have you tried the dating app I suggested?"

Vanessa shook her head. "It wasn't working for me."

Emma cleared her throat, placing her fork down. "Why?"

"I had some interest, but nothing caught my attention." Vanessa eyed Emma, staring as Emma took her bottom lip between her teeth.

"Maybe you're looking in the wrong place…" Emma's voice came to life, wrapped in silk.

Vanessa offered a single nod. "Maybe I am. But it doesn't matter right now. What matters is Lauren is happy and thriving." She reached out a hand, taking her daughter's. "I'm so proud of you."

"Thanks, Mum."

"And I think that is my cue to leave," Emma said, standing and pushing her chair back. "You two have a lovely night together, and I'll see you in the morning."

"No, stay." Lauren frowned. "You're a part of this family, too."

Vanessa's heart constricted when she looked up at Emma to find a sadness in her eyes. She was the cause, it was clear as day to see, but Vanessa didn't know how she could make this right. Of course, she wanted to see more of Emma. God, she wanted to lie in bed with her until the end of time, talking and holding one another, but Lauren had hit the nail on the head. Emma, in many ways, *was* a part of this family. Vanessa's pulse quickened. She'd well and truly damaged everything this evening.

"Mum, tell Emma to stay. We can all hang out together for my last night."

Vanessa cleared her throat. "Emma knows she's welcome to be a part of our night. But if she wants to let us be, she's perfectly entitled to do so." It was all Vanessa could offer. If Emma sat around with them this evening, Vanessa was going to fuck her senseless, regardless of who was around.

"I think I'm ready to call it a night. I'm still not sleeping properly." Emma eyed Vanessa once more, her jaw clenched slightly. "No idea why, though."

"Okay, well, I'm making breakfast in the morning. Be down for nine at the latest, and I'll make you those pancakes you love."

Emma leaned down and hugged Lauren. "Wouldn't miss it for the world."

CHAPTER EIGHT

This was it. The day her best friend left her alone to fend for herself.

Emma couldn't be happier for Lauren, they'd worked hard to get to where they were now, but the idea of being alone with Vanessa weighed heavy on her mind today. It didn't matter if they knew it was wrong, the pull was too hard to deny. It was only confirmed yesterday before dinner when Vanessa lunged at her, kissing away every thought she'd ever had about her lips. Because no matter how hard she strained to imagine it, it was better than every scenario she'd played out in her mind. Vanessa Middleton had ruined her for any other woman. But this morning and this afternoon…it was as though it hadn't happened. Emma felt like a stranger in her own body.

The car came to a stop outside the airport. That element of loneliness Emma had felt all morning was beginning to skyrocket. Lauren deserved every moment of her trip to Australia—she worked hard and deserved a break—but Emma was starting to wish she was back in Ghana. Away from the trouble she could potentially cause. Instead of climbing from the car, she sat quietly in the backseat of Vanessa's Audi Q8. The leather interior was pristine, like most other elements of Vanessa's life. Emma wouldn't be the one to turn it all upside down. She couldn't imagine losing the family she'd been taken in by.

It was the comment Lauren made last night during dinner which reminded Emma of how she was perceived by the Middleton's, and it was the deciding factor when she got up and left the dinner table. She couldn't sit around pretending to be a part of something so meaningful when she still had the taste of Lauren's mother on her lips. Nothing about that situation could be considered right.

"Are you not going to hug me goodbye?" Lauren spoke from the boot as she took her luggage.

Emma snapped out of her thoughts, shaking her head. "Of course. I was giving you a minute to get your shit out."

"Well, my shit is beside me so get your arse out of the car."

Emma released a breath. This wouldn't be as emotional as when she left for Ghana, but it was going to come in as a close second. She eased herself out the car, smiling. "Don't forget to text me once you're through security."

"I won't."

Emma tucked a strand of dark blonde hair behind Lauren's ear. "And when you land, don't forget to text me then, too."

"Again, I won't."

"And if you need anything, a friend on the end of the phone, I'm available all hours of the day. It doesn't matter if it's the middle of the night…I *will* answer."

"I think I'll be okay."

Emma nodded, hugging Lauren and then stepping back so Vanessa could say goodbye. "Miss you already."

Lauren smiled with tears in her eyes. "Miss you more."

Emma exhaled a breath, shoving her hands in her pockets as she rested back against Vanessa's car. She'd never been a fan of goodbyes, regardless of how long Lauren would be away for. If something happened, how was Emma supposed to be there for her best friend? *Nothing is going to happen. She's going to be with the love of her life.* Emma cast her gaze on the floor. *While you try to get yours off your mind once and for all.*

"Alright, no crying." Vanessa brushed her thumbs under Lauren's eyes, pulling her into a strong embrace. "I want you to have the best time, okay?"

"Y-yeah." Lauren's bottom lip wobbled. "And I want you to look after yourself, Mum."

"I'll be fine. I have plenty of work to keep me busy until you're home."

"Are you sure you'll be okay?"

Vanessa held Lauren's face in her hands. "I wanted the world for you. You have it now. Go and have fun with Rob."

Lauren stepped back, gripping the handle on her suitcase. Neither of them wanted to part, but Lauren needed to get herself through security. Emma pushed off the car. "*Go*. You'll miss your flight."

"I'm going, I'm going."

Emma opted for the passenger seat for travelling back, opening the door as she gave one final glance in Lauren's direction. "I'll see you soon, okay?"

"You will."

Emma ducked into the car, closing the door while Vanessa waved her daughter off. Emma was suddenly feeling a little empty inside, so Vanessa was surely beside herself. Maybe that could be the one thing they kept in common while Lauren was away. If they focused on her, everything else could take a backseat.

Vanessa cleared the emotion from her throat as she slipped into the driver's seat, gripping the wheel as she watched Lauren and her luggage vanish from sight.

"She's going to be fine." Emma offered a sympathetic hand on the shoulder, satisfied when Vanessa didn't shrug it away.

"She will be fine. But I'll miss her so much…"

"You and me both." Emma sank back into her seat, sighing as Vanessa pulled away from the drop-off point. Now she just had to manage the fifty-five minute journey back with the woman who held her heart firmly in her hands. A woman who could never be anything more.

"Since we're stuck with one another, why don't I apologise for last night?" Vanessa spoke suddenly, the hairs on the back of Emma's neck standing to attention. "I wasn't supposed to kiss you."

"Could have fooled me."

"No, I mean...I've been trying to stay out of your way. I know it's for the best, but last night, I don't know what came over me."

"Probably a mistake," Emma said, shrugging. "Since everything else feels that way lately."

"I-I wanted it to happen, if it means anything to you." Emma felt Vanessa side-glance at her, but she couldn't meet those crystal blue eyes. "And I know we agreed to keep things strictly friendly between us, but it just happened. You looked incredible last night...I couldn't keep my hands to myself."

Emma rested her head back, closing her eyes. "Please, stop talking."

"Emma..."

"No, I need you to stop talking." Emma's voice broke. She couldn't do this anymore. "You have no idea how I feel about you, do you?"

"I do. You told me if you remember."

"But I don't think you realise the severity of it all. This isn't normal, Vanessa. You can't tell me nothing can happen and then pin me up against the kitchen door. It's fucking with my head. And of all the people in the world, you're the one I don't want to fall out with."

"I'm sorry," Vanessa said, sniffling. "This wasn't ever my plan, Emma."

"What plan?"

"To fall for my daughter's best friend."

Emma snorted. "I doubt you've fallen, but I appreciate you trying to placate me."

Vanessa squeezed the wheel as they stopped at a red light. "It's happening, and I need it not to."

"Maybe if you stopped kissing me, you'd stop fucking with your own head, too."

"No more kissing. Got it."

Emma turned her head, watching the world go by outside as they drove down the motorway. Vanessa's perfume hugged her, made her feel safe, but the woman wearing it was only going to break her heart into a million pieces. And from this moment on…Emma had to prepare herself for the inevitability.

CHAPTER NINE

Vanessa stepped out of the shower, wrapping herself up in a fluffy robe. She'd spoken to Lauren on a few occasions since she landed in Australia, but Vanessa felt lost. Nothing seemed right. Emma came and went with minimal conversation; they didn't even share dinner with one another. Of course, when Lauren called, Vanessa lied and told her she was watching TV with Emma. *If only it were true.*

She turned off the lamp, lighting a few candles on the nightstand before climbing into bed. Vanessa had never felt so tense, her entire body in desperate need of a massage. Perhaps it was time to call her regular masseuse; she hadn't spent time on herself in quite a while. Work always got in the way, but Vanessa knew she had to slow down and take care of herself. Nobody else was going to do it for her.

Her phone vibrated on the nightstand. She was surprised to find Richard's name on the screen. "Hello?"

"Hi, Vanessa. How are you?"

"Great," she lied. "You?"

"Oh, you know. Work and no play."

Vanessa snorted. "I find that hard to believe. Isn't the secretary keeping things spicy for you?"

"I haven't called to discuss my sex life."

"Thank God." Vanessa paused. "Anyway, what can I do for you?"

"I left a few suits at the house. Could I collect them? I have a business trip in a week or so. I'm sorry, I didn't realise I hadn't brought them with me."

"Oh, those suits?" Vanessa winced. "I assumed you didn't need them anymore. I gave them to the local charity shop."

Richard exhaled a heavy breath. "Do you have any idea how much they cost me?"

Vanessa had been close to burning them at one point.

"They can't have been important to you if you left them. Or did you leave them on purpose so you could come back here and hope to find me a wreck on the floor?"

"N-no. Not at all. I want you to be happy, and you have to admit, we weren't happy."

"I'd have had no qualms with you walking away because we were unhappy, but to do what you did to me…I deserved better. We have a daughter together. We lived a life with one another. Was I really making you so unhappy you had to find love in someone else before you could admit we were falling out of love?" Vanessa paused. "I suppose it's my own fault for staying the first *and* second time it happened."

"I never wanted to hurt you, Ness."

"Well, you did." Vanessa chewed her lip. This was the first time Richard had owned up to his misgivings. It was the first time she'd heard sincerity in his voice since the end. "But you've moved on, and now I'm doing the same."

"You've met someone?"

"Sort of. I think…I don't know." Vanessa could just about recall what day it was. Her head was well and truly up her arse.

Richard cleared his throat. "Who is he?"

"It's actually a she." Vanessa waited for the laugh, but it never came. "But it's not going to work out. Too many obstacles."

"What kind of obstacles?" Richard asked, his voice honest and genuinely interested. "Surely it's nothing you have to work yourself up about."

"She's a friend…a family friend." It wasn't quite the truth, but Vanessa couldn't confide in her ex-husband. She'd like to think Richard could one day be a friend, but Vanessa still harboured too much anger towards him right now. Besides, she couldn't be sure he wouldn't call Lauren and tell her. "Never mind. It's nothing."

"Which family friend?"

"Oh, I shouldn't say. You don't need to know."

"Well, if you've found someone…I think you'd be a fool to turn it down. We may have ended, but I still care about you. You were my wife for thirty years."

"Lauren wouldn't understand."

"Lauren?"

"You know, me falling in love with a woman. It would knock her for six." Vanessa knew that wasn't the problem here. Lauren wouldn't have an issue with her mum being bisexual, but it was who she chose which would cause ructions. Major ones. "She'd be completely confused."

"Lauren is the most open person I know. Her best friend is a lesbian."

"Yeah, I know." Vanessa internally chastised herself. She'd just given herself away with the tone of her voice. She knew it.

"Vanessa."

"Yeah?" She chirped up. "I'm still here."

"Is…Emma back from Ghana?" Richard asked. "I haven't spoken to Lauren, she won't answer my calls, so I don't know what's going on lately."

She chose to bypass the question regarding Emma. "Well, Lauren landed in Australia six days ago…"

"Damn it. I didn't know. I should have known."

"And you shouldn't have broken her mother's heart and then we wouldn't be having this conversation."

Richard fell silent. Had he finally realised the hurt he'd caused?

"You may have been getting your kicks elsewhere, and that's fine by me, but you forgot about Lauren in all of this, didn't you? While you were spanking your secretary, you didn't stop to think about how it would affect our daughter." Vanessa kept her tone even. She wouldn't give Richard the satisfaction of knowing she was still angry, perhaps slightly hurt. "I think she needs time to settle down. She'll come around to the idea of speaking to you again when she's good and ready."

Vanessa didn't know why Richard's affair hurt so much. Perhaps it wasn't hurt, but jealousy instead. Because while Richard was happy, Vanessa was miserable and wishing for something that couldn't be. Surely after his behaviour, he deserved happiness less than she did.

"Look, we're getting off track here."

Ah. The good old response from Richard when he knew he was wrong.

"If you're sleeping with Lauren's best friend, you should be upfront with her about it. Both of you. I love Emma like a daughter, but if Lauren is kept in the dark, it will ruin everything."

"Don't be bloody ridiculous. I'm not sleeping with Emma." Vanessa wanted to add *yet* onto the end of that sentence, but she couldn't get her head to match up with her heart. While she fantasised about everything they could have, she knew how wrong it would be. "You're out of your mind."

"Oh, I think it's you who is out of their mind, sweetheart. I saw how you used to look at Emma. I'm not soft. But this would kill Lauren if you don't tell her."

"I'm going now, Richard. You have no right to a say on my life anymore. That ended when you fucked the pretty blonde who used to bend over your fucking office desk!"

Vanessa ended the call, frustrated as she dropped her phone and pressed the heels of her hands into her eyes. Why did she have to fall for someone forbidden? Vanessa should be content with her life as it was, but it was hard to feel that way when she longed to be with Emma.

Emma. The only one to ever look at Vanessa as though she had a purpose in life. The only one to kiss her like the world was blazing around them.

She needed to release the tension building inside her.

As she got to her knees, removing her robe, Vanessa settled back on the mattress, running her hand down her stomach. Alone time...was exactly what she needed. Though she couldn't touch Emma, she could certainly think about her and all the ways she wanted to make her scream.

Because if Vanessa ever got her way, she would take Emma to an entirely different planet.

Emma quietly turned the key in the lock. She'd returned later than she thought she would—Emma had spent the last several days catching up with friends—but she was an expert when it came to stealth mode. She didn't want to wake Vanessa; she had work to get to tomorrow. She also wouldn't be one of those house guests who rocked up all hours of the night. She had more respect. Especially for the Middleton family.

As she gently pushed the door shut, bolting it, Emma crept up the stairs. The house was in darkness, not a flicker of a light anywhere, but that was the beauty of living out of town. It meant no streetlights to disturb your sleep. Or neighbours. Emma couldn't ask for anything more.

And then the reality settled in. She desperately needed to find a place to live. Lauren had only been gone for six days, and Emma already felt herself beginning to struggle. It was easier if the transition started sooner rather than later. Vanessa needed her own space, and Emma needed a reality check.

She had a meeting next week at her old high school for a position in the physical education department, and provided she didn't cock up the interview, Emma knew she had it in the bag. But the panic of preparing could wait until tomorrow. Right now, her body craved sleep.

When Emma's foot hit the top step, her body immediately froze at the sound coming from down the hallway. Mrs Middleton...had company? Her body's immediate reaction was to curl up and sob until her heart felt empty, but Emma noted that the bedroom door was cracked open slightly. She shouldn't move towards it, should she?

A low, throaty moan had wetness gathering between her thighs. Fuck, those moans were incredibly arousing. Surely, someone else had to be causing them. Nobody was *that* vocal when they were alone.

Emma took a hesitant step forward, the door within reach. If she tapped it, it would open. But if she turned around and minded her own business, everything would stay the same. Sometimes that was best for everyone. Emma made the respectful decision to head for her own room. She would kick herself tomorrow, but Vanessa was only doing what Emma should be. A little self-care.

"F-fuck, Emma."

Emma froze again. She surely hadn't heard right. Had she? God, she wished she hadn't heard it at all, because now she was stepping painfully close to the bedroom door that didn't belong to her, light gasps filtering out into the hallway.

With the tip of her finger, she pushed the door ever so slightly. There Vanessa was, the side of her face buried in her pillow and turned towards the door, backside up in the air, hand between her legs. And her body was a thing of absolute beauty. The holidays while they lay around wearing bikinis didn't compare to a completely naked Vanessa, only the moonlight shining down and silhouetting such impeccable skin. *Holy fuck!* Emma's body shuddered. If she moved, she was likely to come. If only Emma could see those incredible eyes...

Vanessa released a frustrated moan, her free hand fisting in the pillow beside her. "God, I want you to fuck me..."

Emma's mouth fell open, disbelief overpowering her arousal momentarily. Did Vanessa know she was in the room or was this all pure, unadulterated fantasy? It didn't matter what it was, it was fucking hot! One step closer, and Emma could be doing the one thing she'd dreamt about. Touching Vanessa.

I shouldn't...

But Emma couldn't hold back.

She got to her knees beside the bed, gently brushing Vanessa's hair from her face. "You are the most beautiful woman in the world." Emma stroked her fingertips down Vanessa's spine and over the curve of her arse. Her skin was the softest Emma had ever touched. But it was the lack of shock from Vanessa that Emma focused on as those pretty blue eyes opened. "Tell me what you need."

Vanessa's eyes filled with tears. They slipped to the pillow as her lips parted. Emma dragged her nails up the back of Vanessa's thigh, pleased when she received a gasp. "M-more," Vanessa whispered, her voice barely audible. "D-don't leave."

Emma placed her hand to the inside of Vanessa's thigh, overcome with the need to feel this woman. All of her. Vanessa moaned when Emma brushed the back of her hand against her sex, dripping...Emma needed more, too.

"Y-yes." Vanessa forced herself back against Emma's hand, her entire body shaking. "Please."

Emma gathered unimaginable wetness on her fingertips, sinking into Vanessa from behind. She'd dreamt of this moment from day one, she'd fantasised about touching her best friend's mother for so long, but *nothing* could have prepared her for this moment.

The bed creaked as Emma pushed in and out, harder with each thrust, the whimpers and moans too much for her to take any longer. She slipped her free hand into her jeans, met with her own soaked underwear. She didn't once take her eyes off Vanessa's. This, she could do. Because if Vanessa didn't touch her, Emma could never crave more. She would never know what she was missing. If Vanessa's hands didn't reach her skin, Emma could walk away tonight and never look back.

As Emma's fingers connected with her sensitive clit, her mouth fell open. Vanessa was freely fucking her fingers, and God, it felt good. Too good. Vanessa's walls squeezed Emma's fingers, her orgasm evidently roaring towards its peak.

Emma leaned forward, lowering her mouth to Vanessa's ear. She ran the tip of her tongue along the shell, placing a gentle kiss to Vanessa's neck as she whispered, "Come for me, Mrs Middleton."

A strangled cry erupted from Vanessa's throat, her hand tightening in the pillow. Tears fell freely from her eyes; Emma's own were working their way to the surface as she came undone in front of Vanessa. As intense as this moment was, it was also devastating. This was the end of the line for Emma.

The kiss last week had tipped things, but this one act had destroyed everything. Still, she found herself fucking Vanessa regardless. Emma would never see the inside of this home again after tonight, but she could leave knowing she'd accomplished one of the greatest things in life. An intimate moment with Vanessa Middleton.

Emma coaxed the last of Vanessa's orgasm from her, her fingers forced out by Vanessa's throbbing walls as her lower half collapsed onto the bed. And then the realisation of what had happened sunk in. Emma had fucked her best friend's mum.

Vanessa lay breathless, her eyes firmly on Emma. Neither said a word for several moments, only the ever-present longing between them. And then Vanessa squeezed her eyes shut. "E-Emma."

"Don't say anything." Emma choked back a sob, her world slowing as Vanessa stared back at her. "You are *everything* I could ever want, but it's time to let you go." She brushed Vanessa's hair from the side of her face. "You deserve more than this. A secret. You deserve the most intense love with someone who won't complicate life for you."

Vanessa's tears continued to slip down her face.

"I love you," Emma whispered, pressing her lips to Vanessa's temple. "But I'll go. Y-you won't have to see me again."

Before Vanessa could respond, Emma fell out of the door, her face stained with tears.

It was time to leave.

Perhaps a new city was a good place to start.

CHAPTER TEN

This was the only place Emma had ever wanted to be. It was the one thing that kept her grounded and feeling loved. Her family didn't matter, the past had no bearing on who she was now, and when she was inside Vanessa's home, everything came full circle. It always had. But as Emma sat outside the Middleton residence this evening, a week on from making the biggest mistake of her life, she no longer felt whole, complete.

Everything was hollow.

Vanessa's car sat on the path beside Lauren's, the lights up the drive shone as they always had, but being here felt alien to Emma. The manicured shrubs which ran along the edge of the Indian stone driveway would lead Emma to Vanessa, but she couldn't climb from her car. Instead, she sat quietly, exhaustion creeping through her as she struggled to keep her eyes open.

Emma glanced into the back seat where a few blankets sat folded. For a week now, they had kept her warm while she slept in her car, finding a new layby she could park up in each night. Yeah, this was her life now. She'd gone from spending the most amazing eighteen months in Africa to being back home and sleeping in her car. Pathetic was all she had to describe the direction her life was taking.

As she focused her eyes back to front of Vanessa's home, a light lit up the front bedroom. The one Emma had fled from last week. She could just about make out Vanessa between the gaps in the open blinds, but even that didn't feel as good as it once had. Because every waking moment since *the* night, Emma could *only* feel Vanessa. Her every sense was consumed by the woman she'd so freely taken last week without any regard for the consequences.

When Vanessa looked into her eyes, desire coursing through her, Emma couldn't do anything other than give in. Because Vanessa was Vanessa. She was the only woman in the world to ever make Emma feel this way. And it was powerful. Far too powerful for Emma to deal with. But did Vanessa know? Was she waiting for the moment when Emma would be at her weakest so she could pounce? Emma knew that wasn't fair to Vanessa, but she was angry. At herself, at the woman who'd called out her name during a lust filled haze of masturbation, and at the world for ever introducing them to one another. As much as Emma had loved creating every memory she had with Vanessa and Lauren, the pain she now felt wasn't worth all those years of happiness… and longing. Emma wasn't sure anything would ever be worth the turmoil she felt.

She pressed her forehead to the steering wheel. The urge to cry wasn't convenient right now. And what was she crying for? She'd brought this all on herself when she made that call to Vanessa. She'd continued to create problems for herself by agreeing to stay with Lauren until she found a place to live, and she'd put the final nail in the coffin when she didn't push Vanessa away during their kiss. Emma knew she should have. She'd gone over every possible consequence in her head for too many years. But the selfish side of Emma pulled her deeper into Vanessa's world, and now there was no going back to her life before.

Emma lifted her head, exhaling a deep breath. She didn't know why she'd chosen to drive here this evening; it wasn't as though she had any intentions of knocking on the door. She thought she would, bravery was on the agenda today, but she'd sat in this very spot for over an hour…unable to move. She felt paralysed whenever she imagined Vanessa opening the door to her. Maybe it was the idea of saying goodbye, perhaps it was the thought that maybe Vanessa would refuse to let her go. Whatever it was, the fear continued to rise inside Emma. Each breath she took seemed tighter, every flicker of her eyelids heavier.

She knew what she had to do.

She had to start her car and pull away.

Turning the key in the ignition was the easy part. It was removing the handbrake and applying her foot to the accelerator which seemed to be the issue. Taking a few breaths, Emma closed her eyes and cleared her mind. This wasn't healthy. It would never be simple, and she couldn't put herself through it any longer.

When Emma opened her eyes, her chest tightened.

Vanessa was standing at the end of the driveway, her hands shoved in the pockets of her black high-waisted pants, the sleeves of her white shirt rolled up just below her elbows. *God, she always looks remarkable.* Emma's bottom lip quivered as Vanessa offered a soft smile and lifted one hand to wave. "Please, go inside," she muttered to herself. "Before I get out this car and do something fucking stupid again."

Emma gripped the steering wheel, her knuckles white. As much as she knew driving away was the right thing to do, she remained rooted to the spot…staring. At Vanessa. Through Vanessa. Every thought, every smell, it was all Vanessa. It always had been.

Vanessa took a step closer, her ash blonde hair bouncing around her shoulders, and motioned for Emma to lower the window. Emma considered it for a moment, but she couldn't do it. Instead of giving in to what Vanessa wanted, she released the handbrake, turned the wheel, and drove off towards another layby for a night of sleeping on the backseat of her car.

And then she looked in the rear-view mirror, tears brimming in her eyes. Vanessa stood in the middle of the road, bent forward with her hands braced on her knees, her shoulders shaking. If there was one thing she could say with absolute certainty right now, it was the fact that Emma had well and truly destroyed not only her life but the greatest relationships with the most wonderful people to ever give a shit about her.

Well done. Seems you always were a waste of space after all...

CHAPTER ELEVEN

Vanessa rushed across the street, the rain catching the back of her coat as it fell heavier. Her students were in their final exam, Vanessa was close to her breaking point, but coffee would fix everything. Wouldn't it? Coffee, lately, was her only friend. *God, how depressing.* But Vanessa wouldn't complain. There were people out there who had much worse days than she was having.

She placed her usual coffee order, a blueberry muffin on the side, and took a seat. The barista would bring it to her when it was ready, and honestly, she needed to take a seat. She needed more than a seat, but it was the only thing on offer at the moment.

Emma had...vanished. There wasn't a single method of contact from her since she rushed from Vanessa's home two weeks ago, only the brief sighting of her outside the house last week putting a stop to any fear Vanessa had about Emma being hurt. But could she blame Emma for not calling or answering a text message? For driving away last week? No, she couldn't. In a moment of completely unbridled passion, Vanessa had caved. It was one thing to know your daughter's best friend had caught you masturbating, but to finish the job for you…well, that was something else altogether.

Vanessa knew she should have gone after Emma, but the pain in her voice on top of what they'd shared had been overwhelming. Vanessa hadn't wanted Emma to leave, she wanted to spend the night with her, but Vanessa found herself in a place she'd never been. She couldn't comprehend what had happened.

"Come for me, Mrs Middleton…"

Vanessa shuddered. For two weeks, those words played over in her mind. If Emma stood in front of her right now and demanded the very same thing, Vanessa would drop her pants and take anything Emma gave her. Because that moment, the second Emma slid her fingers inside her, God…it had been one of the greatest moments of her life.

Only in Vanessa's wildest dreams could she imagine Emma taking control of her, demanding something so intimate. And only for Emma would Vanessa ever give in to such a demand. Just the mere thought of Emma's hands between her legs, her breath washing over her ear, it had Vanessa's body fired up.

"Your coffee, Vanessa." Carl, the barista, offered her a smile as he set down her cup. "And as always, the blueberry muffin. Last one, too."

"Thank you, Carl." Vanessa couldn't make full eye contact. She was too busy thinking about fucking her daughter's best friend. Carl didn't need to see the look in her eyes. Nobody did. "I'll take another to go when I'm done here."

"Whatever you want, Mrs M."

Carl had once been a student of Vanessa's, leaving school and setting up his own bistro once he was able to. And now, because of the hard work he'd put into his business studies, he had a thriving coffee shop to add to his list and was well thought of in the community. "Say hi to your brothers for me, won't you?"

"Sure will."

Carl left the table. Vanessa was once again only keeping

herself company. It was commonplace lately, but Vanessa only had herself to blame. If she'd shown Emma a hint of how much she wanted her to stay, this day could have been entirely different. The last two weeks wouldn't have happened.

Vanessa wanted Emma. There were no two ways about it.

Even Lauren wasn't deterring her thoughts anymore. They were worrying about something which may not even produce the expected results. For all they knew, Lauren may be perfectly fine with her mother and best friend being in a relationship.

But then Vanessa realised Emma wasn't to be. If she was, Vanessa wouldn't be sitting here alone, going out of her mind, wishing for contact. She had fulfilled one of Vanessa's greatest fantasies, and then she was gone. Her bags and all. The house was deserted, along with Vanessa's heart.

No longer able to stomach her blueberry muffin, Vanessa pushed it away and sighed. She hadn't eaten much at all since that night two weeks ago. Nothing she chose was satisfying enough.

Vanessa got to her feet, taking her coffee with her. "Hey, Carl. Can I have this in a takeout cup?"

"Sure, Mrs M. I'll get right on it for you."

"Thanks."

Vanessa stood at the end of the counter, glancing around while she waited on her coffee to go. But then her heart fell directly into her stomach at lightning speed. Sitting in the window of the coffee shop, perusing a menu, was Emma. Vanessa's first reaction was to rush over there, but then she decided to hold her position at the counter.

Vanessa thought hard about her next move. The last thing she wanted was to cause a scene in her local coffee shop. Least of all in front of an ex-student. She turned when Carl cleared his throat. "You see the woman in the window?"

Carl smiled. "Emma Bradley."

"You know her?"

"She used to date my sister. A long time ago now, but she was actually at my mum's a few nights ago," Carl explained. "I think, and I don't want to get my hopes up, maybe they could get back together."

Vanessa bristled. The thought of Emma with another woman…*no!* "Well, that was information I didn't ask for…"

"Sorry." Carl held up a hand. "I'm very fond of Emma. She was good for my sister. Really good."

"Anyway." Vanessa reached into her purse and pulled out a twenty. She didn't need Carl to put *those* thoughts in her head. It was messed up enough. "This should cover anything she orders. Bye, Carl."

Vanessa moved away from the counter, her step faltering slightly. Emma looked tired and worn, her usual long black hair dragged up atop her head in a messy bun. Honestly, it was hard to witness. Especially when Vanessa knew she was the cause of Emma's anguish. But if it mattered at all, she felt the same way.

As she approached the door, Vanessa thought about getting out as quickly as she could. But when she side-glanced in Emma's direction, she found dejected eyes staring back at her.

Oh, please don't look at me like that. She couldn't bear it.

"H-hi," Vanessa said, aware the coffee shop was filled with people. "I didn't expect to see you here."

Emma smiled weakly, lowering her eyes back to the menu.

"How are you? I haven't seen you in a while." What the hell kind of question was that? The last time she'd been in the same room as Emma, the poor girl was fingers deep inside Vanessa. "I mean, are you okay?"

Emma looked up briefly, unable to hold Vanessa's eyes. She nodded and looked away. "Fine. Thanks."

"Good, that's…good." Vanessa was turning into a mess. For every second she stood in front of Emma, she wanted to drag her out of the coffee shop and directly into her car. This was about to go down like a lead balloon, but Vanessa thought it best to say, "I think we should talk, Emma."

Emma's bottom lip trembled as she focused on the high street outside the window. "I have nothing to say, Mrs Middleton."

Her voice, the way Emma said her name, it took Vanessa straight back to the bedroom. She closed her eyes briefly, exhaling a calming breath. "But I have things I'd like to say to you."

"Then you can say them here."

Vanessa cocked her head, smiling. "I don't think it's appropriate, do you?"

"Have you spoken to Lauren lately?"

She's deflecting. I need more.

"I have, yes. Rob has this week off work so they're doing some tourist things. It sounds like she's having a wonderful time."

"Nice."

"Has she called you?" Vanessa asked, pulling out a chair and sitting directly opposite Emma. "She said she was planning to…"

"She has, but I've been unable to answer. Busy, you know." Emma shrugged.

Vanessa reached a hand across the table, taking the menu from Emma. "Please, can we go somewhere private to talk?"

Emma focused on her fully for the first time, tears streaming down her cheeks. "Why didn't you stop me?"

Vanessa swallowed. It was a perfectly acceptable question. But she didn't want to talk about this here. They needed privacy and time to discuss things. A coffee shop was never the place to talk about such intimacy. Vanessa leaned in, her voice low. "Because I didn't want you to stop."

Emma squeezed her eyes shut, shaking her head. "And I didn't want to spend these last two weeks desperate to call you and holding back, but I did. It's called self-control, Vanessa."

Vanessa ran a hand through her hair. "Well, it seems I lose all self-control when I'm with you, Emma. But you can't lay the blame solely on me. You willingly came into my room."

"It's hard to stop yourself when the woman you're in love

with is fucking herself and calling out your name." Emma got to her feet, her chair screeching against the tiled floor. "I can't do this. I can't be around you, trying to justify my reasons while you think it's nothing."

Vanessa watched Emma leave. Suddenly invigorated by her speech, she rushed out of the coffee shop behind Emma, gripping her wrist and pulling her into an alleyway. "You've no idea how I feel." She pushed against Emma, pinning her to the wall. For every second she was in Emma's company, Vanessa craved more. And in such close proximity, she yearned for Emma's touch. Her lips. Just…Emma. "You think this is all one-sided, and I'm out to find someone to prey on, but it's not like that. I see how you look at me; I feel your stare when I'm in the same room as you. And you know what? Nobody has ever made me feel this way before. You, Emma Bradley, have stolen my heart."

"Then have it back. I don't want it." Emma pushed forward, unsuccessfully. "Vanessa, please."

"Come home with me right now, and we'll talk."

"About what? How we can't do this. It's the same old thing, and I'm tired of hearing it."

"I actually wanted to talk to you about working through this." Vanessa dipped her head, her bottom lip brushing Emma's. "Because as wrong as this feels, I can't stop thinking about you. I can't get the thought of you out of my head."

But Emma turned her face away from Vanessa, shattering any hopes she had of fixing this. "We can't do this."

"Why should we deny each other because it may hurt someone's feelings?"

"Because it's your daughter's feelings, Vanessa. I don't give a fuck about anybody else, but Lauren is going to hate me when she finds out about this."

"Please…come with me?" Vanessa asked, her forehead pressed to Emma's. "I only want to talk to you."

"You and I both know talking is the last thing on the agenda when we're alone. And as much as I want to work through stuff... I'm at the end of my resolve. I don't think it's a good idea. I want it to be, God...I really do, Vanessa. It's just—"

"So, let's be adults and discuss this. As we should have in the beginning."

Emma hesitated, but then nodded, sending Vanessa's heart rate soaring.

"Thank you."

CHAPTER TWELVE

Emma blew out a bracing breath as Vanessa turned the key in the lock. She'd spent too long thinking about knocking on this door and begging Vanessa to give them a chance, but Emma knew better than to hope for something she couldn't possibly have. While giving Vanessa exactly what she wanted that night in the bedroom had been incredibly fulfilling for Emma, it had been a mistake.

She couldn't sleep. She couldn't eat. And she couldn't face hearing her best friend's voice on the phone. Everything was far too complicated now that she'd given in, and Vanessa had to know it, too. If she was at least the tiniest bit hopeful, she would have called Emma and demanded to see her before now. If Vanessa had one ounce of decency, she would have chased after Emma that night.

But she hadn't. As Emma had suspected.

"Sit down. I'll put the kettle on." Vanessa moved into the kitchen. Emma chose to follow her. "Go through to the living room."

"I'm fine here." Emma took a seat at the dining table, her eyes focused on the light pouring in from the bi-folding doors at the back of the house. She'd missed it here; this house would always commandeer a huge space in her heart. It was a shame things had escalated. "How's work?"

"Almost over for the summer."

"Any plans?" Emma lifted her leg, resting her ankle on her knee as she sat back. "Holiday?"

"No. Nothing this year. With Lauren going away, I thought I'd spend time at home instead."

"Fair enough."

"Tea or coffee?" Vanessa glanced in Emma's direction, her eyes bright. Too bright. Enough to tip Emma over the edge in all honesty.

"Whatever you're making."

"Okay, look." Vanessa braced her hands against the counter, sighing. "I know you hate me, and it's perfectly understandable, but I can't talk to you if you're going to give me short, pointless answers."

"Vanessa, I don't know what you want me to say. Whatever we decide today, it's not going to end on a good note, is it?"

"I...don't know."

"Yes, you do. So me being here is a waste of time. More so for you. You're the one who has a busy life, not me."

"Any luck with a job yet?" Vanessa asked, dousing the flames of anger within Emma.

"Yeah. September start for me. At Bellfield Comprehensive."

"You got the job? That's amazing." Vanessa hesitated as she rounded the counter, frowning slightly. "Can I give you a hug to congratulate you?"

Emma hesitantly got to her feet, smiling as Vanessa opened her arms. Their embrace was soft, nothing too untoward, but Emma's body responded regardless. As she tried to pull away, Vanessa held her. "Vanessa, I—"

"Please let me hold you." Vanessa nuzzled into the crook of Emma's neck, inhaling deeply. It felt good to be wanted by a woman like Vanessa, but Emma couldn't put herself through the turmoil anymore. It was too painful. "I've missed you." Her fingers stroked the back of Emma's neck, sending a shiver down her spine. "And I don't know how we fix this, but I need to try."

"You have to know I want every second with you, Vanessa. But you and I both know it's going to complicate things."

Vanessa pulled back, her hand wrapping around the back of Emma's neck. She pulled their foreheads together, Vanessa's eyes fluttering closed. "Lauren isn't here right now. Can we not try?"

"Try what?" Emma had fucked Vanessa already. In terms of trying, they were way past the point.

"To see if we're truly compatible and it's not lust we're giving into?"

"Trust me, it's not lust on my part." Lust had never been in mind for Emma. When it came to touching Vanessa, it was far more than anything she could make sense of.

Vanessa blushed. "Nor mine. But I think it would be sensible to at least…explore."

Emma quirked an eyebrow. Where was Vanessa going with this? "Explore?"

"Mmhmm." Vanessa took her lip between her teeth, glancing down at the exposed skin of Emma's chest. She'd caught Vanessa eyeing her up over the years when she left a few buttons open, and when a woman like Vanessa was looking at you? It was one huge ego boost. "I can't stop thinking about you, Emma."

"I have one particular image that's burned into my memory for the rest of my life." Emma knew exactly how Vanessa was feeling. It had been one hell of an experience for them both. And as hard as Emma tried to push this woman from her mind, she couldn't. Just one look was enough to repeatedly hammer down the walls she was unsuccessfully building around her heart.

"Yeah?" Vanessa slowly trailed her fingertip up the middle of Emma's throat, drawing a light gasp. "What image would that be?"

Feeling bold, Emma gripped Vanessa and dragged her back towards the dining table. Perched on the edge, Vanessa came to rest between her legs. "You, naked, and so fucking beautiful on your bed. Begging me to fuck you."

"When you touched me," Vanessa paused, taking the hair tie from Emma's hair, her tresses cascading down her shoulders. "I've never felt a touch quite like it. It was raw, passionate, but soft." She fisted her hand in Emma's long locks, tilting her head back and kissing her way up Emma's throat. "And when you demanded that I come for you... God, you're a fucking dream come true."

"Vanessa?" Emma swallowed, placing a gentle hand to her chest. "C-can we talk?"

Vanessa pressed a soft kiss to Emma's lips. "If you promise to at least consider the possibility of us, then yes. I'd love to talk."

Emma settled against Vanessa, her shoulders no longer tense. "I promise."

"Unless you don't care for the possibility..."

Emma craned her neck, capturing Vanessa's mouth. "You know I do.

Vanessa wrung her hands in her lap as she watched Emma take a seat on the opposite end of the couch. In an ideal world, they'd be sitting side by side, but Vanessa understood Emma's reservations. They were the same as her own, but she was trying not to think about them. What would that achieve? Nothing more than a broken heart.

Vanessa eyed Emma, but she couldn't read her. She seemed distant, cautious, but Vanessa needed to get it all out before Emma walked out the door again. "So, I..." Vanessa calmed herself, taking a long slow breath. "I wanted to say thank you for coming back here with me today."

Emma wore a shy smile, her eyes not quite holding Vanessa's.

"And I should have asked you to stay last time, but—"

"Look," Emma interjected, scrubbing a hand down her face as she sat forward in her seat. "This is a mess. The biggest. And I know I'm not the person you saw yourself getting involved with, so I can leave and—."

"That's not what I want." Vanessa knew with one hundred percent certainty that Emma leaving was the last thing on her mind. "And I don't know where we go from here, but I'm not willing to lose you, Emma."

"I wish I could tell you I'm worth the hassle, but I'm not."

Vanessa's forehead creased. Why did Emma suddenly think so little of herself? This wasn't the woman she'd spent years attracted to. "I know that's not true."

"I actually think it is true. And I know if this goes further, you'll discover it yourself and then resent me for encouraging you to seek more with me. So, I think it's easier if we don't do this. I don't want you to lose your friends or family because of me, Vanessa. And I think it's exactly what could happen."

"Is this all because of Lauren?"

Emma shoulders sagged. "Of course it is. I don't particularly care for anyone else's opinion. But Lauren is going to be devastated when she finds out."

"How can you be so sure?" Vanessa was genuinely intrigued. In reality, neither of them knew the outcome. Lauren could be thrilled for all they knew. "I mean, has Lauren ever given you the impression that she'd hit the roof?"

"No. But that doesn't mean she wouldn't."

"And it doesn't mean she would, either." Vanessa took her chance, shifting closer to Emma. Once she was within arm's reach, she rested a hand on Emma's thigh and sighed. "I don't want to get to the end of this year only to discover I lost you. And I don't want to always wonder what if. We both know this is far more than what we're making of it. Unless I'm seeing and feeling things which are not there." Vanessa swallowed. Was that what was happening? Surely not. Emma had been more than forward with her own feelings. "But I don't think that's true. I think you want this as much as me."

"It's...more."

"More?"

Emma smiled faintly. "I want you more. I always have. And I need to figure this all out in my head because it's driving me to distraction."

Vanessa's body thrummed with a nervous energy. When Emma was open and honest, it was one of the hottest things Vanessa had ever experienced. "So, why are we sitting here like this? Why aren't we dating?"

"Because...Lauren."

It always came back to Lauren. And for the first time, truly, Vanessa wasn't accepting it as an excuse. "Okay, so, if Lauren wasn't in the picture?"

"I'd be waking up in your arms," Emma said, her voice barely audible. "I'd be cooking dinner for you. And taking you to the cinema. And walking around town with my hand in yours. I'd be doing so much more than this, sitting on your couch, terrified to touch you."

Vanessa's heart fluttered. Why couldn't they do those things? "I'd love to be doing that stuff with you. The simple things, you know?"

"I do know. I've thought about it all since the day I realised I was in love with you. He never gave you any of that. I mean, you've spent the entire time I've known you dressed immaculately. Hair done, makeup pristine, a particular look about you. Now don't get me wrong, I love all of it, but you never seem relaxed. You never look as though you're truly enjoying life."

"Because I'm not," Vanessa confessed. "Not until recently, anyway."

"What changed?" Emma asked, her voice shaking.

"You coming home." It was all the truth. From the moment Vanessa stepped inside her home after Emma arrived, she knew everything would change. The dynamic of their relationship being the biggest. "Because even though I knew I shouldn't want you, how I thought it wouldn't be right, you were the one I lay in bed thinking about. Even when Richard and I were still together, I thought about you."

Emma's eyes brightened with Vanessa's admission, a tinge of blue colouring them so beautifully.

"And I know we have to figure things out with Lauren, but is it worth refusing one another when it's what we want?"

"I…don't know."

"I know you want to do the right thing, Emma. But what *is* the right thing?"

Emma laughed. "I don't know that either."

"And neither do I. No one does…ever. But isn't it worth going for it and hoping for a perfect result in the end? Because that's how it feels to me. I feel as though it's all going to come together in the end."

"And when your daughter disapproves? Potentially disowns the both of us?"

Vanessa's stomach lurched at the prospect. "I haven't thought that far ahead. But I'm sure it won't come to that. She's going to be surprised, perhaps shocked, but if she wants me to be happy like she claims she does, then she'll understand."

Emma shifted closer, turning her body to face Vanessa fully. And then their hands found their way to one another's, fitting as though they were meant to be. "I've spent so long praying you could be mine to the point where it seems impossible."

"I know how you feel."

"But you're right. Nobody knows what the future holds. Lauren could jump with joy. I doubt it, but it's a possibility."

"It is a possibility."

Emma cleared her throat. "And if it doesn't happen? What then?"

"I don't know. But I'm not going to let you go because my daughter doesn't like it. So, if that's what you're worried about, please don't be."

Emma smiled weakly, lifting Vanessa's hands and kissing her knuckles. "I love your enthusiasm, I genuinely do, but I wouldn't expect you to throw away your relationship with Lauren for me."

"I wouldn't be throwing it away. I'd be stepping back until she came to terms with it."

Emma nodded. "Okay."

"Okay, what?"

"Let's…give it a go." Emma winced. "Wait, that sounded really unenthusiastic. But you know what I mean. I'm worried, okay? I'm struggling with the thought of losing my best friend and ruining her family all at once."

"That's not going to happen," Vanessa said, leaning in and pressing a hesitant kiss to Emma's lips. If she was going to change her mind, Vanessa had to keep her attachment level low. If she lost Emma, she'd also lose her mind in the process. "Will you stay the night with me?"

"You mean…together?"

Vanessa smiled into another kiss. "Yes, I mean together. Let's get into bed, put the TV on, and spend some time together. No stress."

"You know what? I can absolutely do that. I'd *love* to do that."

"Perfect."

They hadn't made it to the bedroom yet, Emma was far too comfortable as she lay on the couch, her back pressed against Vanessa. How could something as simple as spooning feel so good? And why, after the promises she'd made to herself over the last fortnight, was Emma here tonight?

Because Vanessa was right. Neither of them knew the reaction Lauren would have.

And honestly, being here felt too good to pass up. Quite frankly, Emma was sick to death of fighting their connection. They were both adults. Though it may be frowned upon by some because of her friendship with Lauren, they weren't *actually* doing anything wrong.

As if sensing that Emma's thoughts were turning heavy, Vanessa lowered her lips to the spot below her ear and smiled against her skin. "You doing okay?"

Just having Vanessa's breath against her skin had every desire whooshing through Emma. Add the hand on her stomach into the mix, and she wasn't sure she could deny Vanessa's touch for much longer. Sooner or later, Emma was going to beg Vanessa to sink inside her. "I-I'm okay."

"I'm glad you're here." Vanessa spoke low, rubbing gentle circles against Emma's belly. "And I know things aren't ideal right now, but it'll all be okay."

"Yeah." It was all Emma could offer. Vanessa was touching her bare skin, so nothing else mattered. The house could burn down around them, but Emma wouldn't budge an inch.

She shuddered when Vanessa smoothed her palm across her lower stomach, a light gasp slipping from her lips. Her fingers pushed past the waistband of Emma's joggers, but Vanessa didn't move any lower. Honestly, it was killing Emma.

"Sorry." Vanessa attempted to move her hand, but Emma covered it with her own.

"No. Stay there," Emma rasped. Having Vanessa's hand placed where it was dulled everything else around her. "You're driving me insane."

Emma felt the wetness gathering between her thighs. It didn't matter that they'd simply been lying here. This was the exact reaction her body always had in Vanessa's company. And then every time Emma closed her eyes, seeing Vanessa with her ass in the air infiltrated her mind. Honestly, it was the greatest image she could have chosen to keep there.

When Vanessa removed her hand and shifted behind Emma, it took all Emma's strength not to groan her disapproval. If they were ever going to get on with this relationship, Vanessa needed to take the lead. There would certainly be no complaints from Emma. Not in this lifetime.

The left arm which rested between the cushion and Emma's head flexed beneath her, Vanessa's hand slipping inside the front of her vest top. Emma wasn't wearing a bra, she hadn't been since a few hours ago when she changed into something comfortable, and Vanessa knew it. As she tweaked a nipple, Emma arched her back. "Oh, shit."

"If you want me to touch you," Vanessa whispered against her ear, pinching Emma's hardened nipple, "you only have to ask."

Emma clenched her jaw as Vanessa's hand made its way back to where she'd needed it a few moments ago, her pulse pounding in her ears. "I do want you to touch me, but the second you do, I'm going to explode."

"I'm not sure what the problem is." Vanessa smirked when Emma glanced over her shoulder. "If my woman needs to come, then she will come."

"Sweet fucking Jesus." Emma let out an audible groan, her eyes closing as Vanessa urged her legs apart, her right one now draped over Vanessa's hip. "You're too much."

"Mm." Vanessa palmed the skin of Emma's thigh beneath her baggy joggers. Just when Emma thought she had a moment to breathe and compose herself, Vanessa pressed a finger to Emma's underwear, pushing the material between her lips. "Relax, and let me take care of you."

Emma inhaled a deep breath, surprised but aroused when Vanessa pushed her underwear to one side and gathered her wetness on her fingertips. Fucking Vanessa had blown her mind, but having Vanessa return the favour was a whole other experience. Her touch was determined, but this woman had the power to melt Emma in a matter of seconds.

"You know…" Vanessa drew slow circles around Emma's swollen clit. "There is nothing I enjoy more than being with women. And knowing you're the first and *only* in thirty years… it's a different kind of special."

Emma whimpered when Vanessa teased her entrance.

"And feeling how wet you are for me…" Vanessa whispered as she nipped at Emma's earlobe. "God, I'm struggling to hold back. Because right now, I want to fuck you senseless."

Every thought Emma had dissolved into thin air, only Vanessa's hot breath washing over the side of her face reminding her she was alive and breathing. Emma lifted her hips, encouraging Vanessa to slip inside. "Do you have any idea how many nights I lay in bed thinking about you being inside me?"

Vanessa pushed one finger in, only to pull out again. "Tell me," Vanessa teased once again, this time pushing deeper and curling her finger.

"F-fuck."

When Vanessa pushed a second finger into her, the heel of her hand pressing against her clit, Emma's eyes slammed shut. She wished this moment wouldn't end so prematurely, but she could barely hold on for another second. Between Vanessa's voice and what her fingers were doing, Emma was close to losing her mind completely.

"Fuck, you're so warm." Those words pushed Emma closer to the edge. "And tight. Mm."

Vanessa trailed open mouthed kisses down Emma's bare arm, only stopping when she picked up her pace between Emma's legs. The sound of Vanessa's heavy breathing and the pressure building in the pit of her stomach had Emma desperate to come. All she wanted was to drag Vanessa up the stairs and spend forever making up for every moment they'd spent dreaming of being together.

"S-so close."

Vanessa stared into Emma's eyes, a third finger slowly but surely finding its way inside her.

"O-oh, fuck!" Emma's eyes rolled shut, every nerve pulsing through her body. "S-shit."

"Open those beautiful eyes." Vanessa spoke so low the vibration travelled through Emma. When she opened her eyes, Vanessa's were the bluest they'd ever been. "That's better. I want to watch you when you come for me."

Emma's mouth fell open, a silent scream her only response as her body shook against Vanessa Middleton. Her life would never be the same again. "Y-yes. Don't stop."

"Oh, baby…I'm never going to stop."

Emma trembled when Vanessa teased her sensitive clit, easing her dripping fingers out of her reluctantly. She pulled her hand from Emma's joggers, slipped her fingers into her mouth, and sucked.

"You taste like heaven." Vanessa moaned, climbing out from behind Emma only to land on all fours above her. With one hand braced against the couch, the other gripping Emma's jaw, they fell into a heated kiss. Vanessa rolled her tongue against Emma's, fully aware of what she was doing. "Wouldn't you agree?"

Emma simply nodded, unable to comprehend how sexy this woman was. She'd always known it, Vanessa exuded everything a gorgeous middle-aged woman possessed, but to see Vanessa so free as she cleaned Emma from her fingers…holy shit.

"I think it's time to take this upstairs. I need you naked for the rest of my plans." Emma allowed herself to be dragged up from the couch by Vanessa, their bodies colliding as she got to her feet. Vanessa gripped the back of her head, fisting her hand in her hair, and trailed her tongue up Emma's throat. "We have *a lot* of making up to do."

CHAPTER THIRTEEN

Emma woke to the shrill of her phone's ringtone; she'd forgotten to silence it last night. She cracked one eye open, groaning as the clock read 7:30. And then she froze when an arm embraced her, pulled back against a soft, warm, *naked* body. Emma tried to get her bearings, focusing on the ceiling as she breathed through the intensity of everything she was feeling this morning. She was in bed…with Vanessa.

Holy fuck!

She closed her eyes for a few seconds, accepting that everything had changed in her life. Would Lauren be a part of her future? God, she hoped so. Would it be wise to discuss all of this over the phone with her best friend? Emma didn't believe so. That kind of news couldn't be broken via a simple text message or long-distance call. No, it needed to be face-to-face. And if Lauren punched her, then so be it. Vanessa was certainly worth the upheaval of her life.

Her phone started to ring again. This time, Vanessa released her grip on Emma's waist.

As she lifted the handset and stared at the screen, dread filled her.

It was Lauren.

"Shit."

Vanessa leaned up, pressing her lips to Emma's shoulder. "What is it?"

"My phone. It's ringing."

"I know," Vanessa said, purring as her lips moved towards the back of Emma's neck. The sensation was far more than arousing. "Why don't you silence it and lie back down? I was having the most amazing dream..."

"I-it's Lauren."

Vanessa stilled but her lips remained pressed to Emma's skin. "She wouldn't expect you to answer this early in the morning."

Emma glanced over her shoulder. "I shouldn't answer it?"

"Do you *want* to answer it?" Vanessa asked, one eyebrow quirked.

When her phone silenced, Emma flopped back onto the mattress. This morning, Emma was on cloud nine. As anxious as she felt regarding Lauren, Emma had spent the night sleeping beside Vanessa. This moment, the decade and more of longing... Emma couldn't imagine being anywhere else. Vanessa peered down at her, her fingertips gently feathering over her collar bone, those heavenly blue eyes telling her everything would be okay.

But would it?

It didn't matter this morning. Nobody else existed in Emma's perfect world.

"Baby," Vanessa whispered, sending a roar of arousal straight to Emma's core. "I know this is difficult, but there is no use worrying about something that isn't going to come to a head until September."

Emma frowned. Vanessa had clearly read her facial expression wrong as she lay daydreaming. She turned on her side, smiling as she ghosted her hand up Vanessa's thigh and towards her hip. Vanessa quaked, a light gasp escaping her lips.

"I'm...not worried," Emma murmured, resting her head on

Vanessa's shoulder. "And maybe I should be, *we* should be, but this morning, I just want to be with you. I don't want to think about *anything* other than you." Emma's hand gently palmed the skin of Vanessa's belly, a low throaty moan rumbling from her.

"The night when you called me..." Vanessa paused, clearing her throat. "When you told me you loved me..."

"A night I'll never forget."

"I wanted to pack a bag and follow you to the ends of the earth. To spend the rest of my life making love to you."

Emma frowned, her hand stilling.

"Even though I'd never shown it, I felt all those things too. I wanted to be with you, happy with you, but it wasn't the right time."

"I-I never knew."

"I know. And when you left, I sat alone in this very room wondering how I could possibly be in love with someone I'd never touched. Someone I'd merely spent time with, while with my family. Nothing made any sense to me. I just knew I was unhappy when you weren't around."

Emma's entire body thrummed with love. She appreciated Vanessa being honest with her. If this was going to work, they had to remain on that level with one another. A level of understanding and communication. "I know you used to flirt, but I thought it was something you did with everyone."

Vanessa closed her eyes. "The times I wanted to sneak into the bathroom when you were showering. Or the nights we sat up when Lauren and Richard had gone to bed. It...was the wrong time. And perhaps it's my fault for being a coward and sticking with what I'd always known, but I've never felt so free, and I want you to still be here when this is all over, Emma."

"How do we tell her?"

Vanessa side-glanced at Emma. "I'll tell her the same way I would if I was dating someone else."

"You've never had that conversation with Lauren, though. You've never dated anyone other than her father."

"Still," Vanessa sighed. "Let me handle it, okay?"

Emma fell silent. She couldn't expect Vanessa to take the brunt of this while she stood back and watched her relationship with her daughter fall apart. If this was happening, and it definitely was, they would have to stick together. When the time came to sit Lauren down, Emma would be beside Vanessa without a second thought.

Vanessa threw back the cover, rolling over and settling on top of Emma. "Do you have any idea how happy I am to have you in my bed?" Vanessa braced her hands either side of Emma's head, straddling her stomach and rolling her hips.

"Well, I mean…I could give it a good guess." Emma smirked, burying her head deeper into the pillow as Vanessa's slick arousal coated her stomach. "God, this is my ultimate dream."

"In that case, why don't we have a wonderful morning together before you make me breakfast?"

Emma lifted her head, feigning shock. "Huh. I thought I was the guest here?"

"The times I've watched you walk around my kitchen, doing your own thing…" Vanessa smiled into a kiss. "Now I can *really* admire you while you do it."

"Mum, where the hell have you been? I called twice this morning." The worry in Lauren's voice didn't go unnoticed by Vanessa. But truly, she couldn't quite explain the morning she'd had.

"Sorry, love. I've had a lot on." It was all Vanessa could offer for the time being. Emma was looking at her from across the kitchen with a frown on her face. "How's it all going?"

"Amazing. But I'm so tired tonight."

"What time is it there?" Vanessa kicked her feet up onto a chair, relaxing with her coffee. "It must be late."

"Just gone ten at night." Lauren yawned, her voice trailing off. "But it's been a lovely day. We spent tonight at a friend of Rob's."

Vanessa placed her phone down on the table, hitting the speaker button. "What's the weather like?"

"Cold, but it doesn't matter. It's still gorgeous."

"Well, I'd rather be where you are. It's rained all morning here." Is this what Vanessa's life had come to? Talking about the British weather? Christ! "Enough about the weather."

"Hey, Mum...have you seen anything of Emma? I've been calling, but she lets it ring out. I've had a few texts from her, but she's been distant."

Vanessa looked over at Emma who was resting against the counter. She held her coffee cup to her lips, her eyes focused on nothing in particular. "She's fine, I think."

"Could you check on her for me? See if she's doing okay? She probably wants to be back in Ghana, especially with me going away so soon after she got home. I...I'm worried about her."

She eyed Emma again. Was she having second thoughts about this? After the day they'd had so far, Vanessa wasn't entirely sure she could deal with the potential of losing Emma.

"Oh," Vanessa perked up, giving Emma a knowing look. "Here she is now. I think she was in the shower."

Emma approached the dining table, giving Vanessa an apologetic look. "Hey, kiddo."

"Ems, how the hell are you?"

Vanessa watched as Emma morphed into her old self—pre-Vanessa. "Good, yeah. Busy getting stuff sorted here."

"How did the interview go?"

"They called me a few days ago. I got the job. I start in September when the new school year kicks off."

"Friend, that's amazing! I'm so happy you got the job. And I'll be home soon after, so we'll celebrate, okay?"

Emma ran a hand down her face. She did have a look of uncertainty in her eyes, but Vanessa would deal with it once the call had ended. She needed a moment to prepare for any eventuality.

"Yeah. Celebrating sounds good." Emma drained her coffee, her voice not quite as enthusiastic as Vanessa would have liked. "So, I have to go. I was on my way out. But I'll talk to you soon, okay?"

"Miss you."

Emma's eyes welled with tears. "Miss you, too."

"Miss you more."

Emma sighed, shaking her head as her eyes closed. "Not possible."

She walked away, disposing of her cup and heading out the back door towards the stairs. But Lauren was still on the end of the phone, so Vanessa composed herself and cradled her chin in her palm. "Hey, sweetie. Can you call me tomorrow whenever it's best for you?"

"Sure."

"I have a class until eleven. Would it be too late on your side if you call me around then?"

"No, Mum, that'll be fine. I think we're out to dinner tomorrow, so I'll call you when I'm back. Do you have a class after lunch?"

"Mm. I have another at two."

"Okay, but if you're going to be unavailable, let me know." Lauren paused. "Is everything okay?"

"Of course. I wanted to hear your voice." Vanessa was going to reveal her sexuality tomorrow. Adding Emma into the mix could wait a while longer. She may want her daughter to know about the feelings she'd hidden for so many years, but she wouldn't hit her with a double whammy. What good would it do? "I'll speak to you tomorrow, okay?"

"Goodnight, Mum. Love you."

"I love you too, my beautiful girl."

The call ended, leaving Vanessa with her head in her hands as dread filled her. Vanessa wanted to believe her bond with Lauren was unbreakable, but this was big. Huge. *Only if we make it so.*

"God, this is all a mess."

"Babe?" Emma spoke from the doorway.

Emma's soft voice, those eyes...Vanessa couldn't turn to meet her gaze. Her emotions got the better of her, tears slipping freely down her face. "I'm going to lose you, aren't I? I-I can't have both..."

Emma rushed across the kitchen, dropping to her knees in front of Vanessa. Her palms gently caressed up and down Vanessa's thighs, soothing away her tears. "What's going on? Did you tell her something?"

"No. But this is going to end in tears. And you don't deserve to wait around for it to happen..."

"I'm not leaving if that's what you're expecting." Emma said, not a hint of hesitancy in her voice. "When it comes down to it, I'll be by your side, okay?"

Vanessa stared down at Emma. Did she truly mean it? Emma would willingly put herself in the line of fire for Vanessa...for them? "You will?"

"We're in this together, no?"

Vanessa nodded, exhaling a deep breath. "I'd hoped we would be, but I also don't expect you to hang around if this gets ugly."

"It won't. Bumpy, maybe, but not ugly." Emma leaned up into a kiss. "Now, I want you to relax today. Stop worrying."

As Emma climbed to her feet, Vanessa noticed that Emma looked ready to head out. She had mentioned to Lauren that she was on her way out, but Vanessa had thought it was an excuse to get off the phone. "Are you going somewhere?"

"I am. I'm visiting a friend. But I won't be long. And I thought maybe I could cook dinner for us tonight?"

"I'd love dinner with you."

"Okay, well call me if anything changes or you need me for something."

Vanessa narrowed her eyes. "Anything at all?"

Emma shook her head, laughing. Vanessa loved the playful nature Emma had always seemed to thrive on, but that had been missing recently. She wanted to get back to those moments. Emma grinned. "Anything."

CHAPTER FOURTEEN

Emma wasn't sure why she'd spent the day walking around aimlessly, Anna had been expecting her for over two hours, but here she was, unaware of what she'd spent her day doing. She recalled sitting in the coffee shop while she enjoyed a cappuccino, and she remembered texting Vanessa to see if she wanted anything from the local store, but the rest of the time seemed a blur.

Honestly, Emma couldn't quite believe that she'd woken up beside Vanessa…and would climb into bed with her again tonight. Of course, it felt good, but she would also admit to a slight terror that washed over her occasionally. Could she be enough for someone like Vanessa? Could she make such an intellectual and well-respected woman happy? Emma wasn't sure this would all have the desired outcome, but she was sure as hell going to try.

Emma looked up at the house she'd landed outside. Anna Matheson had once been Emma's world, way back when. But she wasn't here to rekindle old flames; she was here because Anna had been a friend to her when Lauren couldn't be. Her ex didn't exactly know the ins and outs of what Emma felt, or who it was directed at, but she'd always been a good listener. And it was exactly what Emma needed right now.

She curled her hand and knocked, startled when the door suddenly flew open.

"What time do you call this?"

Emma shoved her hands in her pockets, wincing. "Sorry. Did you have plans?"

"No. I thought you'd been dragged off the street into the back of a van."

"I'm fine. I was only walking around."

Anna pulled Emma inside by the front of her jacket. When the door slammed shut, Anna turned to face her. "Is everything okay?"

"You know what, it is."

Anna breathed a sigh of relief, her hand placed on her chest. "Good. Thank God."

"I mean, things weren't okay. Not at first."

"Explain."

"I've been up and down for the last couple of weeks. Spent the night in my car a few times."

"Y-you've been sleeping in your car?"

Emma nodded, her eyes cast on her feet. "When I couldn't sofa surf, yes."

"No. That's not right. I-I thought you were staying at Lauren's mum's place?"

Lauren's mum. "I was. But I had to leave."

"And your mum?"

Emma lifted a shoulder. She couldn't bring herself to stay at home. It never worked out. "She doesn't even know I'm back from Ghana."

"Wow. Okay."

"You know we don't get along. And she's the last person I want to see right now." Emma shrugged off her jacket, draping it over the back of a dining room chair as Anna ushered her through the house.

"Then talk to *me*," Anna said, laying a gentle hand on Emma's shoulder. "You know I'm always here for you."

"You remember I told you I was in love with someone when I was here the other week?"

"I do remember. Are you ready to tell me who it is, or…"

Emma exhaled a deep breath. She couldn't keep it all in any longer. "Vanessa Middleton."

Anna's eyes widened, and then she frowned. "Shit. You fell in love with your best friend's mum."

"I'm aware."

"Crap. Lauren is going to…God, I don't know what she's going to think when she finds out," Anna paused. "Unless she *did* find out and that's why you're here."

"No, she doesn't know. But I think I have to tell her before this gets serious."

"Or you could forget about it all and maybe avoid Vanessa."

If only Anna's suggestion was that simple. To forget about Vanessa Middleton? No. It wasn't possible.

"Vanessa knows," Emma said, clearing her throat. "She's known since I left for Ghana. But now I'm back, and everything has changed. I spent the night last night."

"O-oh."

"I mean, when we're together, it doesn't feel like we're doing anything wrong. And I know she wants to be with me, she says she has since before she divorced her husband, but I need someone to either tell me I'm out of my mind to consider it or that everything is going to be fine and I'm worrying for nothing."

The frown lines in Anna's forehead deepened. "Why would you be out of your mind?"

"Anna."

"No, I'm serious. You forget we spent three years together.

And I know it was a million years ago, but you're still the lovely person I fell in love with. Anyone would be lucky to have you."

Emma smiled weakly. She was so happy her and Anna had ended on good terms. "Thank you. That means a lot."

"So, tell me. Why does this seem like such a bad idea?"

"Because it's Lauren's mum?" Emma chanced.

"Meh. Could be worse." Anna shrugged. "Lauren is big enough to come to terms with it in her own time. But why should you deny how you're feeling if it's what you want?"

"Is it that easy? Really?" Emma couldn't begin to imagine what would go through Lauren's mind the moment she discovered the truth.

"It's only hard if you make it hard." Anna ran a hand through her light brown hair. "Don't spend your life pushing down how you feel. We never know when our time is up, and if you can fall in love with someone who loves you in return, I'd say that's the most important thing. If Lauren is your best friend, she will fully support this. And I know it's going to be hard for her to understand, but I'm sure she only wants her mum to be happy."

"I know she wants Vanessa to be happy; it's all she talks about. But I'm not sure it extends to *me* making her happy. I'm her best friend, Anna. We've spent so long being joined at the hip. I just don't know."

"I guess there is only one way to find out." Anna placed a supportive hand over Emma's.

Anxiety rolled around in the pit of Emma's stomach. And then she thought back to this morning when Vanessa's eyes held tears as she asked if she was going to lose Emma. God, this was heartbreaking. She never wanted to see Vanessa cry.

"And if Lauren never speaks to me again?"

Anna offered a sympathetic smile, her honey-coloured eyes soft. "Then I guess she doesn't love you as much as you thought."

Okay, that wasn't very fair to Lauren. No one would expect her to be okay with this. Not immediately, anyway. It didn't mean she didn't love Emma; it meant Emma had disappointed her beyond belief.

"If she's the best friend she claims to be, she'll love you regardless."

"Yeah, I'm not so sure about that." Emma wrung her hands in her lap, calming the whirring in her head. She needed to relax. "She doesn't even know Vanessa is bi."

"I guess she's going to find out eventually." Anna grinned. "And may I say, you picked *the* hottest woman in town."

"Don't I know it. I can't stop thinking about her." And Emma really couldn't. From the moment she'd sank to her knees beside Vanessa's bed, life hadn't been the same.

"She taught our Carl. I think he still has a crush on her now."

"Yeah, well, he can back off," Emma laughed. "She's all mine."

"Whatever the outcome, Lauren *will* be okay. Maybe it won't happen overnight, but in time, you two will be okay."

"Thanks for being there for me." Emma got to her feet. She couldn't walk the streets forever. It was time to get back. "And I know we were supposed to hang out for a while, but I do need to leave."

"If I find out you've slept in your car again, I'm going to smack you upside the head."

"I won't."

Anna pulled Emma into a hug, gripping her tight. "Where are you going to go?"

"I should head back and see Vanessa. I hadn't planned to be out this long. She'll be worried."

Anna held Emma at arm's length, offering her a knowing look. "Okay, but if it all goes wrong, you come back here. I have plenty of room for you."

"It's going to be fine," Emma said, squeezing Anna's shoulder. "I don't want to lose her."

Vanessa eased back against the mass of throw cushions on the couch, the TV playing in the corner of the room. She sat in darkness, only the flicker of the screen sending flashes of light through the room intermittently. All this alone time was becoming tedious; she needed company. Conversation. She needed…Emma.

Her phone suddenly started vibrating on the couch beside her, but it wasn't her usual ringtone. No, it was a FaceTime call coming through, and it was Lauren. Vanessa cleared her throat and ran a hand through her hair, smiling fully when the call connected.

"Are you calling this way to make me jealous?" Vanessa grinned, thrilled to see Lauren looking so healthy. They hadn't had the opportunity to video call before now. "Because I'm already jealous."

"Nope. I wanted to see my mum's gorgeous face."

Vanessa got comfortable, sinking further down and hugging a cushion to her chest. "I miss you so much."

"I miss you, too. It's why I called."

"It's only 7 a.m. isn't it?" Vanessa frowned, confused as to why Lauren was awake so early. Unless she was working, she wasn't usually up at this time. "Why aren't you in bed?"

"Couldn't sleep." Lauren propped her head on her hand, staring down the screen. "And when I spoke to you this morning, or last night, you kinda worried me."

"Why?"

"Asking me to call you tomorrow…or today," Lauren said, her brow furrowed. "God, this time difference is confusing. But anyway, was there something you needed to talk about? Because even though I'm not at home, it doesn't mean I'm too busy for you, Mum."

Vanessa's heart sank. She hadn't expected to do this face-to-face…or as close to that as possible. If it was an average call, she couldn't see how horrified Lauren was. "I do want to talk about something, yes."

"Okay, well I have all the time in the world." Lauren smiled one of her sweet smiles. "And I even have coffee ready, so I'm in no rush to get off the phone."

"I appreciate that."

"Is it about Dad?" Lauren asked, her gentle face morphing into one of sadness. "You know, with everything happening for you right now?"

"You *can* say it's a divorce, love. I'm not frightened of the word."

"I know. But I don't think you like talking about it. So, I never know how to approach it."

"It's not about the divorce. The sooner it's all over, the better. You know I don't like being tied down to something I have no control over."

Lauren smiled and sipped her coffee. "I know. So, what's this about then? You're not pregnant, are you?" Lauren laughed, but Vanessa sat in shock. "Oh, are you?"

"I'm not sure if you're aware of this or not, but I'm fifty, love. I'm not sure anything works anymore."

"Okay, so you're not pregnant. Thank God!"

Vanessa barked a laugh. "You're a nut!"

"I wonder who I get it from." Lauren quirked an eyebrow, mirroring Vanessa's trademark stare. One hint of it in the classroom, and her students fell silent. "Okay but come on. Tell me. I wanna know."

"Before I met your father..." Vanessa paused. She needed to ease this into the conversation. "Well, I dated a few people before him. Yes, I was young. But I still knew what I was doing. I still *wanted* to date those people."

"As you're entitled to do."

"Those people were women, Lauren."

Lauren paused her coffee cup in front of her mouth, falling

silent. Vanessa's heart slammed against her chest. She didn't need silence. She needed some encouraging words, positivity from her daughter. Because after all, only Lauren's opinion mattered.

"And now you're ready to end the call." Vanessa's voice broke as she closed her eyes. "I don't expect you to understand, I was married to your dad for so long, but he was who I loved back then. I wouldn't change anything we had."

"You…dated women." It wasn't a question. It was merely Lauren trying it out.

"Yes. I dated women."

"So, you're…bisexual?"

Vanessa nodded, pleased Lauren had actually responded. "Always have been, love."

"Why didn't you tell me?"

"It's not something I felt needed discussing. I was married to your dad. I also never thought it was important, so I didn't mention it."

"Well, I, uh…congratulations?" Lauren chanced.

"I wanted you to know. If you come home and see me with a woman, I think you'll wonder what the hell is going on."

"*Are* you with a woman?" Lauren asked, a slight smirk curling on her mouth. "Because it's totally fine if you are. The house would always be tidy, and it'd always smell nice. I hated that aftershave Dad used to wear. And he left the toilet seat up. Women don't. And I don't know, I think you'd look amazing with another woman. I mean, you *are* absolutely gorgeous, Mum."

"I've had a couple of dates." Vanessa chose her words wisely. "But that's all."

"Well, you could always ask Emma if she knows any friends who are looking. Obviously, they'd have to be good enough, but she wouldn't want you to date someone who wasn't worthy, so I'm sure she'd help you out."

"Oh, I don't know."

"I'll call Emma later. Have a word with her. You know?"

"No, Lauren. Please don't." Vanessa suddenly felt flustered. Now that her daughter had an idea in her head, she wouldn't let it lie. "I'm not ready."

"Mum, you don't have time to waste." Lauren suddenly frowned. "And why are you sitting in the dark? Where's Emma? I thought you two had been hanging out."

"She's out."

"Oh. Well, I checked the weather earlier, and it says it's pissing down at home. She hates the rain."

Vanessa laughed. "You don't miss a thing, do you."

"Are you sure everything is okay with her? She's being super weird. I mean, she's weird anyway," Lauren said, grinning, "but this is a different weird. It's a *weird* weird."

"That's a lot of weird, sweetheart."

"Well, she is. I don't know what the hell is wrong with her. I texted her last week, and she was with Anna. I thought it was kinda odd, but I don't know, maybe they're getting back together. Emma probably has a lot on her mind."

"Anna?"

"Yeah. Her ex. I don't know her much. They were together before we became close, but she speaks highly of her, and they seem to be spending a bit more time together."

Ah! Carl's sister. Vanessa bristled. Emma had been gone all day. Was she with this Anna woman? "Didn't know she'd been seeing an ex."

"Oh, I don't know if it means anything, but it'd be nice if she did meet someone."

Vanessa cleared her throat. "Yeah."

"Anyway, I'm sure she'll speak to me when she's ready to. It's not like I can force it out of her while I'm all the way over here. And she'd tell me to bugger off anyway."

A weight suddenly settled in the pit of Vanessa's stomach. Emma hadn't told her about this ex of hers, but why? Was it because they were getting back on track, and Vanessa was just a fantasy to pass the time by? What if…Emma was sleeping with Anna right now? *No!* Emma wouldn't do that to her.

"I-I have to go."

"Mum? You good?" The concern in Lauren's voice melted Vanessa's heart. Her daughter would always be there for her, no matter what.

"I'm fine, honey. I think I'm ready for bed."

"Okay, well you'd better warm it up so you can find a nice lady to keep you company." Lauren winked, and then suddenly burst into a fit of laughter.

"I'm glad you find my sexuality so funny."

"No. I'm not laughing because of your sexuality." Lauren splayed a hand across her chest, still laughing. "I…oh my God! Can you imagine?"

"Imagine what?" Vanessa's brow knitted.

"If I came home and found you and Emma together. Hilarious."

A nervous laugh escaped Vanessa's lips as she looked away from the screen. At least Lauren found it funny rather than infuriating. "Yeah. Imagine."

"Wait!"

Vanessa sighed. "What now?"

"That's not going to happen is it, Mum?" Lauren's voice changed, the seriousness sending a shiver down Vanessa's spine. Okay, not so funny anymore. "Because it wouldn't be okay. Any other woman in the world, but not my best friend."

Vanessa had nothing to offer. Every moment she'd shared with Lauren flashed before her, the prospect of losing her daughter now at the forefront of her mind.

"M-Mum?"

"Lauren…" Vanessa swallowed, tears welling in her eyes. How the hell did she admit to this? She couldn't exactly deny it; Lauren wasn't stupid. "I—"

"No! No way." The anger in Lauren's voice was startling, but who could blame her for feeling that way? "Don't you dare tell me you're sleeping with Emma!"

"I'm sorry."

"Sorry?" Lauren spat, disgust written all over her beautiful face. "You're sorry?"

"Please don't speak to me like that. I'm your mother!"

"My *mother* wouldn't sleep with my best friend." Lauren scoffed, shaking her head. "I mean, are you *so* desperate to not be alone that you'll take anything on offer?"

"How dare you!"

"No, Mum. How dare *you!*"

Lauren ended their video call, the silence in the room deafening. Everything had been going so well, and then Vanessa, once again, wasn't able to control herself. But on the flip side, she didn't want to have to control how she felt. She wanted everyone to be on the same page while she fell head over heels in love with Emma.

Who are you trying to fool? You're already there.

CHAPTER FIFTEEN

Prepared for an evening with Vanessa, an expensive bottle of red cradled in her arms, Emma turned the key in the lock and nudged the door open with her shoulder. Vanessa's familiar perfume soothed her, but anything involving her usually did.

Emma kicked off her shoes by the door, poking her head into the living room. "Hey."

"Hi," Vanessa said, her tone even.

"Just putting these bits in the kitchen." Emma threw a thumb over her shoulder. "Want anything?"

"No." Vanessa didn't make eye contact. She sat on the couch, staring blankly at the TV.

"Right, okay." Emma rushed into the kitchen, quickly placing down the wine and the bag of ingredients she'd collected for dinner. She wanted to shower before she got comfortable with Vanessa, but she got the impression Vanessa didn't want any company this evening. She approached the living room door. Vanessa was standing with her arms folded across her chest. "I'm going for a quick shower before I make dinner, okay?"

"Any particular reason why?" Vanessa frowned, her eyes

taking in Emma's entire form. "Been somewhere that would *require* you to shower?"

"Well, no. I figured I'd shower now, and then I'm free for the rest of the night."

"You've been gone all day."

Emma sighed. She should have called Vanessa. They'd only spoken once today, and it had been not long after she'd left the house. "I know. I'm sorry. I went for a walk and then called in to see a friend. I didn't realise how long I'd been gone. But…I'll make it up to you."

Vanessa beckoned Emma closer, her eyes cold. "Come here."

Emma moved closer. She had every intention of kissing Vanessa for the rest of the night. Emma stopped in front of her, frowning as she leaned in only to be rejected when Vanessa turned her face away. "Uh, that wasn't what I expected, babe. Is everything okay?"

And then Vanessa bent forward, inhaling deeply.

Emma shot back a step or two. She knew what Vanessa was doing. She was checking for another woman's perfume. "Are you for real?"

"Spend the day with Anna?" Vanessa's stance would usually be intimidating, but Emma just felt sad. Vanessa turned her watch towards her, scoffing. "Well, most of the night, too."

"Are you asking me what I think you are?" Emma couldn't begin to imagine why Vanessa thought she'd been with another woman. And okay, she had, but not in the way Vanessa seemed to be imagining.

Vanessa's bottom lip trembled as she lowered her chin to her chest. "I-I'm sorry. I didn't mean it. Tonight has been…awful."

"Yeah, that's not good enough for me." Emma shed her coat, taking her phone from her pocket. Honestly, she had no words for what had happened. Vanessa truly believed she was the type of woman who would cheat on her? *Wow.* "I'm showering. If you don't want to have dinner with me, I'll say goodnight now."

"I'm sorry," Vanessa whispered, reaching out her hand. "Please don't leave."

"D-did you just ask me if I'd been sleeping with another woman?" God, that was hard enough to say, let alone imagine. "Really?"

Vanessa swallowed. She looked truly dreadful tonight. "I'll see you when you've showered, okay?"

Emma wanted to resolve this now, not after she'd showered, but giving it a minute or two would be for the best. She didn't know where to begin with trying to explain herself. She simply frowned, watching Vanessa for a moment. "Sure."

Disappointed, she turned and left the living room, taking the stairs two at a time. When Emma reached the bedroom door, her phone vibrated in her hand. *Lauren.* She couldn't avoid her best friend's calls any longer. Lauren was a million miles away, and the one thing they'd always stuck at was long distance calls.

"Hey! You're up early. Did you shit the bed?"

"You were like a sister to me," Lauren whispered, her voice shaking. "The memories I have with you…are those someone would have with a *sister!*"

"You okay, friend? You sound kinda upset." Emma didn't like Lauren's tone. She'd definitely been crying. "Do I need to get a flight out and kick the arse of whoever pissed you off?"

"I loved you like a sister!"

"Whoa. What's going on?" Emma's pulse thrummed in her ears. Whatever Lauren was talking about, she wasn't making any sense. "Lauren?"

"Y-you're sleeping with her."

"With who?" Emma's throat dried. She hadn't known what would happen when the time came, but she thought she may have been better at composing herself. She needed more time to figure this all out in her head. "I'm not sleeping with anyone." *Liar!*

"Get your shit, and get out of my house. You're not welcome

there."

And that was it. Emma didn't need to admit to anything; Lauren already knew. "Lauren, please…"

"I'm not interested in *anything* you have to say. I just…I can't believe you'd do something like this to me. S-she's my mum, Emma. My fucking mum!"

Emma hung her head, tears flowing from her eyes. "I-I love her."

"Oh, give me a break. I've only been gone for weeks, not years. You can't possibly love her!"

Emma cleared her throat. She had to gain some control of this conversation. Lauren had no idea what she'd gone through over the years, and more so, recently. "I'm not doing this with you over the phone. When you get home, we'll discuss it."

"There's nothing to discuss. Touch her again, and I'm getting the first flight home."

Okay, that was a little dramatic. Did she think Emma was forcing Vanessa into having sex with her? It couldn't be further from the truth. "You sound a bit ridiculous right now."

"You know what?" Lauren blew out a deep breath, the phone line crackling ever so slightly. "Fuck you, Emma."

Emma stared down at her phone when the line went dead, disbelief plaguing every other thought she should have. She didn't know whether to actually do what Lauren had asked and pack her stuff up or whether to continue with her plans to cook dinner for Vanessa. *She's just accused you of cheating on her. Dinner is the least of your worries.* Emma squeezed her eyes shut. She knew what she wanted in her heart, but she hadn't expected to come back here tonight to Lauren's call *or* the accusation before it.

And how the hell did Lauren know?

She set her phone down on the bed, stripped her clothes from her body, and stood in her underwear. A hot shower was her first port of call, and whatever else followed was anyone's guess.

But then Emma looked up. Vanessa was standing in the doorway. "So, she had plenty to say to you too?"

"I don't know what the hell has happened tonight, but I feel like I'm about to lose my mind." Emma flopped to the edge of the bed, dragging her hair tie from her hair. "I..." She ruffled it, exhaling a calming breath as she eyed the hold-all on the floor. Most of her stuff was still packed. "She wants me to get my stuff and leave."

"This is my house." Vanessa got to her knees between Emma's legs. "You're not going anywhere."

"That may be true, but I don't know why you care if I'm here or not." Emma scoffed, still annoyed by Vanessa's accusation. "You think I've been shagging someone else."

"Please, forgive me." Vanessa's voice shook, devastation clouding her piercing eyes.

"Do you have any idea how ridiculous it sounds when you accuse me of something like that? I mean, I woke up with *you* this morning. Why the fuck would I need anyone else?"

Vanessa dipped her head, her hands resting on Emma's thighs. "It was something Lauren said. And maybe I wanted to hurt you back for avoiding me all day, but I am sorry. So sorry."

"I'd never do *anything* to hurt you, and I wasn't avoiding you. I was visiting a friend." Emma lifted a hand, caressing Vanessa's cheek. "I don't know what to do. I need you to tell me."

"You're not leaving. Lauren knows now. I think she needs time to come to terms with it. And she can take all the time she needs to do so."

"I wasn't prepared. And you said we'd do it together." Emma's forehead creased. Vanessa should have told her what was going to happen. "Why did you tell her without me here?"

Vanessa ran her hands up Emma's thighs, leaning up as she silenced Emma with her lips. When she pulled back, placing sloppy kisses along Emma's jawline, Emma's body suddenly thrummed. Vanessa would *always* take her to the heights of ecstasy. No woman could ever come close. When Vanessa pulled back, tears fell down her face. "I'm so sorry for accusing you. I-I know you'd never do anything to hurt me."

"Babe." Emma cocked her head, wiping away Vanessa's tears. "You do know that, don't you? I'd never do anything to fuck this up with you. I've wanted this for so long; I'm not stupid enough to break your heart *or* my own."

Vanessa got to her feet, guiding Emma backwards on the mattress. When her back was pressed to the headboard, Vanessa climbed onto the bed beside her. "I know. A moment of panic which will *never* happen again."

Emma pulled Vanessa down to the mattress, and they held one another. This was always where she felt safe. Emma slipped a hand under Vanessa's shirt, ghosting her fingertips up and down her back. "Did you tell her?"

"Not quite. No."

Emma narrowed her eyes. "Why don't I believe you? She can't have figured it out for herself."

"I told her I was bisexual. And she was great about it. Didn't faze her at all."

Emma smiled. That was something positive if nothing else. "Good."

"And then she made a joke about coming home to find us together, and I guess my face gave it away. I couldn't lie to her when she asked me. I don't want *anything* to be built on lies."

"No. I couldn't lie either. It's why I've been avoiding her. But you could have warned me when I walked through the door that she knew. I could have prepared myself better for the call."

"Sorry."

"Then again, you were too busy assuming I was with another woman all day."

Vanessa blanched, her cheeks reddening. "Sorry again?"

"What *was* that about?" Emma got comfortable, pulling the comforter over them. "It was a bit unexpected."

"Lauren said you'd been friendly with your ex. Anna. And when I was at the coffee shop, Carl mentioned you'd been to visit recently."

"She's only a friend, Vanessa. We haven't been together in thirteen years."

Deep down, Vanessa knew she had no reason to worry; Emma could see it in her eyes. But Lauren must have caught her off guard when she was already feeling vulnerable. She'd simply focused on that element of the conversation with her daughter instead of everything else.

"Do you trust me?" Emma asked, running a hand through Vanessa's soft hair.

"I trust you."

"As you should," Emma said, lowering her eyes between them. "The times I've dreamt about this. Lying with you. Kissing you. God, I don't know how I didn't combust in the past. It will *always* be you, okay?"

"And it will always be you. No matter what happens in the months to come."

"Yeah?" Emma offered a shy smile, shifting closer to Vanessa. "You're sure you'll still want me around?"

"Depends."

"On what?" Emma's forehead creased.

"On how good you are at sharing a long hot bath with me."

Vanessa's eyes darkened when Emma slipped a hand beneath her shirt. This was what she wanted. The intimacy, the opportunity to make up for the longing they'd both felt. Nothing, not a single thing, could replace *this* right now.

Emma took her bottom lip between her teeth, her fingertips brushing Vanessa's nipple. "Why don't you run us a bath, and I'll *show you* how good I am."

"What about dinner?" Vanessa asked, gasping as Emma grabbed a handful of her breast.

"Dinner will be ready when I'm finished with you."

Vanessa groaned, squeezing her thighs together. "Fuck."

Emma sunk down into Vanessa's jacuzzi bathtub, sitting face-to-face with the woman of her dreams. Vanessa always looked catwalk ready, and even now as she sat naked and exposed, her face free of makeup, she still looked exquisite.

"How's the temperature?" Vanessa asked, their legs tangled together as she pulled Emma closer.

"Perfect." Vanessa's eyes appeared bluer than ever. "You're so beautiful."

"So are you." Vanessa dragged her nails down Emma's back.

Emma smiled against Vanessa's ear. "Who'd have thought I'd be sharing a bath with Mrs Middleton, huh?" Whispering, Emma grazed the sponge across one of Vanessa's nipples, garnering a gasp. "And I have to say, you've exceeded my expectations already."

Vanessa's eyes closed. "Mm. Keep talking."

"I think you exceeded them the night I watched you fucking yourself." Emma pinched a nipple, palming the other. "Hearing you call out my name..." She paused, nipping Vanessa's earlobe. "God, I was wet for you."

"If I'd known you were there..."

"No. If you'd known I was there, none of it would have happened. I needed you to not know I was watching. Because it lived up to *every* fantasy I'd ever had about you."

Vanessa gripped a handful of Emma's hair, tilting Emma's head and exposing her neck.

"The times," Vanessa kissed her way down Emma's throat, "I've wanted to fuck you..." Her mouth moved lower, Vanessa's lips enveloping a sensitive nipple. "You've no idea."

But Emma did. She knew *exactly* how Vanessa was feeling. The nights she'd laid in bed wishing for things to be different.

The times she'd considered laying it all out on the table. It had all come down to this point in their lives. And now, Emma could never let Vanessa go. "I wanted you, Vanessa. God, I wanted you like I've never wanted anything else in my life."

Vanessa kissed her way down Emma's stomach as Emma got to her knees, her hands holding Emma's hips firmly in place. Her tongue took a slow pace around her navel, sparks bursting into flames inside Emma. "Your skin tastes incredible." Vanessa's soft whispers tickled Emma's skin, her body shuddering as Vanessa lowered her hand only to trail it up the inside her thigh. "And I know you're wet for me." Vanessa smirked against Emma's ribs, and two fingers pushing past her soaked lips.

Emma steadied herself, her hands on Vanessa's shoulders. "I need you inside me." Emma bucked against the hand between her thighs, gritting her teeth when Vanessa pressed her fingertips to her clit. "Fuck, please."

One finger slipped inside. Then another. "Mm. So tight."

"Oh, fuck." Emma's mouth fell open, her breath catching when Vanessa curled her fingers, finding that spot which would send Emma to the moon. "Shit."

Vanessa wrapped an arm around Emma's waist. "You don't come until I say you can."

Oh, no. No, no, no. Emma was about ready to explode, and knowing she couldn't…well, Vanessa was going to be sorry when it did happen. "I'll try, " Emma whispered, her voice dripping with arousal.

"No." Vanessa gripped her backside, spreading Emma open. "You won't *try*. You'll *do*."

Okay, this was fucking hot. From Vanessa's tongue grazing Emma's ribs, to the hoarseness in her voice, every sensation was heightened. Emma felt as though she couldn't breathe in this woman's company.

Vanessa pressed the heel of her hand to Emma's clit, smirking as she craned her neck and took another swipe at her nipple.

"Fuck, babe." Emma clenched her jaw, her nails grazing the back of Vanessa's scalp. "Y-you..." Emma breath caught when Vanessa added a third finger, her body instinctively sinking down against them. "Oh, shit. P-please..."

Vanessa released Emma's nipple with a pop, her eyes shining as she looked up at her. "You want to come?" Vanessa quirked one of those sexy eyebrows.

"Y-yes."

"Ask me." Vanessa got to her knees, still three fingers deep, and swiped her thumb across Emma's clit. "Go on. Ask me."

"Please let me come."

Vanessa's hand stilled, her head cocked. "Ask me how I *know* you want to ask me."

Oh, fuck. This woman was going to end Emma's life one of these days. She stared into Vanessa's eyes, her lip between her teeth, her knees shaking. "Please let me come...Mrs Middleton."

Vanessa captured Emma's mouth, her free hand gripping her jaw. She thrust, hard and deep, her own body shaking against Emma. She pulled back, breathless. "One more time."

"Please," Emma gasped, her orgasm roaring towards its peak. "Mrs Middleton, m-may I come f-for you?"

"Always," Vanessa said, whimpering when Emma suddenly parted her slick lips and pushed two fingers inside her. "O-oh." Vanessa's mouth fell open against Emma's, her breath catching with each thrust.

And then Emma's world turned black, her legs turning to jelly as she gripped Vanessa with her free hand, her nails digging into Vanessa's shoulder. But it only spurred Vanessa on, a hiss escaping her mouth as a silky moan followed.

Vanessa held Emma upright, her fingers slowly massaging her walls. Throbbing, Emma needed a moment or two, but she still craved so much more. "S-stop," she whispered. "I need a sec."

"Mm. You and me both."

CHAPTER SIXTEEN

One month later...

Emma took the stairs, landing in the hallway with a spring in her step. For the next six weeks—minus a day or so—she had Vanessa to herself. And what a feeling it was this morning waking up to that thought. Vanessa, those incredible lips, her intellectual mind, and those hands. *Mm, the hands.* It always came back to the bloody hands. Truly incredible.

"Babe, you here?" Emma poked her head around the kitchen door, smiling when she found Vanessa sitting in nothing but a short, silk, royal blue robe. "Hey."

Vanessa held up a hand, smiling as she mouthed, "One minute." She was on a call, so Emma poured herself some coffee and waited for Vanessa's delicious voice and superb eyes to focus fully on her.

"Well," Vanessa sighed. "It's been a wonderful 30 years, regardless of how it ended."

Emma spied the paperwork in Vanessa's hand, the manila envelope.

"I know. I know. And we have a daughter together. One who isn't speaking to either of us, but we still love her."

Emma leaned back, her coffee cup resting on her chin. She watched Vanessa's body language. She appeared…calm.

"Well, I'd better go," Vanessa said, lifting her feet onto the empty chair beside her. "Take care of yourself, Richard." Vanessa nodded. "Yeah. Goodbye."

Vanessa placed her phone down on the table, staring at the screen momentarily. Emma would give her a couple of minutes to adjust to whatever had happened, but she suspected she knew. Vanessa's divorce had been finalised. *Thank God.* She'd always been fond of Richard, but she hadn't held the same respect for him as she did for Vanessa over the years. Not because he was an awful person but because he had what Emma wanted. She'd grin and bear it in his company, but the moment he was gone, Emma would breathe a sigh of relief. It meant she had Vanessa to herself. In her mind, at least.

"Well," Vanessa spoke, spinning in her seat. "Coffee or champagne? Decisions, decisions…"

Emma turned her watch towards herself, smiling. "I mean, it's 5 o'clock somewhere, babe."

"I think I'll settle for a coffee for the time being."

Emma grinned. "Good choice. We can drink all the champagne we like tonight."

Vanessa got to her feet, prowling towards Emma, her gorgeous thighs on show. She was certain if Vanessa lifted her arms, that pretty little V shaped tuft would be visible. "Oh? Did you have something in mind?"

"Well, first of all, I want to ask how you are. I know you and Richard haven't been together in a while, but it must still feel strange to you. So, are you okay?"

"I'm fine." Vanessa rested beside Emma, her arms folded across her chest. "I'm glad it's all over. And now we're together, I feel like I'm finally free."

Emma took Vanessa's hand, kissing her knuckles. "You know I love you, but I want to say it finally for the first time with no obstacles in the way." Emma had wanted to truly tell Vanessa how she felt, how she lit up her world, but it never seemed to be the right time. They still had Lauren to contend with, but they had another five weeks before she returned. "I don't want you to say it back until you mean it, but I do, Vanessa. I love you."

Vanessa caressed Emma's cheek. "I know, baby."

"No, I don't think you do." Emma ran a hand through her raven hair. "It's not an *I love you* said on a whim. It's an all-consuming *I love you* I need you to hear. Since you told me how you felt, it's like my heart is getting bigger in my chest, and I don't know what to do with any of it. And I don't expect you to feel the same way any time soon, that's not what this is. It's just... you make me feel like nobody else in the world ever has."

Vanessa took Emma's coffee cup and pulled her against her. "I'm so grateful that you never backed down. And I know we still have a lot to work through, but I feel the love you have for me." Vanessa paused. "I just wonder if I'll always be enough for you?"

Emma quirked an eyebrow. "Enough?"

"If this, what we're doing, is just sex and a good time, I need you to tell me."

"Sex and a good time? Really?"

Vanessa shrugged, but Emma saw the insecurities in her eyes. "I don't want you to think you still have to feel the way you did before you left."

"This is not that. Just sex and a good time? Not. At. All."

"And it doesn't feel like it is." Vanessa ran her fingers through Emma's hair, sighing. "But I want you to know that if you ever realised this wasn't working for you, you know?"

"No, I don't know." Emma pulled back, frowning.

"You still have a lot to do. You're young. I'm...*older*."

"You're fucking gorgeous is what you are."

Vanessa blushed, lowering her eyes. "I've just left a marriage which spanned three decades. I have a daughter. And I'm much closer to the age of retirement than anything else."

Emma nodded. She completely understood Vanessa's point, but it didn't change anything for her. "The only regret I'll ever have in life is not winning you over sooner. But now is the right time. I don't care about your age. I just want *you*. The woman I fell in love with. And to be honest, I feel like I'm falling all over again. Only this time, it's completely different."

"Everything is different."

"And I wouldn't change a thing. Never. Whatever happened has brought us to this point. Right here, right now."

Vanessa wrapped a hand around the back of Emma's neck, smiling into a soft, lingering kiss. "You're absolutely right."

"Now, what plans do you have today? Because I kinda had something for us." Emma settled her palms against Vanessa's chest, stopping for a moment to appreciate the natural beauty of this woman.

Vanessa's eyebrow rose. "Oh?"

"Plans first," Emma countered.

"I was going to open all my end of year gifts from my students. It's closure for me. You know, for the ones I won't see again. At least, not in the classroom."

Emma loved that Vanessa was dedicated to her job and her students. "Can I get in on it? I'd love to see the gifts they got you."

"Of course. Maybe you could bring some fresh coffee in for us."

Emma cleared her throat as she turned her watch towards herself. If they were to get going with the plans Emma had made, they'd have to leave in the next few hours. "How long does this usually take you? Roughly?"

"However long it takes. Do you need to get somewhere?"

"We'll...discuss it later." Emma leaned up, kissing Vanessa as her hand connected with her backside. "Go on, beautiful. I'll bring the coffee in."

Emma watched Vanessa saunter out of the kitchen, her impressive ass begging to be squeezed to within an inch of its life.

I can't believe she's mine. Emma grinned, her cheeks heating as she privately blushed. Vanessa Middleton was everything she'd ever wanted. And more.

Vanessa relaxed in front of the fireplace, surrounded by bottles of wine, quirky artisan gifts, and a tonne of chocolate. Basically, her plan this summer was to pile on the pounds. Or her ex-students hoped for that, at least. It was always a sad occasion when the end of the school year came around, but Vanessa could say with one hundred percent certainty that her students were ready to take on the world. Surprising, given the year she'd had herself. But work was always separate from her personal life; it was her number one rule.

"Oh, you have one more." Emma reached into a pink sparkly gift bag, taking out a gift-wrapped box with a card pinned to it. "Ooh, this looks fancy."

"How can I receive so many gifts?" Vanessa took the box from Emma, scooting closer to her. She smiled when Emma placed a gentle hand on her thigh.

"It means they love you, and they're going to miss you."

"The pile grows each year. I don't want my students to spend all this money on me. I'm only doing my job."

Emma grinned. "If you'd been my teacher, I'd have spent *every* penny I had on you."

"Why?" Vanessa side glanced at Emma, slipping her finger under the lip of the envelope.

"Because you're hot, and I'd want to be the one giving you the best gift. You know, so you'd notice me."

Vanessa barked a laugh, shaking her head. "I don't think it's the reason my students lavish me with gifts. But thank you."

"Open the present. I'm excited to see what it is. They've taken their time wrapping it."

"They have." Vanessa opened the card, her brow knitted as she read the neatly written note.

I've had a wonderful time with you lately, V. I'm hoping you'll call me during the summer so we can get together and enjoy ourselves. If I'm lucky enough for it to happen, bring this gift along with you. Dani x

Vanessa swallowed, glancing down at the box in her lap. She couldn't exactly avoid opening it; Emma was sitting right beside her. "Okay, so this is a gift from someone at work."

"That's nice," Emma said, resting her head on Vanessa's shoulder. "Are you going to open it, or…"

She cleared her throat, shifting uncomfortably. "I can do it later. I feel like you have plans you want to discuss with me."

Emma wrapped an arm around Vanessa's mid-section, snuggling into her. "Just open the present. I'm too comfortable to move right now. And you smell delicious, so it's kinda hard to want to dress at all."

"Emma, I—"

"Unless it's from your *other* girlfriend."

"I-I don't have another girlfriend," Vanessa said, unsure if Emma actually meant it or not. "You're the only one in my world."

"Babe, I'm joking. Chill out and open the friggin' thing."

Vanessa slid the card into Emma's lap. If she was going to open a gift from another woman, Emma should at least know who it was from first and the gist of it. "It's from Dani."

"Ah. The famous Dani with an I not a Y?"

"Yes." Vanessa frowned as she peered down at the gift. Why would Dani give her something? And why would she do it so secretly? "So, I don't know if I want to open it. Because whatever it is, it won't mean a thing to me. Maybe it's best if I give it back to her. Still wrapped."

"She went to the trouble of buying you a gift." Emma sat upright, the loss of body heat felt immediately by Vanessa.

"Unless it's a proposal, I don't think you have anything to worry about."

"But it's you I want to open gifts from. Not Dani."

Emma landed on all fours in front of Vanessa, her dark hair cascading over one shoulder as she leaned in and captured her lips. "Babe, there are going to be so many gifts from me that you can open over the years. Dani felt the need to give you this, so open it. I'm not going to be mad, whatever it is."

"Promise me?"

"I promise."

Vanessa exhaled a deep breath, ripping the paper from the gift. A plain rose gold box sat in her hands, but she was none the wiser as to what was inside. When she removed the lid, her eyes widened. A strapless dildo sat encased in black velvet with a note slipped in behind it. "Oh, wow."

It's time we had a little fun, Mrs Middleton...

Vanessa closed the box and placed it down on the floor. "I, um..."

"How close were you two exactly?" Emma asked, her eyes narrowed. "Because considering you'd been on a few dates, that's a *big* gift to send to someone you haven't seen naked."

"We're not close. *At all.*"

"I think maybe I need to have a little word with Dani." Emma cleared her throat, getting to her feet. "You know, explain how you're *kinda* unavailable, and I'd appreciate it if she didn't send you shit like *that.*" Emma pointed to the gift that lay on the floor, scoffing.

"You said you wouldn't be mad."

"With you. I wouldn't be mad *with you.*"

Vanessa closed her eyes, pinching the bridge of her nose. Dani really had overstepped, and Vanessa would tell her colleague that. "I'll sort it out. Don't worry."

"And what's all this Mrs Middleton thing about?" Emma scoffed again, shaking her head. "Fucking weirdo."

Vanessa suppressed a smirk, following Emma into the middle of the room. She didn't need her girlfriend to be pacing; there was *nothing* to worry about. "If it makes you feel any better..." Vanessa embraced Emma, nipping her earlobe. "When you call me that, I feel sexy...*wanted*."

"And when *she* does it?"

"It makes me feel old." Vanessa laughed, but Emma lowered her eyes. "Baby, look at me." She curled her fingers, lifting Emma's gaze. "What she's done is not okay. And I'll tell her."

"But are you going to tell her *why* it's not okay?"

Vanessa frowned. What did Emma mean? "It's not okay because it's not okay. It's that simple."

"Never mind." Emma untangled herself from Vanessa, but Vanessa held her grip.

"Talk to me. You're upset."

"I thought maybe you'd tell her you were unavailable. You're not interested anymore. I don't know."

"She knows I'm not interested. We kissed *once*. That's the extent of it."

"But you're not willing to tell her you're with me. I get it." Emma peeled Vanessa's arms from her body, taking a step back. "And there was me thinking maybe I could introduce you to a few people. But you can't even bring yourself to tell a woman who wants to fuck you that you're in a relationship."

"It's not like that."

Emma nodded, a weak smile on her mouth. "Sure."

"No, it's not. I'm not hiding you. I just need some time."

Vanessa watched on as Emma took her phone from the coffee table and her rucksack from the floor. She basically had her life in it. And it could only mean one thing: Emma was about to walk out.

But then she reached into her bag, taking out a gift box and an envelope before lowering her rucksack to the couch. "Here. This is for you. It can mean whatever you want it to mean. Probably nothing at all, but I understand." Emma dropped the gift into Vanessa's waiting palm. "Did you ask me earlier about my intentions because you were hoping they were the same as yours?"

"I-I don't—" Vanessa was confused. She'd asked Emma if this was only sex earlier so she didn't get too attached.

"You're not looking for a relationship, Vanessa. I realise that now. You want the sex but not the attachment. And I don't blame you. This is your time to find yourself, to see where life takes you. You're not looking for something serious."

"I am," Vanessa countered.

Emma lifted a shoulder. "But not with me. Because what would people think of you fucking your daughter's best friend? All those people I've met over the years…how would they react? The same way as Lauren. I don't want you to be the talk of your circle of friends. I'm honestly not worth it."

"Oh, you are. And you're perfect for me." Vanessa took a hesitant step closer. All she ever wanted was to be glued to Emma. In every situation, she wanted Emma's hand in hers, their bodies moulded. This space between them was far too much for Vanessa.

"Yeah?" Emma grinned, her eyes boring into Vanessa. "You mean that?"

"Since you came home, have I done anything to suggest otherwise?"

"N-no."

"We knew coming into this that it would be hard, I'm sure you agree, but I pursued you, Emma. After that night, the way you touched me as you cried against my skin…I couldn't let you go. I'm not sure I can *ever* let you go."

Emma leaned in, her lips caressing Vanessa's with a softness that had the capacity to knock her off her feet time and time again. "I've never been crazy about anyone in my life but you." Emma took Vanessa's bottom lip between her teeth before slowly releasing it. "You've no idea."

"That's all I need to know." Vanessa held Emma by the waist, one arm slipping around her back. "I don't care what other people think. I've never cared. I only care that you and I are happy together."

"I don't think I can do this with you and never fully have it all. Richard had you on his arm, and now I want you on mine."

Vanessa toyed with the giftbox in her hand, her eyes searching Emma's face. "I had no idea you felt this way. I'm sorry."

"I didn't either until today."

"But I'll make it right. For us, okay?" Vanessa dipped her head, finding Emma's eyes. "You mean the world to me, and if I have to do the whole coming out thing again, I will."

"I don't want you to do anything you're not comfortable with. I just want some kind of acknowledgement that we're in this together."

"We are."

Emma reached out, tucking Vanessa's hair behind her ear. "You really are the love of my life."

Those words tore through Vanessa at the speed of light. She was the love of Emma's life? But…how? Right now, she had no words. Emma Bradley was all she needed and more.

"Open the box."

Vanessa did so, tears welling in her eyes when she stared down at a white gold bracelet with a date inscribed. Tucked behind it was an address with booking confirmation. *A lodge*. Her fingertip grazed the date as she frowned.

"Do you know the date?"

Vanessa cleared her throat. "I was hoping you'd tell me what it meant to you. It's ten years old; I barely remember what I did ten minutes ago."

"The day after your birthday," Emma said. "I'd been into you since the year before. But it was the night you came home alone from a meal with Richard and friends."

Vanessa listened intently, wearing a slight frown. How did

Emma remember all this stuff? Dates, occasions, particular situations. *Because she's in love with you.*

"Lauren had gone to bed. I was catching the end of the Olympics. And you came home upset. You told me he was more interested in discussing a client than spending the evening with you. And you'd been left alone with the wife of his friend while they went off to drink whiskey."

Vanessa lowered her eyes. She remembered the night Emma was talking about. Emma had been so sweet in offering to sit with her, to listen. "I remember."

"You had a black evening gown on that dipped to the base of your spine. God, I couldn't take my eyes off you. But it wasn't only me admiring you. It was the night I wished for the first time that I could make you happy. Because I'd never entertain other people if *you* were by my side."

"You even remember what I was wearing?"

Emma flushed. "Sorry. I have a very good memory when it comes to you."

Vanessa curled her fingers under Emma's chin, beaming a smile at how perfect this woman was. "I love the bracelet." Vanessa leaned in, pressing her forehead to Emma's as she kissed her slowly. And then she inched back ever so slightly, holding Emma's gaze. "And I hope you know how I feel about you."

Emma's eyes fluttered closed momentarily. "Sometimes I feel like I do, but then...I don't know. I don't know if we're just passing time, you know?"

"Hey," Vanessa feathered a thumb across Emma's bottom lip, replacing it with a languid kiss. "I love you, too. More than I thought possible. You...you make me feel alive, Emma. You make me excited to come home at night. I know you'll be here waiting with open arms, ready to kiss me like the world is going to end. And that's all I've *ever* wanted in life. Someone who sees me for me. Not someone who is only seen as an object, looking pretty."

"I've never seen you that way."

"I know."

Emma pulled Vanessa against her. "And I never will."

Vanessa brushed Emma's hair from her face, smiling at her with tears in her own eyes. "Nobody could come close to how you make me feel. Never."

"I keep wishing I'd known how you felt before I left…"

"Don't think about what could have been. At that point, I wasn't in a position to make anything more of the feelings I had. And honestly, I had no idea how I *was* feeling. It'd been so long since I'd felt loved, cared for. When you looked at me as though we were the only two people on this planet, I didn't know how to deal with it."

"Thank you." Emma craned her neck, kissing Vanessa like she meant it. God, her body always reacted in the same way. *Awakened*. "For being honest. For understanding…for being you."

"I do love you, and you're *so* worth it."

"Then we should get some things together and head off. If you fancy the lodge."

Vanessa absolutely wanted to be at the lodge. "Do I get you all to myself?"

"Every last inch of me."

CHAPTER SEVENTEEN

Vanessa stared into the open fire at the lodge as she placed her phone on the coffee table, the sound of Emma humming in the kitchen making her smile while she watched the flames dance higher. Being here, alone, was everything Vanessa could have dreamed of.

"Here," Emma said, holding out a cup of coffee for Vanessa over the back of the couch. "Get this down you."

"Thanks."

Emma's hooded eyes stared back at Vanessa; she definitely had something on her mind. And then Emma cleared her throat. "I know you want to unpack, but could we sit for a minute?"

Vanessa nodded as Emma rounded the couch, sinking down beside Vanessa. "This is incredibly difficult for you, I know, but everything I said before…I meant."

"I know you did." Emma took Vanessa's free hand, their coffees resting on their knees. "But I want to ask you something."

Vanessa swallowed. She didn't know where this was going. "Okay."

"I want to know more." Emma turned, tucking her legs beneath her.

"More?"

"I'm not asking you to justify anything, but I left not knowing you felt the same way. And I don't know, I think it would be nice to know more. Maybe how you came to realise you were into me. Or the day you knew you wanted something more..."

Vanessa set her cup down on the table, taking Emma's too. She opened her arms, pulled Emma into her body, and sighed lightly. "I don't think I'll ever forget the day."

"Why?"

"I mean, I'd wanted you before this particular day, trust me, but it was the moment for me when I knew I was in too deep. But I didn't know what to do or how to tell you."

Emma relaxed in Vanessa's arms, holding her hands against her stomach. "Tell me."

Vanessa held Emma close, her mind cast back to a day some six months before Emma left the country. Back then it hurt, but right now...pure bliss.

Vanessa leant against the counter, smiling as people milled about in her kitchen. It was her birthday, but she barely knew the people here. They were Richard's friends. Business associates, but he called them friends anyway. She spied her husband in the corner by the patio doors, discussing something with his assistant.

Rosanna had been with him for a few months now, but something about her had Vanessa's back up. Whenever she called the office, it was her voice Vanessa was met with. Not her husband. She didn't know why it bothered her so much, but if Richard was dabbling again, Vanessa wasn't sure she could continue their marriage a third time around. It had been generally perfect, but Vanessa knew about the women he'd overstepped with in the past. She scoffed. How could she claim her marriage was perfect when Richard currently had his hand on his assistant's backside?

She needed air. Richard may not care who saw him, but Vanessa did. She didn't want to be in the room when his friends noticed how infatuated he was with his assistant.

"Enjoying the evening, Mum?"

Vanessa plastered on a fake smile. "Of course. It's lovely."

"Then could you tell that to your face?" Lauren barked a laugh. "You look like you're waiting to visit a mortuary."

Vanessa rolled her eyes. "Am I that obvious?" She had to try harder. Richard had gone to a lot of trouble to put this on tonight. Even if it was all guilt related. He couldn't even manage to separate from Rosanna. That said a lot when it was supposed to be Vanessa's evening. "Sorry, love."

"Mum, you and I both know we'd rather be sitting in a bar, sipping cocktails."

Vanessa stepped closer to her daughter, lowering her voice. "So, why exactly aren't we doing that?"

"Because...Dad." Lauren lifted a shoulder, but Vanessa knew she sympathised. They'd done this plenty of times over the years. It was another excuse for Richard to mingle with the big wigs. "But I'm sure we can go out to a bar this week. Just you, me, and Emma."

Vanessa smiled at the thought. Emma was supposed to be here this evening, but something must have cropped up. Wherever Lauren went, Emma did too. But not this evening. Disappointment settled in Vanessa's stomach; Emma was the only guest she wanted to lay eyes on tonight. Out of everyone in this room, Emma was the one she felt most comfortable around. Their conversations were always light and honest, but it was the way in which Emma listened intently to everything Vanessa said that thrilled her.

"I thought she was coming tonight."

"She is. She's going to be a bit late."

Vanessa fought back the urge to squeal. Over the last few months, her attraction to Emma had grown. And by grown, Vanessa meant that it was hard to think of anything else. They'd spent last Sunday together working in the garden while Lauren was out with work colleagues, and it had meant so much to Vanessa. Emma always seemed to be around to keep her company. But Vanessa knew she had to curb how she felt. Nothing good could possibly come from the emotions surging inside her whenever her daughter's best friend was around. Which was pretty much daily.

Vanessa needed a moment.

And she still needed air.

"Okay, well, I'm sure I'll see Emma about when she arrives. I need to pop outside for a few minutes."

"Everything okay?"

"Migraine."

Lauren nodded. Vanessa seemed to have a 'migraine' every other day lately. "Let me know if you need anything."

"I'll be okay." Vanessa stepped past her daughter, making a beeline for her husband. She tapped him on the shoulder, an eyebrow raised. "Can you not!"

"Not what?" Richard asked, his brow creased.

"Mentally fuck your assistant in our kitchen. It's distasteful."

Richard straightened, his hand falling from Rosanna's backside. "Don't be absurd."

"Just...keep her out of MY bed." Vanessa cleared her throat. "And you may want to be less handsy. If Lauren catches either of you, she'll have no qualms with throwing her arse out onto the street. And what would the neighbours think then?"

Vanessa stepped away, blowing out a deep breath as she slipped off into the garden. She dipped her hand into a small box which sat beside the dining furniture, pulling out a cigarette and a lighter. She hadn't smoked for a long time, but, lately, the need seemed to creep up on her unexpectedly. And quite frankly, it was a cigarette or time inside for murder.

She lit it, blowing the smoke high into the night sky. The temperature was pleasant this evening, but Vanessa didn't want to be standing outside alone at her own party. She rested back against the wall out of sight, allowing everything she felt to slip from her mind. Emma would be here soon. She would be more than occupied then.

A throat clearing startled Vanessa. She turned, her entire body trembling when she saw Emma stood in front of her. Lauren's best friend usually arrived dressed quite casually, but tonight? Oh, tonight Emma was the most beautiful woman in Vanessa's world. "E-Emma, hi."

"Hi." Emma frowned, her eyes shifting to the cigarette Vanessa held.

"Sorry," Vanessa said, offering a weak smile. "Terrible habit."

"I...didn't know you smoke."

Vanessa shook her head, stubbing it out under her heel. "I don't. Usually."

"Mrs Middleton, are you okay?"

"Of course. I'm fine. And I'm so happy you could make it this evening."

Emma blushed. "Lauren said you'd be out here." She stepped forward, wrapping her arms around Vanessa. Their bodies pressed together so seamlessly. "Happy Birthday."

"Thank you." Vanessa held Emma at arm's length when she pulled back, drinking in her incredible features. "Wow. You look...wow. I almost didn't recognise you."

Emma blushed again, lowering her eyes. "I didn't want to show up in jeans. Everyone would have talked about it."

"You can show up here however you like. This is my house; they can like it or lump it." Vanessa realised she'd been holding onto Emma for too long, so she quickly let go, gathering herself. "I see Lauren got you a drink?"

"Yep. Beer."

Vanessa suppressed a smile. Emma was standing in a little black dress, knockout heels, her hair and makeup sending Vanessa's blood south...but she wanted to drink beer. She shouldn't love that, but Vanessa did. She loved everything about Emma.

"So, have you had a nice day?" Emma sidled up beside Vanessa. "You have a lot of friends."

"They're Richard's business associates, not my friends. The wives of said business associates, yes, but they're not here for me."

"Oh."

"But you and Lauren are here. That's what matters."

Emma shifted from left to right, holding her clutch bag in one hand as she set her beer down on the table. "Could I speak to you for a moment? I don't want to disturb your evening, but it'll only take a few minutes..."

"Of course." Vanessa made the mistake of glancing inside the house. Richard still had his hands all over his assistant. She took a moment to breathe. It was one thing to know Richard was up to no good again, but to see him so freely touching Rosanna in her kitchen left an anger dripping inside her, waiting to be unleashed. "W-what's up?" Emma wanted to discuss something, and Vanessa wouldn't for one second give Richard the headspace while she had Emma's attention.

"I've had a job offer."

"Wow. That's great." Vanessa beamed a smile; Emma had been between jobs and working for agencies for a while now. She never seemed to want to settle in one place. "I know you were looking at a school placement, so which one is it?" If Emma were positioned at the same school as Vanessa, she may lose her mind.

"It's...Africa."

Vanessa hadn't expected Emma's news to hit her so hard, but it did, deep down in the pit of her stomach. She studied Emma's eyes, bright and excited. It didn't matter how Vanessa felt—devastated—it mattered that Emma was stupidly happy. "You look thrilled."

"I am. I've always wanted to do something like this. And I don't know, I guess I wanted to ask what you think about it. Lauren doesn't know yet, and even though she's going to tell me she's happy for me, I know she won't be. We always promised to be here for one another."

Vanessa smiled weakly. If Richard continued his foolish games, Lauren would need Emma a lot sooner than either of them knew. "Lauren is going to be beside herself for you. She loves you and will only want the best for you. When do you leave?"

"December."

Okay, so Vanessa had another six months or so of watching Emma from afar. It wasn't so bad. "You're going to be amazing over there. I know it."

"Thanks. That means a lot." Emma reached into her clutch bag,

clearing her throat. "And this is for you. I didn't want to give it to you inside because I get a bit nervous when it comes to giving gifts. But if you don't like them, it's totally fine. I have the receipt so you can choose something else."

Vanessa frowned.

"I saw you looking online a few weeks ago at the dining table." And then Emma sighed, shaking her head. "Shit. You already bought them. Crap."

Vanessa grinned. Emma often seemed flustered around her, but it was something else to add to the growing pile of things she loved about her daughter's best friend.

"Anyway," Emma said, her hand shaking as she handed a small gift-wrapped box over. "Pretend you don't have them and then take them back when I'm not here. I'll never know."

Warmth spread through Vanessa when Emma placed the box in her hand, closing her fingers around her skin. God, she'd miss Emma's touch when she left. And for most of the years she'd known Emma, her touch had been just that, a touch. But as time passed, it ignited Vanessa's entire body.

"Happy Birthday, Vanessa."

The way Emma spoke her name had a shiver coursing through Vanessa. Her voice, when they were alone, was velvet. "Thank you."

Vanessa tugged at the tiny gold string wrapped around the box, an overwhelming sense of gratitude rolling through her. Emma always bought her a gift for her birthday, but this one seemed to mean more. To both of them.

When she removed the wrapping around the box, Vanessa's breath caught. The Cartier logo sat across the lid in gold, Vanessa's heart hammering in her chest. "Oh, Emma. T-this is too much."

"Honestly, after how you've made me feel over the years, welcoming me into your home without a second thought, I fear it's not enough."

Vanessa noted how Emma's voice cracked ever so slightly, and when she opened the box, her own voice betrayed her. "O-oh. These are the Légers earrings I was looking at."

"You bought them, didn't you?"

Vanessa frowned, clearing her throat. "I didn't. I asked Richard for them, but, well..." Vanessa paused, closing her eyes momentarily. Richard hadn't picked them up for her birthday. Instead he'd handed her an envelope for a weekend spa break with Lauren. Thoughtless, really, since he always sent them on spa breaks. Chances were, he was getting a good business deal with the ones he was booking with Rosanna. "They're beautiful." And then the cost of them flagged up in Vanessa's mind. "But I can't take them. It's far too much."

Emma shook her head. "No. Please. Don't give them back to me. Unless you hate them."

"I don't hate them." Vanessa placed the lid on the box, pulling Emma into her arms. She breathed in deeply, Emma's perfume alluring but a familiar comfort to her. "I love them."

"They'll look great on you," Emma whispered, turning her head into Vanessa's neck as she tightened her grip on her waist. Okay, this was new. Very new, and...Oh, Lord, it was incredibly fulfilling to have Emma against her in this way. "Beautiful." And then Emma shot back, clearing her throat. "Sorry. That was far too much."

Vanessa cocked her head, smiling. "I'm going to miss you when you go."

"I'll be back. Don't worry."

Vanessa drew in a shaky breath, holding Emma against her. She needed to feel their connection, body to body. Because for all the time she'd missed Emma, Vanessa feared all the years to come would never make up for the longing. "I just knew," she whispered. "You went out of your way to give me something so beautiful for my birthday, but he couldn't even manage to hold back with his assistant."

"Babe, I wish you'd seen it sooner."

Vanessa laughed. "I knew all along. I saw the credit card statements, and I watched him with other women. Richard was having affairs a long time ago."

"I know." Emma cleared her throat, shifting in Vanessa's arms.

"But I didn't think it was my place to say anything. Not back then."

Vanessa stared down at Emma, pressing a kiss to her forehead. "It wouldn't have changed anything."

"Perhaps not, at least not for us, but you deserved so much more. I mean, he's a bastard for what he did to you. But then the selfish side of me is kinda glad, you know? I mean, I never wanted him to hurt you, but now I get you. And I get to love you forever...because I'm not going anywhere, and I don't care how long it takes to prove it to you. I'm all in."

"Oh, Emma. You have *nothing* to prove. Believe me."

"Maybe not." Emma lifted a shoulder, turning and curling her body around Vanessa. "But you're going to know how much I love you every day. I promise you."

"I felt it...in the past."

"Felt what?"

Vanessa dragged a blanket over them, sinking down onto her back as Emma rested against her. "Your love."

"You did?"

"Of course. But I had to push it away. My life was slowly turning upside down, and I couldn't have you contending for my heart. As much as I wanted it, wanted *you*, I wasn't in the right place."

Emma took Vanessa's hands. "But you definitely are now?"

"Without a shadow of a doubt."

Emma leaned in again, her arms wrapped around Vanessa, until her phone started to ping incessantly. "What the hell is going on?"

Vanessa sat forward, taking Emma's phone and handing it over. "No idea. You'd better check." Vanessa watched as Emma's eyes widened, then she frowned. "What is it?"

"Y-you changed your relationship status on social media."

"Mmhmm. I did."

"A-and everyone is commenting." Emma stuttered, her thumb scrolling down the page. "Wow. You have a lot of friends."

Vanessa shrugged. "And not a single opinion is relevant to me. My real friends will support me."

And then Emma stopped scrolling, tears rolling down her cheeks again.

"Okay. No more crying. I can't bear to see you upset. And this is a good thing, no?"

"It's not that." Emma pulled Vanessa closer. "Lauren left a comment."

"Oh." Vanessa's heart suddenly tumbled into her stomach. "I, uh...I'm not sure I want to see it."

Emma turned the screen to her. It simply read: *I love you both.*

Vanessa's entire face lit up, the feeling of her life coming together hitting her with force. She couldn't say she'd ever been this happy, but it was a wonderful memory she would keep close to her heart. Whenever she was worried, panicked by the changes in her life, she would remember this second, alone and in tremendous love with Emma Bradley.

CHAPTER EIGHTEEN

Roused from her sleep by a warm hand on her shoulder, Emma turned to find Vanessa staring back at her. Her royal blue silk robe covered her delectable skin, a sweet smile playing on Vanessa's lips when Emma stretched, yawning. "What time is it?"

"Time you woke up so we can have breakfast in bed."

Emma's eyebrow rose. She couldn't say she'd ever had breakfast in bed. Unless it was a euphemism. "Breakfast in bed?"

"Mmhmm."

Emma sat up against the headboard, sun streaming through the floor to ceiling window in the bedroom. She looked down at the foot of the bed, surprised to find all kinds of delicious food ready and waiting for her.

"I hope you're hungry..."

Emma was always hungry when Vanessa was around. The woman certainly knew how to work up an appetite. And then Emma's stomach growled, answering Vanessa's question for her.

"Yep. You're ready to eat." Vanessa grinned, getting to her feet and balancing the tray on Emma's lap. Once she'd joined her in bed, Vanessa shifted closer, her bare thigh resting against Emma's. "I wasn't sure what you felt like, so I basically cooked everything. I'm surprised I didn't wake you with the noise I made in the kitchen."

"I'm a deep sleeper." Emma swept her hair from her face, side glancing at Vanessa. "Is there a reason why you've done all of this?"

"Well, this is our first morning as an *official* couple. I thought perhaps we could enjoy some food and take today at our own pace. Yesterday was…emotional, to say the least."

Vanessa was absolutely right. Emma wasn't sure what day it was in all honesty. From yesterday when she expressed her worries, everything seemed to roll into one. And to have Vanessa here this morning after Emma had so readily told her she wasn't happy about the fact she felt she was being hidden was astonishing. Still, Emma was thankful Vanessa was with her. It meant she wanted this to work.

"About yesterday," Emma started. "I'm sorry if it felt as though I was giving you an ultimatum. It wasn't like that, and I'd never expect you to turn your life upside down for me."

"No, you were right. I was worried about what people would think of me. And I've never been that type of person, so when you told me how you felt about Dani, I knew you were right. My life is of no concern to anyone else. It's something I have to remember."

Emma slathered butter on a bagel, adding bacon to it. She didn't know about fancy breakfasts, but she loved a bacon butty. "Please don't think I don't sympathise with everything you're going through. I do. But I let things get the better of me, and I shouldn't have reacted how I did. I wasn't convinced you were all in."

Vanessa offered a single nod, licking her fingers after spreading jam onto a piece of toast. "I can see how it must have looked to you."

"But you're here," Emma whispered, leaning in and kissing below Vanessa's ear. "And that's what matters this morning." Vanessa turned her head, capturing Emma's lips. Soft, sweet, and filled with promise…that's what Vanessa tasted like this morning. "Mm. Stop. Breakfast will be ruined otherwise."

Vanessa offered a shy smile as she pulled back. "Sorry. It's hard to stop when kissing a woman is so much better than I ever remembered."

Emma watched Vanessa. She seemed calmer this morning than any other morning they'd shared together so far. It could be the fact she was basically out, or it could be the unexpected comment from Lauren last night. They were yet to actually speak to one another about it—Emma saw the initial fear in Vanessa's eyes—but Lauren wouldn't have written that comment on social media if she hadn't meant it. Emma knew that much with one hundred percent certainty.

But Emma didn't want to dwell on the past anymore…or what was to come. Here and now was what mattered. "Did you actually bring any appropriate clothes with you? Like, for walking…"

Vanessa feigned shock, swallowing. "You mean, I have to get dressed during this trip?"

Emma grinned. As much as she'd love to spend the next couple of days in bed with Vanessa, they should do some normal things. Like, walking, talking, getting to grips with a relationship. Sex was all well and good, and it *really* was very good with Vanessa, but Emma wanted to venture out of the lodge at some point. "Much to your disappointment, yes."

"Of course I brought *real* clothes with me."

"Okay, good. I thought maybe we could go walking. Grab some lunch at a little pub along the way."

Vanessa swept a hand through her hair. "That sounds like something I could do with."

"Yeah? You're sure?"

"I love walking. And I haven't had the chance to do much of it this year. We used to have a country break once or twice a year."

"I know."

Vanessa cleared her throat. "Right. Yes."

"I don't want us to forget about the past, Vanessa. If we didn't have the past, we wouldn't be here together now. And I won't be offended when you reminisce with Lauren about Richard. He's her dad. I know to expect it."

"Everything feels so raw lately. It doesn't matter what I do or what I feel, nothing seems as good as I want it to."

Emma focused on her bagel. Vanessa had a lot of changes around her lately, but Emma could only be on hand to support her when she needed it.

"Like us, for instance. I want to feel so good when I'm with you, and I do, but I still have things playing on my mind. Or, I did."

"Did?"

"This morning feels entirely different. Because it's not a secret anymore. And I never wanted you to be a secret, Emma. But I hope you can understand in some way why I was wary of putting it all out there."

"Of course I understand." Emma felt terrible for yesterday. The more she thought about it, the faster the guilt ate away at her. She'd pressured Vanessa to do what she did last night. And it didn't feel good. "I'm so sorry. I was a complete bitch. I know what I want, it's been you for so long, but I had no right to react how I did yesterday. And then for you to do what you did, to tell the world...you should have been able to do it when you were good and ready, not because I wanted you to. I feel awful."

Vanessa lifted the tray from the bed, setting it down on the nightstand. It wobbled, but it held. "Please, don't apologise. You had every right to say what you did. And I don't think Dani helped," Vanessa paused. "And yes, I called her while you were packing. She knows I'm not available, *and* she knows about you. She couldn't apologise enough for the gift."

"Dani is the least of my concerns."

"But I did need to put a stop to things with her. I mean, *nothing* has ever happened, but she's very persistent. It was time I told her no once and for all."

"I appreciate that," Emma said, snuggling into Vanessa. "But please don't think I'm worried about her. I'm not."

"You're the only one I've had my eye on since the day I met Richard."

Emma tightened her grip around Vanessa's waist, sighing with contentment. When she got off her flight some two months ago, this hadn't been the expected outcome. Vanessa would always be there in her mind, but beside her in a lodge...no. Not expected. "I'm looking forward to the future. And I know it'll seem too soon for a lot of people, but this has been all I've wanted for so long. I can barely remember a time when I didn't want you."

"I have an idea."

Emma was all ears. She was up for anything Vanessa suggested. "Go."

"Today is starting over for us both," Vanessa explained, her eyes soft. "It's not that I don't want to remember all the longing and craving you, I do, but I want to start again. Here, right now, from this moment on."

"I'd like that."

"Yeah?" Vanessa breathed a sigh of relief. "I feel like I want to know you on a level we've never really known one another. I want to know you as my girlfriend, my lover, not as my daughter's best friend."

"I know what you mean." Emma placed a gentle hand over Vanessa's. "And I'd like to discover who we are, too."

"Then we should get this food eaten, get out of bed, and spend the day walking and talking."

Emma leaned up, kissing Vanessa slowly. Even Vanessa's lips felt different this morning. They didn't feel so forbidden anymore. "Come on. Let's start our own story. One that includes only you and I."

CHAPTER NINETEEN

This was the life. Nature around them, hand-in-hand, the chirp of the birds in the trees for company. Emma kept a tight grip on Vanessa's hand, guiding her through a gate which led to another field. Vanessa had never felt so content. Lauren had certainly helped recently, but it was predominantly Emma who was making Vanessa feel this way. Her genuine nature was all consuming. She wanted to know everything there was to know about Emma.

"You visited your cousin before Lauren left, right?"

"Sharon. Yeah."

"Lauren said you don't get along with your family."

"That's an understatement. I haven't spoken to most of them in around fifteen years. They're…not my cup of tea."

"Care to share?" Vanessa leaned in, their shoulders pressed together as they walked side by side. "I mean, this is the beginning for us, remember."

"Sure, yeah." Emma shrugged, the gravel crunching beneath their feet. "My family are a bit rough. Most of them anyway. Lauren has only met my mum. And that was bad enough."

"You don't speak about your parents much."

Emma snorted. "Not much to say. Mum spent more time with her friends when I was growing up than with me. If it didn't include a bottle of wine and one of the local single men, she wasn't interested."

Vanessa frowned. She had no idea about the relationship Emma had with her parents. Yes, she rarely spoke about them, but she hadn't expected Emma to have so much dislike for them. "And your dad? He wasn't around?"

"He was around," Emma said. "But he was usually shagging one of mum's friends while she was shagging one of his. I used to catch them sneaking someone in when the other was at work. Very strange relationship. One I didn't want to be a part of unless absolutely necessary."

"She must be happy to see you now you're home from Africa." Vanessa could only offer that. She was too shocked by everything else Emma had said. Considering she'd virtually grown up alone, Emma had certainly thrived.

"She doesn't know I'm home." Emma cleared her throat, wrapping an arm around Vanessa's waist as they slowed their pace. "And I have no plans to tell her any time soon."

"She's not contacted you to see how things are going?"

"Nope."

"Oh. I'm sorry." Vanessa cast her gaze on the ground, her walking boots not overly appealing today. But she loved this. Talking freely, no need to dress up and look the part. She hadn't even bothered to put makeup on this morning.

"It's not a big deal. I had to fend for myself a long time ago. Perhaps it was the best thing for me. I've never relied on anyone else in life, and I haven't turned out like my family. I'd say I'm winning in all honesty."

"It's a shame she's not seen you. You look incredible, and Africa really did a lot for you."

"Yeah?"

"You seem different. More confident. Less…unsure."

"Well, flying to Africa and living alone amongst a local community will do that to you. I loved every minute of it." Emma's eyes lit up as she spoke about Africa, her usual grey tinged with a green hue.

Then the reminder of what Emma had said when she returned hit Vanessa in the chest with the force of a thousand bricks. She wanted to go back someday. God, Vanessa didn't know what she'd do when the day came. "Sounds…nice."

"Honestly, it's like another world there. And being alone at night, no drama to contend with, worked for me. I'm quite happy with a simple life; I realised it within a month of being there."

"You want to go back, don't you?" Vanessa asked, keeping her voice in check. If Emma ever considered it, Vanessa wouldn't show she was upset. Even if she would be secretly devastated. This was where the age gap came into play. Emma had so much to do in the years ahead.

"Yeah. It's something I'd love to do. But I couldn't afford it any time soon, and they have no funding left. I think they scrimped just to keep me as long as they did."

"That's a shame."

"Two months ago, it *was* an absolute shame. But today, right now? No. I'm exactly where I should be and where I *want* to be."

That quelled Vanessa's fears for the time being.

"And I don't know. Maybe it wouldn't be the same if I ever went back. I loved being out there with the kids, but I've done it now. I lived the dream, and I wouldn't want it to ruin it if I ever went back."

Vanessa stopped on the path, turning Emma to her. "The night you called me…" She paused. "If I'd told you I felt the same, would it have changed anything? Would you have stayed?"

"Honestly?" Emma quirked a brow.

"Yes. Honestly…"

"No, I wouldn't have stayed. We both know it wouldn't have changed anything. You were married and in love with Richard."

"Married, yes, but not necessarily in love. Let's not forget it was only eight months later when he told me he wanted a divorce."

"So, you'd have upped and left him for me?"

Vanessa smiled weakly. "Since we're being honest with one another…no. And if you want the absolute truth, I didn't think you meant everything you told me that night. I expected a fling, if anything at all."

"Fair enough. It wasn't like you had any idea how I felt prior to the call. It's completely understandable if you thought I was fucking with you. But I don't regret telling you. Not at all."

"Good." Vanessa stepped closer until her body pressed to Emma's. "Because if you regret anything between us, I need to know."

Emma pushed up on the tiptoes, wrapping her arms around Vanessa's neck. "The only thing I regret is not telling you sooner. Because you were unhappy, weren't you? The night I called you… you were alone and unhappy."

Tears welled in Vanessa's eyes. "Yes. I was unhappy."

"Then I regret not whisking you away and making you feel everything you deserved to feel. Loved. Number One. The centre of attention. The centre of *my* world."

"There were times when I felt like the centre of your world before you left. But I thought I was imagining things. You know, I was miserable, so I was seeing things I knew couldn't be real." Vanessa brushed Emma's hair from the side of her face, tucking it behind her ear. "And there were times when I wanted to book the next flight out of here and meet you in Africa because all I could think about was you."

"God, I wish you had." Emma's bottom lip trembled. "I mean, if I'd told you all those years ago when I knew I wanted you, where would we be now? We'd still be together; I know that much. But we'd have had what? Ten years together."

"The time is right *now*." Vanessa leaned in, pressing her lips slowly to Emma's. "And I wouldn't change any of it."

"You know what, me neither. This, being here with you, it's all I could have ever dreamed of. And I'm not greedy."

Vanessa tilted her head, smiling as she studied every feature of Emma's gentle face. "Do you have any idea how beautiful you are?"

Emma dipped her head. "N-no."

"Well, you are." Vanessa feathered her fingertips across Emma's cheekbone, smiling into a tender kiss. Today had meant a lot to her, no pressure to be something Vanessa wasn't. And that's what she'd been missing in her life. Authenticity. Not too much expected of her. Because even though she'd loved Richard for everything he was, the expectation *was* always there. Morning, noon, and night. But with Emma? God, it was a thousand years from everything she'd know with her ex-husband. Emma made her feel. She made her tick. Emma, young as she may be, made Vanessa feel alive. And that was impressive in Vanessa's book, because she hadn't felt alive in a long time. The spark had gone out inside of her, just plodding along while she portrayed the perfect wife for Richard. But no more.

Emma turned her head, kissing Vanessa's fingertips. "I know how hard this might be for you, but please, let me be by your side through it all. Whether it's friends, family, or Lauren, I need to be with you on this journey."

"Journey?"

"*I* know you're bisexual, but most people in your life don't. And that's totally fine, but you should expect some opinions."

"Do I look like the kind of woman who is concerned about opinions?"

Emma narrowed her eyes. "Well, yes. You did tell me you were worried yesterday. But it's understandable. I wouldn't expect you to have this all figured out. Hell, even I don't know what day it is lately. But I know I want *and* need you by my side.

Hand-in-hand. I've waited so long for you, Vanessa. And I don't want to lose you."

"I'm not going anywhere."

"I know." Emma lowered her eyes between them. "And can I say, you look so good today."

"Thank you."

"I don't think I've ever seen you casual. You're always done up and looking stunning. And you look stunning today, but it's a different stunning. It's natural and real. And I really fucking love it."

"It's been a long time since I've felt this way. Laidback, you know?"

"I do," Emma said, wrapping her arms around Vanessa's waist and holding her. Emma's arms always felt so safe. Caring. Protective. Vanessa hadn't ever felt a touch quite like it. "But with me, you'll be so laid back you're falling over, babe."

"I can hardly wait." Vanessa turned her face into Emma's hair, smiling as she pressed a kiss to her head. "Hey…"

"Mm?" Emma pulled back, her eyes lazily fluttering open and closed.

Vanessa sat two fingers beneath Emma's chin, tilting her head as she looked directly into now slightly blue eyes. "I love you."

"I love you, too."

Emma lay back on the bed, her tired body thankful for the comfort. They'd had dinner, showered, and now Emma was ready to lie in her robe in this very position for the rest of the night. The day had been wonderful. Strolling along the uneven paths through the dales with Vanessa had brought them closer after the slight shit storm yesterday. They'd both continued to apologise as the day progressed, but Emma didn't want to think about it anymore. She was here with Vanessa and that was what counted.

The bed dipped at the opposite end, Vanessa's shampoo wafting towards Emma. Vanessa stretched her legs, her head at the foot of the bed, and groaned. "God, I'm destroyed now."

"Me too. Dinner was incredible, but I feel so stuffed." Emma's hands rested on her stomach as she let out a slow, long breath.

"I can't remember the last time I cooked a dinner for two. Since it's usually only me at the weekend, it seemed like a waste of time. Lauren is usually out with friends, or when Rob was home, she was with him."

"Have you heard from her since last night?" Emma asked, sitting up on her elbows and looking down at Vanessa. She wore a matching robe which ended mid-thigh. "I haven't."

"No. But I saw on her profile that she was going sky diving with Rob."

Emma grinned. "She's always wanted to sky dive. She asked if I'd ever consider it with her, but it's not something I could do."

"I'm glad you're not willing to throw yourself out of a plane. I wish my daughter felt the same way."

"You're not keen on her doing it?"

Vanessa sighed, turning on her side and caressing Emma's shin. "Not really. I don't know what would possess someone to do it. It can't be fun. Surely."

"It's not my idea of fun." Emma snorted. She couldn't imagine anything more terrifying.

"Thank God. I don't have to worry about you dragging me along in the future."

"No, babe. Our feet will remain firmly on the ground. I'm all for planes, but I draw the line at hurtling myself from one."

Vanessa's soft laugh warmed Emma throughout. It was a laugh she'd thought about in all the time she was away. But she'd thought about Vanessa entirely while she was away. Every minute if she were being honest.

"Today has been lovely," Emma said, propping her head up on a few pillows so she could look Vanessa in the eye. "And I know it was only walking around, but it was perfect."

"Sometimes the simple things in life appeal to us most."

"And now, lying here with you..." Emma sighed lightly, her hand gently caressing Vanessa's calf. "I've had the perfect day."

"Me too." Vanessa pressed a kiss to Emma's skin. It sent love crashing through her. Those little things, the unexpected kisses, Emma could spend her life feeling this way. And she had every intention of doing so. "Hey," Vanessa whispered, her hand trailing up Emma's leg and beneath her robe. "Open your robe for me. I want to look at you."

Emma tugged at the belt holding it in place, allowing it to fall open and gather against the mattress. Vanessa's soft hand caressed her thigh, a shiver of electricity working through her veins.

"You're so perfect," Vanessa said, dragging her nails down Emma's skin. "I can't believe how lucky I am to have you."

Emma quaked. "I-I never thought I'd see this day."

Vanessa smiled as her lips worked their way down Emma's legs. Emma would do anything for this woman, and that included lying exposed on a bed which didn't belong to them in the middle of nowhere.

"You know when I thought about you," Vanessa spoke low, her breath hot and heavy, "this is exactly what I pictured. Us, just like this."

"Mm. It's certainly a picture I'd happily play on repeat in my head for the rest of my life." Emma's eyes fluttered closed, her breathing laboured. Vanessa only had to look at her and she melted. "I can't believe you thought about me."

"Oh, I thought about you a lot."

"Good thoughts?"

Vanessa's hand crept higher again, her thumb pushing

between Emma's wet, sensitive folds. She gasped, and then took her bottom lip between her teeth.

"Some of the greatest thoughts of my life." Before Emma had time to think about anything Vanessa was doing, her legs were parted, and her knees were bent. A fingertip slowly descended down the outline of Emma's lips, a tremor almost shaking her to the core. "You. Are. Exquisite."

Emma's stomach tightened, the cool air producing goosebumps all over her body. Every word Vanessa spoke was dipped in honey, and Emma was about ready to lose her mind.

"Spread yourself for me," Vanessa demanded, her voice soft.

Emma, with a steady hand, brushed it down her stomach and towards her throbbing sex. It didn't matter what Vanessa asked her to do, or how it made her feel. Emma was ready to fuck herself senseless for this woman. She spread her lips with two fingers, groaning as she brushed her clit. "O-oh."

"Perfect." Vanessa's voice dropped lower as she palmed Emma's thigh. "Touch yourself."

Emma clenched her jaw, her nostrils flared as she gathered her own wetness on her fingertips. And then Vanessa gripped her wrist, bringing Emma's fingers to her own lips and sucking them into her mouth.

Shit! Fuck! What the hell is she doing to me? Emma lifted her head from the pillow, watching Vanessa as she moaned, her tongue running up Emma's fingers. "You taste so sweet." And then she placed Emma's hand back where she wanted it, encouraging Emma to continue. "Go on. Show me how you touched your pussy when you thought about us together."

God. Emma could barely contain herself. Vanessa had always been sexy and intriguing, but the sex was off the scale hot compared to what she'd fantasised about. And the dominance she exuded only made Emma want to lie back and take everything Vanessa demanded. "Vanessa…" Emma wasn't sure if she'd spoken or not. Everything around her felt dulled. Just Vanessa's breath against the skin of her legs holding her in place.

"What is it, baby?"

Emma glanced up again. This time, Vanessa was focused on what Emma was doing, while her hand slid between her own legs.

"God, you're so fucking hot." It was more of a groan than a statement that fell from Emma's lips. "You're driving me insane."

"So give in and touch yourself." Vanessa focused on Emma's eyes, studying her. And then a moan slid from Vanessa's pink lips. "I want to see you fucking yourself. Deep and slow."

Emma pushed two fingers inside herself, spreading her legs further apart. If this was the show Vanessa wanted, then this was the show she would get. She pushed in and out slowly, the muscles in her stomach contracting as she curled her fingers ever so slightly. When Vanessa did the same, sinking two long, slender fingers inside herself, Emma lost her mind. Her best friend's mother was fucking herself while she watched Emma do the same. Of all the fantasies she'd had, this wasn't on the list, but God, she wished it had been. Because as Vanessa's fingers slid out of her, soaked and glistening, Emma wanted to devour her entirely.

Seeing Vanessa so free and uninhibited, Emma sunk her own fingers deeper, pressing the heel of her hand to her clit. "Oh, f-fuck."

"Mm." Vanessa's eyes watched on with interest, concentrated on Emma's hand. But Emma couldn't take her eyes off Vanessa. Everything about this woman was what she'd been looking for in life. Tonight, it didn't matter if she was Lauren's mum, and, tonight, the age difference was completely irrelevant. Because tonight, Vanessa Middleton was rocking Emma's world like no other ever had. "Harder," Vanessa murmured, her voice catching in her throat, those intense eyes a midnight blue. "And faster."

Emma added a third finger, pumping fast and deep. But she

couldn't hold on for much longer, regardless of what Vanessa asked of her next. "Shit, I-I can't..."

"Stop!" Vanessa spoke suddenly, pressing her hand to Emma's. "Hold it."

Emma's thighs shook, her world ready to turn black at any moment. "Babe, I need to come."

"And you will," Vanessa said, smirking as she slowly moved her hand. "But I'm not ready to see this end yet. It's too beautiful. You're too fucking sexy."

Emma swallowed, dropping her head to the pillow. If she could wiggle her fingers, shift them slightly, she would come hard. As she felt movement at her feet, Emma lifted her head again.

Vanessa propped herself up against the foot end of the bed, spreading her legs and pinching her clit as her lips parted. God, it was a sight Emma could have only dreamed of. But this wasn't a dream, and Vanessa was painfully teasing now. Emma needed more.

"Fuck yourself for me." Emma's voice held a confidence she'd never heard before. And judging by the quirked eyebrow Vanessa was wearing, she was just as shocked. "Do it. For me."

"Say please..." Vanessa tugged at her nipple, her fingers slowly rolling over her clit.

"Please. Fuck yourself." Emma didn't lose Vanessa's gaze. "For me."

Before Emma had time to think, Vanessa was sinking into her own wetness, slick and glistening as Emma watched on with an incredible arousal rolling through her. This was a work of art.

"Mm. Yeah, like that." Emma grinned, her own fingers desperate to move. The sound of Vanessa's wetness, her laboured breath, those throaty moans. *Holy shit!* "Fuck, you're soaked."

Those words ignited something inside Vanessa, and her hand moved faster, her breath catching with every thrust of her fingers. "E-Emma."

"You gonna come for me, babe?" Emma spread her legs impossibly wide, her hips rocking against her still hand.

"T-Together." Vanessa cried, her head thrown back.

But Emma shot to her knees and dropped her upper body to the bed—her fingers still inside herself—and latched her lips onto Vanessa's clit.

"Oh, fuck!" Vanessa's free hand gripped a fistful of Emma's hair, her hips bucking as Emma lashed her tongue against Vanessa's clit. "Yes. Don't stop. Fuck, don't stop."

The air thick with sex and desire, Emma couldn't hold back any longer. She sunk her fingers as far as she could reach, enveloped Vanessa's clit with her lips, and tumbled over the edge at the exact moment Vanessa shook in front of her.

As Vanessa's hips slowed, her grip on Emma's hair loosening, she let out a guttural moan. One that had Emma on the edge again. "Fuck me. That was...*wow*."

Vanessa gripped Emma's jaw, encouraging her up her body. "You..." Vanessa said, her chest heaving as she tumbled into a kiss. "God, you've no idea."

Holy fuck, that was an experience.

CHAPTER TWENTY

"Babe, did you want wine or a hot drink?" Emma poked her head out of the back patio of the lodge, her eyes shining bright as the fire crackled in front of Vanessa. "I can get whatever you want."

"I think I'll have a glass of the red we brought with us, please."

"Coming right up. I'll be out in a few."

Vanessa nodded when Emma disappeared back inside the lodge. Tomorrow they had to check out, but Vanessa couldn't imagine being anywhere else right now. She'd lit a fire half an hour ago, the chill in the Yorkshire Dales quite intense once the sun set, but it was flawless. There wasn't a soul around for miles, and for the first time in so long, Vanessa had enjoyed being away.

In the past, it had been hard for her. Richard had always bent over backwards to ensure she had everything she needed. The issue was that Vanessa had never asked for any of it. She didn't want him to try too hard, and she didn't want him to harp on to their friends about how fantastic Vanessa was. She wanted this. Simple, enjoyable, relaxing. *Nothing* beat this.

And even though they'd had many country retreats away, Richard always had things to do. Phone calls, online conference meetings, clients to deal with. While Vanessa would usually sit outside alone, he was entertaining someone through a screen. Vanessa had loathed it all. She wanted to sit and talk until the sun was beginning to rise over the dales. She wanted to toast marshmallows and enjoy fine wine while the person she loved enjoyed those very same things beside her. But with Richard, it wasn't to be. And she couldn't change him, no matter how hard she tried.

"It's the Malbec you opened before." Emma's sudden presence had Vanessa splaying a hand across her chest. "Sorry, babe. I didn't mean to frighten you."

"I was in my own head. It's fine." Vanessa looked up at Emma, those enticing eyes dragging Vanessa deeper into another world. "Come and sit with me. I missed you."

"I was only gone for five minutes," Emma laughed.

"Five minutes too long for my liking."

Emma took a seat and huddled into Vanessa, their wine and beer sitting on the wooden table in front of them. The heat from the fire was instantly warming. It wasn't exactly cold tonight, but it was cosy and romantic. Vanessa couldn't recall the last time she'd had a romantic evening, but God, she'd missed them.

"I don't want to go home tomorrow." Emma sighed, her head falling to Vanessa's shoulder. "But at least I still have weeks alone with you."

"This little getaway has been beautiful."

"I wanted to do something for you. While you're at home, you're on the go. And I know we haven't exactly sat on our arses here, but it's different. You're not pottering around the house for the sake of it. And you had a lie in this morning, something I'm certain you haven't done in a long time."

"I have to get up to make breakfast when I'm at home." Vanessa rolled her eyes.

"For who?"

Vanessa cleared her throat. "Well, it was mainly for Richard. I was his wife, it was expected, but a lie in now and then would have been nice."

Emma lifted her head. "I'm sorry, but wife status doesn't mean you should have to cook for him. Did he not have his own pair of hands?"

"Trust me, heterosexual relationships are not the same."

"Too fucking right they're not. If I catch you climbing out of bed to make me breakfast, I'll withhold sex for a month."

"Oh, sweetheart," Vanessa offered a sad smile, "we both know *that's* a lie."

"No. It's not." Emma stated matter-of-factly. "I don't *ever* want you to get out of bed for me. I'd rather you were in it instead."

"Then I will bear it in mind." Vanessa grinned, a frisson of electricity coursing through her. "I was thinking while you were inside. About how I haven't had a romantic evening in forever."

"Expect more of them with me."

Vanessa tilted her head as she looked up at the stars. "I was always a romantic."

Emma leaned in and pressed a kiss below her ear. "Tell me your ideal night."

Vanessa didn't need to think about Emma's question at all. She knew exactly what she wanted. "At home. A film playing. Snacks on the coffee table while I'm curled up in your arms. We'd be drinking hot chocolate with tonnes of marshmallows and whipped cream, and, obviously, the child in me would come out and I'd smear it all over your face." Vanessa warmed inside when Emma held her. "And then we'd slope off to bed, cuddling one another as soft music played in the bedroom. We'd have silk sheets—they're my favourite—but you'd complain they were annoying you."

"Sounds perfect." Emma sighed.

"And then we'd wake early the next morning. You'd be holding me, I'd be so comfortable I never wanted to move again, but we'd make love until midday. Just you and I. Nobody and nothing to interrupt us."

"You're selling this ideal night for me, I have to say."

"But you didn't need to hear it. You know exactly what makes me tick. You always did."

"I…do?"

Vanessa cast her mind back to a time when this was all in the dark. "Yeah. We did some of that stuff one night when Richard was away and Lauren was with Rob. I'm sure you don't remember."

"I do remember."

"You do?" Vanessa shouldn't be surprised. Emma had been more than forthcoming with other detailed memories.

Emma lifted her legs into Vanessa's lap, moaning when her hand landed on Emma's thigh. Vanessa unfolded the blanket beside them, covering them up. "It was not long before I left for Africa. You came up to my room to see if I wanted some company."

"I did."

"And I was a nervous wreck. I stood in the mirror for ten minutes making sure I looked okay, and then I spent another ten minutes trying to decide whether I should put some perfume on. I know we'd spent tonnes of time together over the years, but that night felt different. You'd never sought me out before to spend time with me. It usually happened by chance."

"I didn't want you to leave," Vanessa explained. "And with Richard gone and Lauren out, I knew if I could pluck up the courage to knock on your door, I'd have you to myself all night."

"Yeah?" Emma rested her head in her hand, propping her elbow up on the back of the love seat they were sharing. "You wanted to do that?"

"That night was the first night I'd ever seriously thought about kissing you. And I really wished I had." Vanessa was admitting it to herself for the first time, but Emma only grinned, those silver eyes staring back at her. "I was at a point of not caring about Richard anymore. He was shagging whatever had a pulse while he was away, and I wanted more. When I was alone with you, I used to think about how good it felt."

"Me too."

"But then I remembered you were leaving, you were Lauren's best friend, and you couldn't possibly be interested in someone like me."

"I was good at hiding my feelings."

"And I think looking back, it was a good thing you *could* hide your feelings. Because if you'd said everything you did on the phone to me beforehand, I think I would have taken it further. I sat at home knowing my marriage was falling apart, and I didn't care at all. When Richard walked in and told me he wanted a divorce, I was relieved. I'd spent so many years putting on a front for Lauren because I didn't want her to hurt, but all the while, I was allowing myself to be put through the hurt Richard was causing." Vanessa felt sad when she thought about how little she'd cared for herself. "And I know Lauren would have understood, but nobody wants to hear their parents are divorcing."

"Mine didn't even marry." Emma snorted. "I just happened to be the unlucky bastard child for them. I'm not sure they ever actually wanted me."

"Don't say that," Vanessa whispered, taking Emma's hand under the blanket. "I'm sure it's not true."

"No, it is. From the age of seven, I used to come home from school and cook my own dinner. Usually beans on toast because I could only work the microwave and the toaster. Sometimes Mum would send me across the busy main road for a portion of chips and a loaf of bread, but I wasn't allowed the bread because she needed it for dad's packed lunches."

Vanessa had nothing to offer. She had no idea Emma had been raised that way.

"Dad only worked around the corner from home, and I never

saw him leaving with a packed lunch. I snuck a piece of bread up to bed one night because I was starving. I lay there, struggling to swallow it because it was so dry."

Vanessa's eyes closed, her nostrils flared. "Did your mum work at all?"

"Yeah, she worked loads. It was one thing nobody could accuse her of *not* doing."

"So, why didn't you have substantial meals at home?" Vanessa frowned. She never understood those who *chose* to see their kids suffer.

Emma shrugged. "I think it all went on the drink."

"I see."

Emma's face suddenly morphed into one of pain. "When I started high school…" She paused, clearing her throat. "Mum hadn't bought me a new uniform."

"But high school uniforms are different…" Vanessa trailed off, knowing precisely where this was going.

"Exactly. I was bullied for three years for being the kid who turned up to high school wearing her junior school uniform. I'd never felt so humiliated in my life. The thought of going back there after the first day was enough to make me ill. I couldn't eat I was so anxious."

In all the time Vanessa had worked as a teacher, she'd never met a child who didn't have the correct uniform. But she knew what other kids could be like when those things did happen. Her heart hurt for Emma. "I'm sorry she did that to you."

"Before my sixteenth birthday, my national insurance number came through the post. I got a job as a server in a local pub."

"You wanted to take care of yourself." Vanessa nodded, pride for Emma coursing through her veins. "And I don't blame you."

"I stayed at home until I could afford to see myself through living elsewhere, but I didn't realise how expensive it would be. So, I stayed with a cousin, and gave him money to go towards bills. I had a bed and a roof; I didn't need much else."

"Is that why your entire life is in that bloody hold-all?"

Emma laughed. "Yeah. I travel light. I don't see the point in spending everything I earn on clothes I won't wear after a few months."

"So it worked out with you and your cousin?"

Emma reached for her beer, offering Vanessa her glass of wine. She took it and smiled. And then Emma sighed. "Not quite. I was in bed one night, and I heard banging on the door. Terrified me half to death since it was the middle of the night."

"Who was it?"

"The police. They'd come to raid his house. I had no idea he was dealing drugs; I was never there because I was always working. And if he was making decent money off it, you wouldn't have known. The place was a tip except for my room."

Okay, this was a lot for Vanessa to take in. She loved Emma, but she had no idea her family involved careless parents and drug dealers. "Wow."

"Don't worry, babe. I don't speak to any of them anymore. They're not likely to come and break into your house."

Vanessa smiled weakly, a slight laugh falling from her lips. "No, I know."

And then Emma sat up, her eyes narrowed. "I've just turned you right off me, haven't I? I mean, what woman wants to hear about her girlfriend who was bullied because she had a shit mother and a cousin who had the door kicked through?"

"Don't be stupid." Vanessa reached out a hand, beckoning Emma closer. "It was…a lot to hear, is all."

"Well, stick with me. I have plenty more where that came from."

Vanessa held up her wine glass. "You know, I think the less I know the better. I love you for who you are, not what family you're attached to."

"And I love you for saying that." Emma leaned in, kissing Vanessa slowly. When she smiled against her mouth and pulled back, Emma had a devilish look in her eyes. "You're so good for me."

"Oh, you're the one who braved her feelings and put it all out there. I had to realise it for myself for the eighteen long months you were gone."

"Painful, huh?" Emma quirked her eyebrow.

Vanessa nodded, squeezing Emma's thigh. "The worst months of my life."

CHAPTER TWENTY-ONE

Two weeks later...

Vanessa reached for her phone, thrilled to see her daughter's name on the screen. They hadn't spoken since Lauren ended her call several weeks ago, but Vanessa wasn't worried. Lauren was busy having the time of her life, and her comment on social media had quelled Vanessa's anxiety about the situation she'd initially found herself in. Now, to see Lauren calling, Vanessa was certain things were looking up.

"Lauren, hi."

"Hi, Mum. How are you?"

Vanessa eased back in her office chair, pushing away the lesson plans she'd been working on. The summer holidays would be over before she had the time to blink, but Vanessa couldn't complain; spending time with Emma had been exhilarating. "Honestly, much better now I've heard your voice."

"Sorry. Things have been a little hectic."

"Don't apologise. You have far too much on your plate to think about me right now. How's Australia? I'm sure you're not looking forward to coming home. You have what? Two weeks left?"

"Yeah, uh…about that."

Vanessa's heart sank. Had Lauren decided to stay? She needed to see her daughter, to figure everything out with one another.

"We're home," Lauren said hesitantly. "Have been for a fortnight."

"What?" Vanessa frowned. Why was she only hearing about this now? Her only daughter was hiding from her?

"Yeah, we found a house online we love. You know how Rob was always planning the last few weeks to himself in Australia? Well, we decided to use those weeks to come home and get everything sorted out for our new place."

Sadness roared through Vanessa. That truly hurt. "Right, well."

"So, I wanted you to know I'm home."

That was it? "And do you plan to come and see me?"

"Of course, yeah," Lauren paused. "Just…getting my head around things, you know?"

"I-I thought we were okay. I mean, I know there's stuff to talk about, but the comment you left on my profile…I thought things were okay."

"I'm sure everything will be okay in time, but I'm not ready to face it all yet."

Vanessa lowered her head to her hand, closing her eyes as her daughter's voice filtered down the line. This wasn't what she wanted, but how did she help Lauren through it all? Life with Emma had been incredibly fulfilling recently, and that was predominantly down to the fact both Vanessa *and* Emma thought Lauren was okay with their relationship. But to know her daughter had been back in the same country—potentially the same city—for two weeks…it hurt a lot.

"Can I meet you for lunch, at least?"

Lauren remained silent.

"Lauren, please?"

"Okay. If that's what you want."

"If it's what I want?" Vanessa's voice trembled. "I want my daughter to stop hiding from me, and I want you to come home so we can catch up, but you couldn't even bring yourself to tell me you were in England."

"I've just told you."

"Two weeks after you arrived, yes."

Lauren sighed. "I'll meet you at the bistro this afternoon. One o'clock. But I can't stay too long. I have things to do. A life to sort out."

"Well, I wouldn't want to put you out." Vanessa may be desperate to see Lauren, but this attitude wouldn't wash with her. First and foremost, Vanessa was Lauren's mother. "So, if you'd rather not see me, that's entirely up to you."

"W-will you be coming with Emma?"

Would she? It wasn't something Vanessa had thought about. Emma was out with friends right now; they didn't live in one another's pockets. "I wasn't planning to, but I can if it's what you want—"

"No! Don't bring her."

"O-okay."

"See you this afternoon."

Before Vanessa could speak, Lauren had ended the call. She stared down at the phone, a picture of Emma looking back at her, and frowned. "So much for everything being okay."

Vanessa slowed her pace as she reached the bistro, her heart currently situated in her throat. It didn't matter how excited she was to see her daughter, everything else was overshadowing it. But Vanessa knew once they'd had lunch and hashed this all out, everything would be perfectly fine between them.

I really need that to happen.

She pushed the heavy glass door open, instantly warmed by

the friendly atmosphere. This was the place Vanessa and Lauren always lunched together. Vanessa hadn't been here since Australia stole Lauren from her, but this felt nice. A safe location.

Vanessa eyed their usual table, her gaze falling to Lauren who was sitting with her back to her. Lauren's dark blonde hair had grown, a slight wave added to it. She looked great. Lauren's arm was propping her head up, her body slumped forward ever so slightly. That wasn't a good sign. Lauren was always so full of life. *Until you ruined it.*

Vanessa cleared her throat, stopping at the side of the table.

Lauren looked up. Those eyes didn't light up the way Vanessa wished they would. "Hi, Mum."

"May I sit?"

Lauren nodded, clearing her throat. "You're early."

"I didn't want to be late," Vanessa said, shrugging her jacket off and hanging it over the back of her chair. "Wasn't sure if you'd bolt before I got here."

"I told you I'd be here. I wouldn't let you down." The disinterest in Lauren's voice sent a chill through Vanessa.

"Well, thank you. I guess."

"I'm sorry I didn't tell you I was home." Lauren's eyes flitted around the room, searching the old bottles hanging above the bar area. She may be here, but she clearly couldn't look Vanessa in the eye. "It seemed easier to get on with the house sale."

"You've actually bought it?"

Lauren beamed a smile, her eyes now on the menu. "We have. We didn't want to lose it."

"Wow. Well, congratulations." Vanessa's throat constricted. She was supposed to know these things before anyone else. She was supposed to house hunt with her daughter, offer the first bottle of champagne to Lauren and Rob. But no, Vanessa wasn't a part of this. "Send my congratulations to Rob, too."

"I will."

"Are you going to sit here and avoid eye contact with me until you leave?"

Lauren closed her eyes briefly, exhaling a deep breath. When she opened them and focused on Vanessa, tears welled. "Mum…"

Vanessa reached a hand across the table, taking Lauren's. "I *need* us to be okay, Lauren. I can't lose you."

"This is *so* hard for me. You're dating my best friend." Vanessa and Lauren had always been so close. To see the disgust in her eyes…it was alien to Vanessa.

"I can't help who I fall in love with. I tried; you've no idea how hard this has been for me *or* Emma, but we tried."

"Not hard enough, clearly." Lauren shook Vanessa's grip from her hand, lowering her head. "I mean, is she my step mum now?"

"Don't be ridiculous. Emma wouldn't be anything other than your best friend."

"This is all too weird for me."

"Why?"

Lauren placed her head in her hands, her shoulders curling as she tried to hide herself from not only everyone around her, but Vanessa too. "I can't believe you're doing this."

"I love her, Lauren."

"Stop saying that!"

The venom in Lauren's voice was enough to startle Vanessa. She straightened in her seat, looking around at the other customers. And then she swallowed hard, frowning when Lauren pushed her seat back and took her coat.

"Lauren, please don't leave."

"I can't do this. I thought I could, but I can't even look at you." Lauren stared down at Vanessa, her coat gripped in her hand. "You've ruined *everything*. You only have yourselves to blame."

Okay, Vanessa was done with this. "What do you want me to do? Leave her?"

Lauren scoffed. "I wish you would."

Vanessa watched with disbelief as Lauren stormed from the

bistro. She quickly threw some cash down for the coffee Lauren was yet to touch and followed her outside. Before her daughter could disappear down an alleyway, Vanessa gripped her wrist and turned her around. "How dare you speak to me like that! The years I put up with him so it didn't break our family apart, and this is the thanks I get?"

Lauren frowned.

"The nights I sat at home alone, the weeks he spent on business trips…I could have been happy long before now. But I chose not to because I didn't want to break *your* heart with the truth. Yet here I am, the bad guy in all of this, because I'm finally putting myself first. I mean, I didn't even have the balls to end things, Lauren. *He* did that. The night when you came home to find out we were divorcing, it was all him. I was willing to stay to keep the family together. I'm sorry for wanting to be happy—"

Lauren cut Vanessa off. "But it didn't have to be with my best friend."

"Except it did. I could drop dead tomorrow, and all I'd have had was a husband who'd been having affairs with younger women. Is that all I'm worth? Being second best to everyone in your father's eyes? Do I not deserve to find someone who loves me and wants to be with me?" Vanessa bit back a sob, releasing Lauren from her grip. "If you truly believe I don't deserve to find someone, I'll go home right now and end my relationship with Emma. And then I'll step away from your life, because I don't think this could ever be repaired. Judging by the way you're treating me, I'm not sure you'd *want* to repair this." The realisation almost broke Vanessa in two. "Tell me what you want from me, Lauren. Everything I've *ever* done is with you in mind, and if you can't accept this…if you can't allow me to be happy with someone who worships every second we're together, then I need to know."

Lauren lowered her eyes as she shook her head.

"Wow. And to think I'm the one who raised you to be such a

beautiful woman. It was only a few months ago you asked me to walk you down the aisle, and now you despise me." The initial anger Vanessa felt as she stepped out of the bistro had been replaced with loss. Because whatever she chose in the coming days, she would either lose Emma or Lauren. *Face it, you're about to lose both of them.* "You seem to care more about who I'm dating than how much your dad hurt me. That speaks volumes."

Vanessa reached into her purse, pulling out an envelope. She had to keep it together for a few more minutes, and then she could slowly die inside. Because that's what would happen. Lauren had been the greatest thing to ever happen to Vanessa. To lose her…Vanessa could barely think about it. "Take this. It was supposed to be a gift from me when you bought your first house. I've been saving it since you were a child."

Lauren reached out a shaky hand, tears slipping down her face. "What is it?"

"My goodbye." Vanessa offered a weak smile. "You and I both know this is a waste of time. You'll never support my relationship with Emma."

"So, you choose her?" Lauren nodded slowly, handing the envelope back over.

Vanessa pushed it away. Of all the scenarios she had in her head, this one hadn't even made the list. This was supposed to be a beautiful start to a new life. But with Lauren's attitude, it wasn't to be. "No. I choose neither." Vanessa took a slight step forward, kissing her daughter's cheek. "Make sure Rob looks after you. And you look after him. It works both ways, always remember that."

"M-Mum?"

"Bye, love." Vanessa chanced a hug, relief flooding her when Lauren didn't back away. Still, she didn't reciprocate. "You have your key for the house, don't you? I'll ask Emma to get her things together this evening. I'm sure she can find a friend to stay with.

And then it'll be free whenever you want to come and collect your things for your new house."

"Where will you be?"

Vanessa lifted a shoulder, her head spinning. She had no idea where she would go. She had the option of visiting her sister down south, but they didn't always see eye-to-eye. And since the divorce, they'd only grown further apart. Apparently, *Vanessa* hadn't tried hard enough. "I'll figure it out."

She stepped back, chancing one last look at her daughter's beautiful eyes, her stunning features, and turned, walking away. Lauren didn't call after her. She hadn't expected her to, but she still wished she was walking away from her this afternoon feeling better. Perhaps Vanessa had been a fool to think it could happen, but she still hoped for a different outcome.

Lauren didn't care if Emma made her happy, and Emma wouldn't continue this if she knew Lauren was dead set against it. So, what was the point? Instead of constantly wishing for happiness on all sides, Vanessa would step back and allow Emma and Lauren to work out their friendship. After all, they'd been friends for so long. Vanessa hated the thought of coming in and ripping it to shreds.

At fifty, she thought she had everything figured out, but reality was sinking in, and Vanessa wasn't sure she could handle a lonely future. In all honesty, she didn't have a clue. She just knew that Emma didn't need her…and Lauren couldn't stomach the thought of sharing a public space with her.

It didn't matter how happy Vanessa felt when she was with Emma. It didn't matter if her future, in the last couple of months, had been mapped out for her. She couldn't continue with something that hurt Lauren as much as it appeared to be. What kind of mother would that make Vanessa?

Vanessa's stomach lurched as she took her car key from her coat pocket.

Her daughter, her reason for breathing, *hated* her.

CHAPTER TWENTY-TWO

Emma took a few calming breaths as she rounded the corner. She'd walked into town an hour ago for some ingredients for dinner, and now her biggest hope was that Vanessa would be home...with Lauren. When she'd found out earlier that Lauren was already home, she'd initially been worried. But then Vanessa told Emma she was meeting with Lauren for lunch today, and Emma instantly settled. If Lauren was still reeling, she wouldn't have agreed to lunch. Her best friend was stubborn. She always had been.

She took her keys from the pocket of her coat, strolling up the drive without a care in the world. If it all went wrong at lunch, surely Vanessa would have called Emma and told her. She had texted Vanessa around forty minutes ago, but there had been no response, and as Emma lifted her head, she frowned. Vanessa wasn't home yet; her car wasn't on the drive.

"Huh. Odd."

Emma slid the key into the lock, the house silent as she stepped into the hallway. Maybe Vanessa and Lauren were actually catching up. Emma lit up at the thought. If there was one thing she could hope for this year, it was that her girlfriend and her best friend could be on better terms. If Emma referred to them as such, it didn't feel so terrible. Mother and daughter didn't have such a positive ring to it in her head. But in time, everything would come together. Vanessa had promised Emma everything would be okay.

"Babe?" Emma didn't know why she'd called out for Vanessa; she clearly wasn't home.

Instead of sitting around, Emma took the ingredients into the kitchen and set them out on the island. She could prepare dinner now and then she wouldn't have to stand in the kitchen for so long this evening. It was only three in the afternoon; she may even manage a nap if she started now.

And then her phone pinged in her top pocket. An email.

Emma read it carefully, recognising the address from the agency she'd travelled to Africa with. They'd secured funding to take her back for at least a year. *Oh, wow.* It wasn't possible, she had too much going on here, but Emma was still grateful they'd offered it to her. It meant she'd left a good impression on them all during her time away.

She would give it a few hours before she responded. She had dinner to make for the woman she loved, and hopefully, her best friend. But first, Emma needed to change into something more comfortable and slouchier. She headed for the stairs, taking them quickly. As she stepped into the bedroom, she grinned when she found a gift box and a note accompanying it sitting in the middle of their super king-size bed. Vanessa had bought her a gift? Emma's heart thrummed.

She took a seat on the edge of the bed, slipping her finger under the lip of the envelope. And then she caught Vanessa's handwriting. She loved it, it was always so neat and pristine. It was very Vanessa.

Emma,

You and I have longed for one another since the moment we met. I could continue lying to myself, but it's been you since the moment you stepped through my door all those years ago. I wish it could be the only factor in all of this, but it can't. You know how I feel about you, deep down I think you always did, but it doesn't change the fact we've hurt Lauren in the process of allowing our hearts to rule our heads.

Sometimes I wish I'd never given in, because then I wouldn't miss the way you touch me, or kiss me, or look at me. And other times, I wish I'd given in many years ago, so I could have felt the love you have for me more fully and freely. I've had my life, my beautiful daughter, and now it's time for you to find someone who can give you everything you've ever wanted. That person cannot be me, but trust me when I tell you how much I wish things could be different.

I wish I'd held you more. I wish I'd loved you harder. I wish I was sitting with you in this very moment. But all of my wishes mean nothing when someone has to get hurt in all of this. I've never wanted to hurt you, I only wanted to love you entirely and with everything I am, but I'll never forget how alive you made me feel. I'll never forget the tears, the laughter, and ultimately the heartbreak I have caused for not only you but my daughter, too. Fix your relationship with her. It's too late for me, I realised it today, but you two have always been the greatest things in my life, and I need to know I walked away with the potential of your friendship being repaired.

Your beauty is breathtaking, and your heart holds so much love, but it wasn't to be for us.

I love you,
Be safe,
V x

Emma held the letter to her chest, pain tearing through her like never before. Every moment with Vanessa travelled through her mind at the speed of light, her body floating somewhere between reality and a nightmare. Vanessa had gone. But how? And why? This morning, everything had been perfect. Just ten minutes ago, Emma was planning on a quiet dinner with the love of her life, a sense of accomplishment pumping through her veins. And now, it all lay in tatters at her feet…along with her heart.

She opened the doors of the built-in wardrobes, gasping when she found them almost empty. As she turned back and her eyes landed on the giftbox, she reached out a trembling hand. Sitting inside was a framed photograph of Emma and Vanessa in the Yorkshire Dales. God, Vanessa's smile lit up the entire room as she peered down at it. But it wasn't real; it couldn't possibly be. Because if Vanessa loved her as much as she claimed to, she would be here right now.

If Vanessa wanted anything she maintained in her letter, she would be here tonight. She would put herself—their relationship—first. Because as worried as Emma had initially been, she was over putting Lauren first. They were all adults; Lauren ought to act like it.

She stared down at the framed photograph again, dejection rolling through her.

Emma didn't know the first place to look, who she should call, nothing.

And then the sound of a key in the lock had Emma's pulse whooshing in her ears. Vanessa…was back! "Babe, is that you?"

Nothing.

"Vanessa?" Emma rushed out of the bedroom, peering down the stairs. But it wasn't Vanessa, it was Lauren. "O-oh."

"Where is she?" Lauren asked, her eyes swollen and red. "I need to speak to her."

"S-she's gone." Emma's voice caught, the realisation hitting her hard as she spoke those words. "What happened? She was so happy going to meet you today."

"I…fucked it all up." Lauren took a step forward, turning and sitting on the stairs. She clasped her hands behind her neck, placing her head between her legs. "God, I really fucked it all up."

"She…left me this letter." Emma stared down at it, the ink

splodging as tears hit the paper. "And I don't know what I've done, but I thought she was happy. I…I thought she loved me."

"She does love you."

"How can she when she's just fucked off?!" Emma hadn't meant to yell, but the shock of the letter was beginning to wear off and she didn't know what else to do. "Did you do this?"

"I…yes. I think so."

"You think so?" Emma scoffed, taking the stairs in record time. When she stopped in front of Lauren, her best friend glanced up at her. "What did you say to her?"

"Not much, to be honest." Lauren wiped her face. Emma noted the embarrassment and the potential devastation, too. "And I think that may have been the problem."

"I don't follow."

"She asked me what I wanted. What she should do. And I froze. Because while I can't fucking believe you're sleeping with my *mum*, I know it's not my decision to make."

Emma had to be honest. She couldn't lose Vanessa. Even if it felt as though she already had. "You're right. It's not your decision to make."

"I—"

"No," Emma said. "You have no right to dictate either of our lives. She's been beside herself with worry, desperate to hear from you and to sit down and talk, but you couldn't even give her an inch. And to be honest, that's fucking sad. I've spent so long worried about hurting you, wanting you to understand, but why should I lose out on this because you've thrown a fucking hissy fit? Why should we do what *you* want when it means destroying *our* happiness?"

"I told her I wished she'd break up with you." Lauren hung her head, her shoulders shaking as she cried into her hands.

Emma wanted to sink to the floor, to pinch herself and wake up, but this felt as real as it actually was. "You got your wish. Well done." Emma moved into the kitchen, dropping into a seat. She couldn't comprehend what was happening this afternoon, but she felt empty. And then anger rose from the pit of her stomach, something she'd never felt around Lauren. "You had no fucking right!" Emma kicked a chair, sending it flying across the open plan kitchen. "How fucking dare you!" She gritted her teeth, overwhelming tears flooding her eyes. "I mean, do you honestly hate me that much?"

"I-I don't hate you." Lauren's voice shook. "Why would I hate you?"

"Because you're doing this to me, and I *never* thought you'd hurt me like this." The pain in Emma's chest left her breathless, her palms tingling as her mouth dried. Was this what a broken heart felt like? "I should get my things together." Emma lifted the letter from the table, reading it over once again. But she couldn't take it; it was far too much. "Fuck." It all hit her at once. Vanessa was gone, Lauren had shoved her hand into her chest and ripped her heart out, and Emma…well, she was close to a breakdown. "She's actually left me."

With those words, Emma rushed to the kitchen sink, emptying the contents of her stomach directly into it. It wasn't classy, but it beat hurling all over the floor. She ran the tap, splashing cold water on her face, and then sunk to her knees. It was all she could do to keep herself from falling down against the pristine marble tiles. Emma brought her knees to her chest, resting back against the kitchen cupboard. She had to think. But she couldn't stay here; she wasn't welcome.

Breathe. Just breathe. Emma felt herself beginning to panic. She hadn't done that in a long time.

But then Lauren was on her knees in front of her, sorrow in her eyes. "I'm sorry."

Emma breathed in deep, exhaling slowly as she placed her hand against her chest. If she could see Vanessa's face for five minutes, if she could touch her hand, everything else around her would calm.

"Emma?"

Emma shook her head, closing her eyes as she rested her head back against the cupboard. She squeezed her knees tighter to her chest, swallowing down the emotion lodged in her throat.

"I don't hate you."

"I…need to leave," Emma said, her hearing dulled. "I shouldn't be here. This isn't my home."

Nothing made sense. Why was Lauren still kneeling in front of her?

She took her set of keys from her hoodie pocket, detaching Vanessa's front door key from the bunch. She didn't even know what the rest of them were for except for her car key. But she couldn't use that either; she wasn't sure it was safe to drive right now.

"Could you give this to her when you see her?" She placed the key in Lauren's palm, trembling as she gripped the counter and managed to get to her feet. "I'll pack. It won't take me five minutes."

Emma braced her hands against the counter. Just another second and she would do what she needed to do. But first, she needed to ask Lauren one question. She turned, eyeing her… friend. "Did you come home early to do this? To split us up?"

"No. I never expected this."

"I get how hard this is for you, I've never *not* understood, but she made me feel as though I had a future. And I know she's your mum, Lauren…but once again, I've been thrown to the side. Tossed into the rubbish like I always was. This was the fresh start I'd always wanted. It was the point where my life *actually* made sense. I wish you could have trusted me to make her happy, because I would have. Over and over again."

On legs that barely registered with her brain, Emma moved through the kitchen and practically crawled up the stairs. She'd never felt so weak and broken. She knew it was complicated, but this? This was a million miles from what she'd expected the outcome to be.

As she reached Vanessa's bedroom, her scent hit Emma square in the chest. Their photograph sat in the middle of the bed, but Emma couldn't bring herself to look at it. And then she reached into the nightstand drawer, lifting a box she'd been keeping safe all week.

She'd take it back to the store, but it would only signify the end of everything. And Emma wasn't sure she'd ever be prepared for that. She opened the box, perching herself on the edge of the bed. The diamond which stared back at her could cover the deposit and two months' worth of rent on a flat, but this would always belong to Vanessa.

Lauren cleared her throat, leaning against the frame of the door.

"I was going to give it to her this weekend," Emma explained, a faint smile on her lips. She glanced back down at the ring, sighing. "It wasn't an engagement ring, I don't think she'd want to marry again, it was more of an eternity ring. And I know those are supposed to be given on wedding anniversaries and stuff, but I saw it in the window and couldn't let it go." Emma closed the box, curling her fingers around it. "It had Vanessa's name written all over it. But she said it herself in the letter. It wasn't meant to be."

"Emma…"

"But I felt as though it was. When we were together, I thought my life was complete." Emma swallowed. She couldn't cry anymore. "I don't expect you to understand, but for one second, imagine being told you couldn't be with Rob. T-that it was forbidden. That you couldn't love him."

"I never wanted it to come to this. Maybe you could call her."

"She's not interested in me, Lauren. How can she be when *you* despise everything about us? She's your mum; she's always going to take your side." Emma scoffed. "Maybe I should have known in the beginning. Because I put my all on the line for her, and where is she? If I meant so much to her, she would be here, willing to work through this."

"Please try."

Emma shook her head. "She's gone, Lauren."

"But she could come back..."

Emma laughed. Even that didn't sound like it had come from her mouth. "Why would she? She thinks she's ruined everything, and when her own daughter has basically disowned her, how else could she feel?"

"I've tried to call her. She won't answer."

Emma got to her feet, taking her holdall from under the bed. She placed the ring safely inside. She needed to grab the essentials. Everything else could be replaced. "I don't suppose she wants to hear how disappointed and angry you are anymore. I just hope wherever she is, she's safe, and she's okay. Because it was all I ever wanted her to feel. Safe, loved...and happy."

"And that's how she felt with you," Lauren said, sitting on the edge of the bed. "I-I read her letter."

Emma frowned. "You had no right."

"But I think I needed to. So I could understand what was going on here. Because while I've been struggling with it, it's none of my business."

"But your approval would have been nice. It was all she wanted from the moment we told one another how we felt. She may not have said it, but I saw it in her eyes. Whenever she was worried, or whenever I had issues with it all, I could see in her eyes how much she hoped you would understand. Long before you even knew. And then you left the comment on social media..." Emma smiled, it felt like a distant memory now. "God, you should have seen how happy she was. Everything changed from that moment on for us. It finally felt real."

"I want her to be happy."

"She will be. I'm sure of it." Emma's stomach swayed at the

thought of seeing Vanessa with someone else. She couldn't say her body had ever physically hurt so much. "But I can't be here when it happens. Knowing we couldn't be..."

"I want her to be happy with *you*."

Emma appreciated Lauren trying, but it was too late. They all knew it was a lie deep down. "I was offered another term in Africa."

"O-oh."

"And the plan was to turn it down," Emma said, folding some clothes and placing them neatly in her hold-all.

"Why? You love Africa."

Emma turned to face Lauren, staring her dead in the eye. "But I love her more."

"You'd give up Africa for Mum?" Lauren seemed surprised, but Emma didn't know why. Hadn't she explained how much Vanessa meant to her? Or had Lauren simply chosen to ignore it all? "Emma, you mean that?"

"Of course I mean it." Emma zipped up her bag, forcing it up onto her shoulder. "But Vanessa couldn't even stick around for me, so I'm starting to realise how messed up all of this is. Africa is the best place for me, and I'm sure you'll agree." She gripped the strap, bitterly disappointed in how this was all ending. "All I've ever wanted was to feel loved. And God, she made me feel *so* loved. But I don't know, perhaps this was all a fling for her. That's how it's beginning to feel. And I don't want to be around here anymore if that's all I am to people. Worthless." Emma cast her gaze on the floor, shaking her head. "I lost my girlfriend and my best friend all in one night. And I know I lost you weeks ago, but I did think everything would turn out okay. Seems I got that wrong too."

"You haven't lost me."

Emma laughed gently, cocking her head. She stepped forward, kissing Lauren's cheek. "I've had the best time with you, truly. But it's time for me to leave and fall out of love with this entire life. It'll take a while, I have a lot of thinking and soul searching to do, but I'll get there."

"Emma, don't go."

"I have nothing else to give you." Emma's shoulders sagged, the weight of her bag only adding to the weight in her chest. "Go and find your mum. Make things right with one another. I know she's devastated by all of this, but I won't be around, and when I do come back…I'll keep my distance."

"I need to talk to you."

"Oh, we're all out of words." Emma lowered her chin to her chest. She'd never felt so defeated. Even her heart barely registered in her chest. Just there…thumping dully.

"Emma, I'm pregnant."

Lauren's news should have thrilled Emma. She'd always wanted kids. But it only crushed her a little bit more. Not only had she lost everything she had here, but now she wouldn't have the chance to be by her best friend's side during one of the most important times of her life. "Wow," Emma said, fresh tears brimming in her eyes. "You're really throwing everything at me tonight."

"I found out last week. I wondered why I hadn't felt great over the last week or so while we were in Australia, but I pushed it from my mind. I didn't think anything of it, but I took a test at Rob's mums, and then I had it confirmed at the GP."

"I'm so happy for you. Both of you." Emma squeezed Lauren's hands. "And your mum is going to be over the moon. Maybe this could be a starting point for rebuilding things with her."

"I hope so. Everything has felt overwhelming lately, and I know it's the reason I blew up earlier at the bistro, but it doesn't excuse what I said."

"Your mum is your mum. You know she'll forgive you in a heartbeat."

"A-and you?" Lauren looked up at Emma with damp eyes.

"Look, there's nothing to forgive." Her love life was the least of everyone's concerns. Lauren was about to take centre stage in Vanessa's life. The way it had always been. And if Emma was being honest, she was glad Lauren had told her about the pregnancy. It made the Africa decision easier to digest. Because regardless of how much leaving would hurt, Emma would never cause unnecessary turmoil within this family. *It's all I'll ever be in life. Unnecessary.* "You have a little one to look after now, and you don't need any stress. Work on your relationship with Vanessa. Nothing else matters."

"But I need you too." Lauren's brow knitted, one hand settling on her belly. "We all do."

"I don't think *anyone* has ever needed me. I'm sure Rob and Vanessa will be with you every step of the way, though."

Lauren shook her head. "You don't understand. I can't do this without you."

"You can." Emma took Lauren's face in her hands. "You're Lauren Middleton. You can do absolutely anything you can put your mind to." With a final kiss on Lauren's cheek, Emma stepped past her, turning as she reached the doorway. "Hey, I'm so proud of you." *Even if you have ruined my life.*

"Where will you go?"

"Wherever my car takes me." Emma smiled. All of this was too bittersweet. "You look after one another, okay?"

"Call her, Emma."

"You call her. Give her the good news. And tell her..." Emma didn't quite know what she wanted to say to Vanessa. "Just tell her...I understand the choice she made."

CHAPTER TWENTY-THREE

Vanessa lay flat on her back, staring up at the ceiling. Three hours since she checked into a hotel in the city...nothing seemed any clearer. The look in Lauren's eyes, the hatred and the devastation for her relationship with Emma, Vanessa couldn't quite believe it. Though she'd *always* expected some kind of fall-out, this didn't feel real. But it was. Vanessa knew it as she wheeled her luggage out of the home she'd owned for thirty years. The home she'd raised Lauren in.

Honestly, her life was falling apart. Big time.

She knew she should turn on her phone, Emma would be worried, but she couldn't bring herself to hear her voice. When she did, she'd call Emma and demand she join her in this very hotel room. When she did, everything Vanessa knew she was doing for the good of everyone else would go out of the window, the selfish side of her succeeding. And God, she wanted the selfish side of her to win out with this one. But it couldn't. Emma didn't need to be subjected to such venom from Lauren. After all, they'd been best friends for too long. Vanessa would accept the blame for this; she never should have given in to her desires.

But then she found herself reaching blindly for her phone,

powering it on. When the screen came to life, showing a selfie with Emma, Vanessa's heart tightened in her chest. Those memories were up there with the very best. They always would be.

And then her phone started to buzz repeatedly. Missed calls. Voicemails. Text messages. She had a whole array of communication this evening. But it didn't matter. *What's done is done.* Until her phone pinged with a new message. One from Lauren.

L: Mum, please tell me where you are. I'm worried about you. And I need to talk to you. About Emma and about other things...

Vanessa frowned. Why would her daughter need to talk to her? She'd left the bistro in a hurry earlier, and she hadn't been interested in a single thing Vanessa had said outside on the street. No, Lauren didn't need her.

She spied the little tape symbol in the corner of the screen. She had a voicemail. She opened her voicemail inbox, closing her eyes as the automated voice explained the options. It would be Lauren, so Vanessa would listen, get a feel for the mood her daughter was in. Lauren's voice always gave her emotions away.

"Hey." Vanessa's lips parted when Emma's voice whispered into her ear. She should end the message right then. But here she was, listening intently. "So, I got your letter. And your gift. It was a really sweet thing you did, putting it together for me. But I had to leave it behind. T-the picture. If I can't have you in life, I can't keep you with me in memory. It's only been an hour, and I already feel like I'm slowly dying inside." *Oh, baby.* Every word Emma spoke broke Vanessa's heart. "But you're doing what's best for you and your family, and I'd *never* stand in the way. I love you so much that I can let you go if it's what you want."

"It's not what I want. Not in a million years," Vanessa whispered into the silence of her hotel room.

"And I don't know, perhaps I was foolish to think we could be together. But when I was with you, I felt it, Vanessa. I guess I thought you did too. I didn't know I could get it so monumentally wrong. I've always felt as though I was missing something, and I know it was you. It was *always* you." Emma paused, sighing. "Don't ever stop being beautiful, and don't ever think you're not worth more than what Richard saw in you. I'd walk over hot coals to make you the happiest woman in the world."

Vanessa drew in a shaky breath, tears slipping to the cover beneath her. She *needed* Emma. She wanted Emma. Her entire life had come full circle the moment she gave in to her desires. To hear that Emma didn't believe Vanessa felt the same way...well, it hurt.

"I should get off the phone. I'm still sitting in your drive while I'm speaking to you. Maybe I'll see you around some time, but don't worry about anything. You're about to have a beautiful life, and I can live with that. Don't ever settle for less than you're worth. You deserve the absolute world. If you thought I could give it to you, you wouldn't have run away. And I'd apologise for making you run, but I don't believe I've done a single thing to show you I wasn't willing to make you happy."

Vanessa closed her eyes, memorising Emma's voice and her soft breath. "Baby, please."

"So, I'll go now. And thanks, for everything. It's been the best couple of months of my life." Emma paused, a sob escaping her mouth. "B-bye, Mrs Middleton."

Vanessa gripped her phone against her chest, a feeling of emptiness hitting her with a weight that stole her breath. And then her thumb started moving as she typed out a new message.

V: I love you.

Turning on her side, Vanessa allowed Emma's voice to infiltrate her world. She replayed her voicemail on repeat, smiling as Emma spoke directly to her. It wasn't the same, Emma wasn't here, but it was the next best thing.

And then her phone buzzed.

E: Just not enough.

Vanessa stared at the screen, her pulse quickening. It wasn't true. *Nothing* Emma was saying was true. Vanessa loved her so much that her body physically ached.

Vanessa needed some kind of sign.

Or did she?

Emma was absolutely right. If Vanessa loved her as much as she claimed to, she wouldn't be lying in a hotel room alone. No, she would be holding Emma, and telling Lauren it was time to grow up.

Vanessa opened her other messages. Every last one from her daughter.

L: I made a mistake. I'm sorry.

L: I'm at the house with Emma. You won't answer my calls. Please, I need to know you're safe.

L: Emma is leaving. She's in a bad way. I'm so sorry, Mum. Please call me.

Vanessa shook her head. None of this was good for the mind, body, or soul. If she could put herself first, to do what *she* wanted to do for once, Lauren would learn to live with this.

And then Emma flowed into her mind. How happy she made Vanessa. The laughs they'd shared, the nights cuddled on the couch, everything. Could she actually give it all up? She hadn't wanted to in the first place, but the vulnerability she'd felt out on the street this afternoon was new to her. Richard may have left Vanessa feeling a little worthless over the last few years, but one thing she *never* felt was vulnerable. Until today.

She scrolled to the next message. Another from Lauren.

L: She makes you happy. I only ever want to see you happy. And I realise now how serious this relationship is for you both. Please, call her. Make things right. And then tomorrow, call me. I want to meet with you and Emma. I have things to say.

Vanessa swallowed hard. Had Lauren given her blessing for this relationship? Vanessa shouldn't need it, she was 50 years old for the love of God, but seeing those words on the screen from her daughter lifted an unimaginable weight from her entire body.

She typed out a message to Lauren.

V: I'm safe. I'm okay.

L: Where are you? I'll come to you now.

V: I need to be alone tonight. I'm at my usual hotel room. But please, don't come here. I need some space. Go home to Rob. I'll call you tomorrow.

L: Promise?

V: I promise. I'm calling Emma. I'm sorry, but I can't lose her.

L: I never wanted it to end this way, Mum. I was awful to you earlier, truly, but I'll explain it all tomorrow. Call Emma. She matters right now.

V: Do you need me? Is everything okay?

L: Everything is fine. And it's going to get better. Your letter to her was beautiful. I don't want you to be anything other than happy. And I know it's with Emma. I love you. Both of you. X

V: I love you, too.

Vanessa rolled onto her back again, exhaling a calming breath. She may have given her daughter far too much rope in all of this, but Lauren had always been her entire existence. Earlier, when Vanessa felt at her weakest, she couldn't see reason. She couldn't for one moment contemplate a way out without hurting Lauren. So, she'd chosen to step away from it all to make life easier for everyone. But as Vanessa lay here this evening, only one constant remained. Emma Bradley.

She lifted her phone, responding to Emma's message.

V: I miss you.

A little bubble bobbed up and down below her message, putting an instant smile on Vanessa's face. She bit the inside of her mouth, her eyes closing briefly. She knew what she wanted. It would never change.

Vanessa focused on the screen; Emma wasn't responding. *Come on.* Vanessa willed her phone to ping, to ring, to do something other than remain silent. "Emma, come on!"

But then Vanessa realised she couldn't blame Emma for not giving in. Her letter this afternoon had been more than self-explanatory. And if Vanessa knew Emma like she thought she did, she would have Lauren's best interests at heart.

Three dots appeared…and then they faded.

"Fuck, I've lost her." Vanessa sunk her head deeper into the pillow, willing herself not to cry. But it wasn't possible. She would cry for the rest of eternity if she didn't have Emma in her life.

Emma frowned as she stared out of her car window, sitting in a lay-by at the edge of the motorway. She had no idea where she was going, there was no one she felt she could turn to, but she had to go somewhere. She'd almost been caught sleeping in her car the last time around; that was embarrassing enough to never want to do it again.

Vanessa wouldn't even be in the city anymore. She was likely lying on a friend's couch and drinking wine while she discussed her family issues. Emma wouldn't be on the agenda; she wasn't important. *God, I've been so fucking stupid.* Emma had never felt this way before. Vanessa always seemed to be one hundred percent in the room when they were together. So, how had she gotten it so wrong?

She pressed her forehead against the steering wheel, her mind working overtime trying to figure everything out. Lauren was going to be a mum…*wow.* Emma hadn't expected it to fall into the conversation earlier, but she was truly thrilled for her. And to know they were about to move into their own place while

Lauren and Rob's life took its own path...Emma would admit to feeling slightly jealous.

But perhaps this happened when it was supposed to. Emma didn't want to get further down the line only for Vanessa to pull away from her. Had she gotten the wrong impression all along? Was Emma so in love with Vanessa that she wasn't willing to see what was right in front of her? This evening, she had no idea. If someone had put the question to her this morning, she'd have laughed. But now, as she sat at the side of a motorway, a hold-all with her life's possessions in the boot, Emma felt like a fool.

Africa had come back into her life at the right time.

A single tear slid down Emma's face. Africa wanted her, but nobody here did. *The story of my fucking life.* And now that she'd cried it all out, she could move forward and forget about the Middleton's entirely. Lauren would be an amazing mum, Rob would be a natural too, so Emma wished the very best for them... and now it was time to leave.

She fixed her hair, wiped the final tears from her jawline, and sat up straight in her seat. What was the point in slouching around, thinking of what could have been?

Then her phone started to ring on the dashboard. It was Lauren.

"H-hello?"

Lauren cleared her throat. "I wanted to let you know Mum is okay. She's staying at the Hilton in the city. It's where she goes when she needs a break from stuff."

"Good. I'm glad she's safe." Emma stared out of the windscreen, a light drizzle blurring her vision. "I need her to be safe before I leave."

"I thought maybe you'd want to know, you know?"

Emma frowned. "No, I don't know."

"She's in room 219. I'm sure she'd love to see you."

"I'm not sure if you remember everything that's happened this evening, but we're not together anymore, Lauren."

Repeating those words physically hurt Emma. She suspected they always would.

"But she said she was going to contact you." Lauren sounded confused. "She hasn't?"

"She sent me a message before, but I'm about to leave the city so I don't suppose it matters."

"Of course it matters." Lauren paused, sighing. "You know she loves you. I'm the one who created this mess."

Emma ran a hand down her face. "That doesn't work for me. She never should have left the letter. She should have looked me in the fucking eye and told me she couldn't be with me. I would have appreciated that a damn sight more."

"Emma—"

"No." Emma gripped the steering wheel. "Don't try to play the hero now. If you'd backed her and what she wanted, this wouldn't have happened. But you know what? I'm glad you said what you did. It's finally shown me the real Vanessa. Because I now know she doesn't love me at all." Wave after wave of devastation rolled through Emma, and then she murmured, "She could never really love someone like me."

"She does!"

Emma shook her head. She didn't have any fight left in her. She'd spent her life fighting for attention and love, and at thirty-three, she was more than done. "I'm going to go now. I hope everything goes well with your pregnancy. Bye, Lauren."

"Em—"

Emma cut the call. She couldn't listen to any more grovelling. It never should have been this way to begin with. And then a message came through on her dashboard. Lauren, again.

L: Room 219. Do the right thing. She needs you.

Emma scoffed. Lauren was fucking unbelievable. But then an intense urge to see Vanessa one final time gushed through Emma. If Vanessa was done, she could tell Emma to her face.

CHAPTER TWENTY-FOUR

The darkness in the room kept Vanessa's migraine at bay, but this had to be the loneliest she'd felt in many years. It hadn't mattered when Richard didn't come home, she knew what he was doing with his time, but this was different. She longed to be with Emma, and for every second they were apart, it was killing Vanessa inside. Honestly, at her age, this wasn't good. And if she wasn't careful, it could end her once and for all.

A gentle tap on the door had her sitting upright, only the light from the moon filtering in through the huge window to her left. Had she dropped off, called room service while she was sleeping, and now a banquet was being delivered to her? Actually, that wasn't the worst idea in the world.

Clearing her throat, she ran a hand through her hair and fastened her robe tighter around her. She turned the lock and squinted as the light from the hall burst through the door. "E-Emma?"

Emma looked broken. "I came here to say goodbye to you."

"Did you want to come in?" Vanessa stepped aside, praying Emma would take her up on the offer. But as Emma stared at her, dark rings around her eyes, Vanessa wasn't sure she would get her wish. Just the mere thought of saying goodbye to one another…God, Vanessa *did* wonder if her heart would finally give out one final time.

Emma glanced around the corridor, nodding slowly. "Sure. I don't want to do this out here."

As Vanessa closed the door, she cleared her throat and turned to face Emma. She had to at least try. "Before you say anything, I have some things I need to say to you."

Emma lifted a shoulder. "It doesn't matter anymore. We both know this is the end."

"B-but it's not what I want."

"You took the time to write me a letter earlier." Emma paused, taking the paper from her pocket. "Is this all I'm worth to you? A shitty piece of paper with a fucking speech on it?"

Vanessa was taken aback. Emma had never spoken to her like that.

"I mean, I've been sitting in my car wondering what the hell I did to deserve this. To lose everything in one night—because you and Lauren *were* everything—when I've done nothing but love you both. What was this? You and I…what was it?"

Vanessa reached out for Emma's hand, but Emma immediately shrugged her off. Fuck, that hurt. Whatever happened tonight, she had to make amends. Because this feeling, the notion she'd hurt the only person in the world she could ever love so unconditionally, it didn't feel right as it pressed against her chest. "Please, sit down for five minutes."

"I can't. I have to go. I wanted you to tell me to my face that I meant nothing to you. I *need* that from you, Vanessa. Because if you don't, I'll spend my life wishing things could have been different. That's how I've spent the last twelve years, and I don't think I have the strength to wish for more any longer."

"You mean the world to me, Emma."

Emma sighed, nodding as she took a step forward, pacing in front of the window. "So, you treat someone who means so much to you this way? You run away because your daughter doesn't like who you're fucking?" The bitterness in Emma's voice sent a chill through Vanessa. "I *know* it's all I was to you. Something to cleanse your pallet and prepare you for some woman who could *never* love you like I do. I see it all now. The daughter's best friend. The forbidden fuck!"

"Please, don't say that." Vanessa's heart slid into her stomach. Emma was more than finished with her. "You know I love you. I have *no* issues with telling you."

"I've spent so long protecting Lauren's heart, and in the process, I forgot all about my own." Emma continued to pace, scoffing as she glanced in Vanessa's direction. "But I never mattered. I was only the prize at the end for a little while. Something to play with. Because deep down, I knew you'd *never* choose me over her. And while I can come to terms with it—she's your kid, after all—it doesn't make me feel any better."

Vanessa caught Emma's wrist, pulling her close. "Look me in the eye and tell me you believe I don't love you."

Emma clenched her jaw, tears threatening in her eyes. "I don't believe you ever loved me."

"Y-you don't mean that." Vanessa searched Emma's face. She knew how much Emma had struggled to say those words. "I'll do *anything* to prove my love for you."

"You had the chance to do so this afternoon, and you didn't." Emma slumped, taking a step back. "You had the opportunity today to show me I was worth more than I've always believed. But...you didn't."

Vanessa remained silent. There was a deeper meaning to what Emma had just said, but should she question it? Would it matter? Emma, tonight, was so distant it was startling.

And then Emma dropped to the bed, her head in her hands. "You're the only person in the entire world who has made me feel like I could be happy. I don't date, it never works out for me, and I don't even sleep around because...what's the point? But when I met you, you looked at me differently. You behaved differently. You...cared."

"Of course I care."

"You didn't even know about who I was until we went to Yorkshire. I'd always asked Lauren not to mention my family in front of you because I didn't want you to take pity on me. So when you seemed so welcoming and genuine, it only attracted me to you more." Emma looked up at Vanessa, a sad smile on her mouth. "I'm so sorry I fell in love with you. All I've done is create problems you don't need. I mean, you and Lauren used to be so close. I loved seeing you with one another. You were more like sisters than mother and daughter, and maybe that's what I focused on. Maybe it made it easier for me to fall for you because you were both so laid back and great. But I am so sorry. I never should have told you how I felt. You're far too good for me. For... this." Emma waved a hand between them.

She wasn't making any sense. How could Emma, for one moment, believe she wasn't good enough?

"But you're going to be so happy once I leave." Emma sniffled, a sad, heartbreaking smile on her lips. "And as much as it's going to hurt me to walk away from you, I know it'll be for the best in the long-term." Emma studied Vanessa's face through the darkness. "God, you really are the most beautiful woman in the world, Vanessa."

Vanessa got to her knees in front of Emma, taking her hands. "Baby, I need to make this right. I don't want to lose you."

"I didn't want to lose you either. I wanted to know we could fix any problems we faced but look at us. You're avoiding your own home because I was there, and I'm about to head off to God knows where."

"I don't want you to leave."

Emma lifted a hand, caressing Vanessa's cheek. Even when they were fighting, her touch was still the gentlest. "You left me, Vanessa. I'm simply here to say goodbye face-to-face."

Vanessa dropped her head to Emma's lap, sobs wracking her body unexpectedly. Emma was right. Vanessa *had* left her. *You fucking coward!*

When Emma placed a hand on her shoulder, squeezing it, she whispered, "Hey, come on. I don't ever want to see you on your knees in front of me."

Vanessa lifted her head, watching Emma for a moment longer. The thought of never seeing her again, touching her beautiful body, holding her...her heart was dying in her chest. "I'm going to spend my life fixing this with you. I'm not letting you go, Emma. I can't."

"Lauren is your world, babe. And in some ways, she was mine too. But I can't be a pushover anymore. I shouldn't have to fight my best friend for the woman I love."

"Lauren wants us to be together. She wants to meet with us tomorrow."

"Lauren...feels guilty. That's all."

Vanessa wanted to defend her daughter, to figure all of this out, but Emma had every right to feel the way she did. Vanessa seemed to make mistake after mistake lately. And Lauren? Well, she had a lot of explaining to do. But this didn't come down to Lauren. This came down to the fact Vanessa had walked away instead of fighting for Emma.

"Look, it's getting late." Emma slowly got to her feet, running a hand down her face. "I should head off."

"Please, stay." Vanessa stood on shaky legs; her knees prepared to give out on her at any moment.

Emma reached down and retrieved Vanessa's letter from the bed, slipping it into her pocket. "I'll take this with me. Maybe it'll remind me why I'm doing this down the line."

Vanessa wrapped her arms around herself, pressing her back to the nearest wall. Emma was *actually* leaving, and Vanessa didn't know where to turn. She wanted to run after Emma, but she knew deep down Emma didn't want that. Vanessa's letter had sealed their fate.

"Hey," Emma said as she turned when she reached the hotel door. "Call Dani. Date her. Get yourself out into the world. A woman like you deserves to find happiness, Vanessa."

Call Dani? That's all Emma had to say? *Wow.*

"And even though it didn't work out for us, I'll always love you. I'll always *be* in love with you."

Emma slipped out of the hotel room, the door closing softly behind her. Vanessa stared, willing for it to open again, but the longer the seconds passed, the more she knew she'd just lost the best thing to ever happen to her.

CHAPTER TWENTY-FIVE

"I'm glad you called me last night, Emma." Anna fell into step beside her, linking an arm through Emma's. "And I know this is hard for you, but things will get better, right?"

Anna was talking to her, but Emma was barely registering the words. Since she'd walked out of Vanessa's hotel room last night, nothing made any sense. Of course, Emma could have stayed and given in, but she was tired of always being second best. To prevent that inevitability, she'd chosen to look after herself for a change. Nobody else was going to do it for her.

"You with me?" Anna asked.

"Sure. Yeah. I have a lot going on in my head today."

"Did you contact the agency about Africa?" They crossed the road, slowing their pace as they neared the bistro. "I know you said you'd do it today, but I wasn't sure if you'd done it yet."

"No, I didn't manage to find the time this morning. With making sure I had everything from Vanessa's, which wasn't a lot, the time ran away with itself. But I'll send them an email this evening."

"And you definitely want to go back?"

Did she? Emma didn't know. "I have nothing here for me, so why not?"

"No, I guess you're right. But I'm here, and I'm your friend, so if you're having second thoughts, you know you have me."

Emma smiled as she side-glanced in Anna's direction. "I know I have you. But she's here so I can't be."

"This has really hit you, hasn't it?"

"Losing the love of my life? Yeah, it's hit me pretty fucking hard."

Anna tightened her grip around Emma's arm, squeezing her. "I'm sorry it never worked out, but at least you're sitting down with Lauren today. That's something, isn't it?"

Emma wished it was something, but it didn't change the fact she felt entirely hopeless in all of this. Lauren may feel guilty, their friendship may get back on track, but nothing would be the same ever again. It couldn't possibly be. And if Lauren thought differently, she was a fool. "We'll see what happens today, I guess."

"Hear her out. It can't have been easy when she found out you and Vanessa were together."

"It doesn't mean I don't deserve to be happy, though. Or does it? Is this all my own fault, because that's how it's starting to seem. Why do *I* feel like the bad guy for falling in love with someone? How is that fair?"

"It's not. And what she did wasn't okay, either. I wouldn't let it slip any time soon."

"She…has stuff going on."

"Then I hope you two can at least part on good terms. You were like sisters, Em."

Emma gritted her teeth. She wished people would stop saying that. It only left her feeling guilty. "Don't remind me."

They came to a stop outside the bistro. Emma's pulse suddenly thrummed in her ears. Was it such a good idea to go inside and meet Lauren when every emotion felt so raw? She hadn't had the time to process the fact Vanessa wasn't going to be in her life anymore. Emma needed more time.

"I'm not sure I can do this."

"You can. It's just Lauren."

"That's the problem. Anything she says, she's going to be right. As much as I love Vanessa, her daughter has every right to be angry. Because it's her daughter, and she clearly doesn't trust me enough with her mum's heart. Which is kinda sad given how close we were. I thought she knew me better than I knew myself."

"Go inside. Sit down. And talk." Anna ushered Emma towards the door, offering a supportive smile. "Once this is over, come back to mine, and we'll binge a series."

Okay, Emma could do that. Something mindless was exactly what she needed tonight.

She peered through the bistro window, smiling weakly when Lauren stared back at her, a slight wave thrown in for good measure. "Right. Wish me luck."

"You don't need luck," Anna said, embracing Emma. "And remember, you've done *nothing* wrong in all of this. Don't let her lead you to believe otherwise."

"I won't."

Emma turned, pushing the bistro door open with a confidence that had appeared from nowhere. However guilty she felt, Anna was right. The only thing Emma had done was fall in love with a beautiful woman. It wasn't a crime.

She approached the table, clearing her throat as Lauren attempted to stand. "Stay there. You don't need to stand to greet me."

Lauren peered up at her. "I'm glad you came. I wasn't sure you would."

"You asked me to meet you, so here I am." Emma eased into a chair, clasping her hands on top of the table. She relaxed her shoulders, lowering her eyes between them. "So, what's up?"

"I wanted to have lunch with you. See how you are."

"I'm fine. But I have a lot to do, so I can't hang around for long."

"Right. I see." Lauren's voice wavered as she wrung her hands.

"Look, you're not in the right condition for stress, so can we not fall out again?" Emma wanted to scream and shout at Lauren, but what use would it be? If anything happened to her unborn child, Emma would never forgive herself.

"I'm pregnant, not dying."

No, but I am. Emma pushed last night from her mind. Dwelling on it wasn't helping. "Still, you should be at home resting. Or doing whatever it is pregnant people do."

"Sitting on the couch eating food."

"Then you should be at home doing that." Emma nodded. "Not sitting here with me for the sake of it."

"I'm not sitting with you for the sake of it. You're my best friend, Emma. I don't want to lose you."

Why was it that suddenly nobody wanted to lose her? Neither Lauren nor Vanessa had given her that impression yesterday. "You have a lot going on right now. The last thing you need is me in your life. Trust me."

A tear slipped down Lauren's face, but Emma had to look away. Lauren looked so much like Vanessa the older they got that it was a struggle for Emma to keep her own emotions at bay. "I made a huge mistake yesterday when I met Mum here. I was horrible to her. I let her walk away. And I need to make it right."

"If it makes you feel any better, we didn't end things because of you. I mean, it played a part, but in the end…it wasn't your doing."

"I find that hard to believe."

"Seriously. I didn't choose to leave because of you, I chose to leave because she didn't bother to fight for me. The letter, the disappearing act…"

"But it was my fault." Lauren ran a hand through her hair,

sighing. "She wrote the letter because of me. She *left* because of me."

"Maybe, but I can't be with someone who is prepared to walk away when it gets a little tough."

"She's heartbroken."

Emma chewed the inside of her mouth. She didn't need to know that. She had enough to deal with without thinking of Vanessa. "She'll be okay. You'll keep her busy once the baby arrives."

"She called me this morning." Lauren's eyes shifted from Emma's, glancing directly over her shoulder and towards the door. "She sounded lost."

"Well, I know once she realises she's better off without me, she's going to find someone who will make her happy." Emma hoped she was convincing Lauren, because she wasn't convincing herself. Lauren eyed the door again. "What are you looking at?" Emma turned, her heart freefalling into her stomach when she saw Vanessa standing a few feet away. "Oh, I don't think so." She shot to her feet, glaring at Lauren. "You only asked me to come here so you could play happy families. You can count me out!"

Lauren got to her feet. "No, it's not like that. I've asked you both here so I could tell Mum I'm pregnant."

"And why do you need me here for such a special occasion?"

"Because you're my best friend."

Emma sunk back down into the chair, exhaling a deep breath. Lauren always had the ability to make her sit up and listen, and it seemed now wasn't going to be any different. She would listen to the good news, and then she would leave. Nothing else needed to be discussed. "Fine."

Vanessa swallowed down the ball of emotion lodged in her throat, her eyes burning through the back of Emma Bradley.

Lauren hadn't told her Emma would be joining them this afternoon, and now that Vanessa was about to come face-to-face with her, she wasn't sure she should take another step.

But then the idea Emma was in on this skipped through her mind. Had she decided to give them another go? Was Emma willing to listen to Lauren and then ultimately take Vanessa back? It hadn't seemed possible this morning, but the smallest sliver of hope had Vanessa's blood pumping harder and faster.

She strode across the bistro, putting on her best smile. "Hi."

"Hi, Mum." Lauren reached over and pulled back a chair, offering it to Vanessa.

As she took a seat, her gaze floated to Emma, but Emma didn't make eye contact. Honestly, it was as though she'd zoned out of the room. That tiny piece of hope Vanessa had sat down with quickly evaporated into thin air. Emma wasn't here to try again. Just like Vanessa, she'd been duped into coming today.

"So?" Vanessa didn't know where to begin. "This house you've bought…where is it?"

"Close to Rob's mums. You know the little quaint street we used to drive past, the one with the trees dotted along the edge of the pavements?"

"I know the one," Vanessa said, smiling. This conversation didn't feel right, but Lauren seemed enthusiastic in her company for the first time in several weeks, so that was something. "You've always wanted to look at the houses there."

"Mum, it's gorgeous. And it has pear trees in the back garden."

"Do you have any pictures?" Vanessa asked, still disappointed she hadn't had the opportunity to gush over Lauren's new home with her. "I'd love to see some."

"Well, we were hoping maybe you would come and visit when we move in next week? It'll be a surprise then if I don't show you any pictures."

"I'd love to."

"Emma?" Lauren aimed her gaze at her best friend. "Will you come too?"

Emma sat with her hands clasped under her chin, her bottom lip quivering. "I…don't think I'll be in the city. Sorry."

"Oh. Well, maybe another time?" Lauren's face paled slightly. Vanessa hated every second of this.

"Maybe, yeah."

Lauren exhaled, rolling her shoulders as she turned her attention back to Vanessa. "Mum, I'm so sorry about yesterday."

"I-it's okay." It wasn't okay, far from it actually, but Vanessa didn't want to cause a scene in here. If they needed to discuss Lauren's attitude, it could be done with a little more privacy. "It's done now."

"And Emma, I'm sorry I caused this mess."

Emma cleared her throat, turning away. "It's fine."

Lauren sighed. "I don't know what the hell was wrong with me yesterday. Well, I do, but my reasons aren't good enough."

"Your reasons?" Vanessa's forehead creased. "I don't understand."

Lauren took a calming breath as she slid an envelope across the table.

"What's going on?" The silence from her daughter didn't do anything to quell the anxiety Vanessa suddenly felt. "Lauren?"

"Open it, Mum."

With a trembling hand, Vanessa opened the lip of the envelope. On the front of a folded white card sat a silver heart, and above it, the words 'scratch here.' Vanessa looked up at Lauren, still frowning, and reached for her purse. Once she had a coin in her hand, Vanessa scratched the silver away from the card, the silence around the table quite terrifying.

Emma didn't even flinch when Vanessa gasped. She had no interest in being here whatsoever.

Vanessa stared. Hard. Her eyes blurred as she focused on the words in front of her.

Hi, Nanna.

With tears streaming down her face, Vanessa opened the card, an ultrasound staring back at her. She studied it intently, her fingertips trailing the outline of the tiniest little dot in the world. And then she lifted her head, looking to Emma, then Lauren. "Y-you…"

Lauren smiled with tears in her eyes. "Sorry, Mum. It looks like the time has come for you to suck it up and be the world's most glamorous *and* gorgeous grandmother."

Vanessa laughed from deep within her belly. It was only a matter of time before she could no longer consider herself young and free. And nothing put a stop to that like a baby. "I'm so happy for you." Vanessa got to her feet, wrapping Lauren up in her arms as they stood in the middle of the bistro. "So happy."

Lauren turned her face into Vanessa's neck, sobbing. "I'm so sorry. I feel like I'm all over the place. And it doesn't make it okay, but I love you so much. And I need you by my side while I do this. I don't know the first thing about being a mum, but you were always so amazing."

Vanessa pulled back, taking Lauren's face in her hands. "It helps when you have a beautiful daughter. But don't worry. I'll be with you every step of the way."

Wow. This was bittersweet. Vanessa had lost the woman she loved but was gaining something incredibly special. Why couldn't she have it all? Now wasn't the time or the place to dissect her life.

She focused on Lauren, narrowing her eyes. "It's convenient how Rob isn't here. I hope he knows I'm going to wring his neck when I get hold of him for doing this to my daughter. And me! Don't think for one second I'm going to morph into some stay-at-home granny. No chance!"

"I wouldn't ever want you to change."

"And I'd like you to make sure Rob's mum knows I'm number one on the babysitting list. I know they live around the corner, but I'm perfectly capable of driving over and picking my grandchild up for the weekend or whatever."

"I'll remember that."

And then Vanessa remembered Emma was sitting at the table. She turned to her, hoping for some kind of mutual happiness. But all she found was Emma sitting with her eyes closed and her nostrils flared, her hands still clasped under her chin.

"Emma?" Lauren interrupted. "I, uh...I had an ultrasound printed for you, too."

Those beautiful eyes fluttered open, a faint smile playing on Emma's lips. "T-thanks. I'll keep it in my wallet." Emma got to her feet and wrapped her arms around Lauren. This was nice; it was what Vanessa hoped for. "Congratulations, kiddo. I'm so happy for you and Rob." Emma paused, turning to Vanessa. "And you, too."

"Not...*us*?" Vanessa chanced. "This is huge for all of us."

Emma stepped back from Lauren, looking down at the ultrasound in her hands. She wiped a tear from her jawline and blew out a deep breath. "I have to go now. But thanks for asking me to come so I could hear the great news. You're going to be amazing, all of you."

Vanessa reached out a hand, desperate to take Emma in her arms, but Emma took another step back, turned on her heel, and left the bistro.

Tears welled in Vanessa's eyes, her entire body aching with a devastation she never once imagined she'd feel. Emma had walked out for the second time in less than twenty-four hours, and it was all her own doing.

"Oh, Mum." Lauren wrapped an arm around her shoulder. "She'll come round, don't worry."

Vanessa smiled weakly. "She won't. She's done with me. But if Emma can't trust that I'm all in, I can't go after her."

"Why wouldn't she trust you?" Lauren guided Vanessa into the chair beside her, holding Vanessa's hands.

"Because I've made a complete mess of everything. But I need you to know one thing before we discuss anything else."

"O...kay."

"I pursued her. This is all my fault." Vanessa took a napkin from the table and dabbed her eyes. "Emma told me it would be a mistake, how we'd break your heart, but I...I love her, Lauren. I feel lost without her."

"Go after her."

If only it was so simple. "She isn't to blame for any of this, okay?"

"Nobody is to blame for anything, Mum. You love one another, and I was having some kind of hormonal meltdown."

"Look," Vanessa calmed her emotions. "You need me, and that's that."

"No. I need *both* of you."

"And you will have us." Vanessa reached out a hand, stroking her thumb across Lauren's cheek. "Emma needs some time to herself, but I know she wouldn't let you go through this alone. She'll be by your side and nothing else will matter."

"But what about you? Your happiness?"

"She gave me enough happiness in the short time we were together to last me a lifetime."

CHAPTER TWENTY-SIX

Emma flexed her fingers, focusing on the screen in front of her. Accepting Africa had taken her almost a week, but here she was, ready to follow up on the email she'd sent four days ago. Emma had initially asked for a couple of weeks to think about it, but she'd discovered staying in the UK was too difficult for her.

Everywhere she turned, she was reminded of Vanessa. Just strolling along the high street was too much. If she bumped into her, Emma would kiss Vanessa until her very last breath, and those thoughts alone didn't do her any good. In fact, they kept her awake at night.

So this, tonight, was an important step in leaving Vanessa Middleton behind. Emma struggled with the knowledge, Vanessa had always been front and centre in her world, but this was undoubtedly for the best.

"You want takeout tonight?" Anna poked her head around the door in the living room. "Chinese? Indian?"

"Indian." Emma smiled. "And make sure you order extra pakoras this time."

"Yes, darling." Anna rolled her eyes. "Anything else?"

"An extra tub of mint raita."

"Okay, got it. Did you want me to order now, or..."

Emma shrugged. She could certainly eat. "Sure. I'm only writing up this email so I'm ready for dinner whenever you are."

The doorbell sounded through the house, Anna's brow creasing. "You expecting anyone?"

"No, but I am expecting a parcel with some new sports gear in."

"Okay, well you get writing that bloody email, and I'll see to the door."

Emma hadn't realised how great it would be living with Anna, but she should have known. They'd always gotten on so well, and it was one of the reasons for their split all those years ago. They were more like friends than partners.

The door closed, but Emma heard voices in the hallway. Anna must have a visitor, so she would mind her own business and get on with something she should have done a while ago. Africa was waiting, and Emma needed to get gone.

She lifted her laptop onto her knees, feet kicked up on the coffee table, and focused fully.

"H-hi."

A familiar voice sent a shiver through Emma's entire body, her stomach tightening as her fingers stilled above the keyboard. She wanted to turn and look towards the door, but her head told her not to.

"Emma?" That very same voice spoke again, this time filled with emotion as it broke. "I know you're busy, but if you had five minutes to spare, I'd appreciate it."

Emma closed her eyes, exhaling a long slow breath. If it really was Vanessa's voice, she was going to hit the floor the moment she got to her feet.

"Em, I'll leave you two to talk." This time, Anna spoke, confirming Vanessa was present in the room. "Go through, Vanessa."

Heels on the wood flooring sent Emma's pulse skyrocketing, yet Emma *still* couldn't manage eye contact. Tears were ready to fall relentlessly.

"Is Lauren okay?" Emma spoke suddenly. "And the baby?"

"Y-yes."

Emma placed her laptop on the coffee table and stood. She cast her eyes on the wall ahead of her, prepared herself to see Vanessa, and turned. "What can I do for you?"

Vanessa strode across the long living room and around the coffee table, holding out the most exquisite roses Emma had ever seen. "I'm sorry. For everything."

"I…thank you." Emma frowned, taking the roses. She stroked the silky petals, her bottom lip trembling. Vanessa was here, but she couldn't fathom why. "I don't—"

"I'm a coward, and I realised this week I always have been. I've always tried to please others before myself. Whether that was Richard or Lauren, I always forgot about taking care of myself. And by doing so, I hurt you. I hurt *us*. I know being here isn't what you want, you're likely sick of looking at my face, but I had to try one more time. If I didn't, I'd always wonder 'what if.' Like you, I've spent too long wondering, wishing for more…"

"Vanessa—"

"I don't deserve you. I don't believe I'm entitled to a single thing you have to offer, but I needed you to know writing that letter is the biggest regret of my life. I wish I could turn back time and do all of this differently. Properly."

"I don't think it would make any difference. It's always one thing or another getting in the way of stuff, and I'm tired of wanting you, Vanessa. I'm done with hiding and lying and pretending this isn't killing me inside. Because it is. It's tearing my heart apart, and all I want is to be happy. In love. But it never seems to work out for me, so I'm leaving."

"L-leaving?"

"I'm confirming details, and then I have a one-way flight to book."

Vanessa's forehead creased. "N-no."

"It's for the best."

"But we needed more time together. I'm supposed to make things right. To prove I love you."

Emma set the roses down on the coffee table and opened her arms to Vanessa. "Come here."

Vanessa collapsed against her, almost knocking Emma to the couch. This was painful, overwhelming, but Emma worried it would continue to be difficult if she tried again with Vanessa.

Vanessa sobbed as she turned her face into Emma's neck. "I've been trying to contact you all week."

"I…blocked your number."

Vanessa suddenly loosened her grip on Emma, taking a step back and creating a space between them. She lowered her eyes, nodding slowly. "I see. So, that's it then, I guess."

"I didn't block you because I wanted to. I had to."

"Are you going back to Africa?" Vanessa lifted her head, devastation written all over her face. "Is that what the one-way ticket is for?"

"Yes."

Vanessa held up her hands, backing away. "Then I won't say anymore. I always promised I wouldn't stand in your way, so I'll go. You have things to do."

"I was turning it down," Emma said. "I received an email for a year long term just before I found the letter."

"Why were you turning it down?"

Emma lifted a shoulder. This would be the last time she saw Vanessa. She had to be completely honest. "For you. Us. I didn't want to leave you."

Vanessa offered a fragile smile. "And instead, I walked out on you. Not only did I push you away, but I'm also the reason you're flying thousands of miles across the world. I'm a real catch, aren't I?"

If only Vanessa knew what a catch she actually was. Emma would never find anyone quite like her.

Emma exhaled a breath. "Since I lost you, I think it's the best thing for me right now. I can't be in the same city, or country, when I know you're around. But I want you to know I wasn't going. I was giving up Africa for you. Because you mean more than any dream job, and you always will. But now it's the right thing to do. I have to fall out of love with you, and it's the only way I know how, Vanessa." Emma laughed, sadness weaved through it. "Even if it didn't quite work out for me the last time around."

Vanessa gasped for breath as her entire body shook with sobs. "You always said you'd return to Africa. But for a split second, you were willing to give it up for me. T-that means the world, okay?" Vanessa reached out a shaking hand, caressing Emma's cheek. "To know someone was willing to make *me* their number one priority…it means the world."

"Vanessa, you were *always* my number one priority. That'll never change." Emma leaned into Vanessa's touch. This was too hard for her. On the one hand, she wanted to leave to prove to herself she could overcome this, but on the other hand, she wanted to stay and work through everything with Vanessa. Because she was here, and she was willing to try. But was *trying* good enough? "You didn't trust me to take care of you. To love you. To work through things with Lauren by your side. And I can't change that for you."

"I've always trusted you," Vanessa whispered. "And I want to ask you to stay, but…"

"But this is the right thing to do." Considering Emma kept telling herself that, it didn't feel like the truth. It felt…ludicrous. They made one another happy. Even before they were together, they were happy in one another's company.

I wasn't content before her.

"Maybe *I* was the problem in my marriage. I always thought I deserved more after Richard and his affairs, but perhaps I drove him to do what he did. I'd say you had a lucky escape, Emma."

What? Did Vanessa truly believe what she was saying? Richard was a prick who deserved nothing from nobody.

Vanessa lifted her handbag higher onto her shoulder, her eyes closing as she shook her head gently. "When do you leave?"

"I'm not sure yet. I haven't confirmed if I'm able to take the position, but I'd imagine in a few weeks or so."

"Can I see you before you go?"

"Tell me what you came here to say." Emma took Vanessa's hand, guiding her to the couch. If she didn't, Emma feared Vanessa would fall down. "You made an effort to come here tonight, so please, tell me."

"I wanted you to know how much I love you. How hard it's been this week without you in my life. I came here to ask for another chance, to ask if you'd consider moving in with me. Just…everything I should have said instead of that letter."

Emma's heart hammered against her chest, her mouth drying. This was the side of Vanessa that Emma loved the most. The honesty, the lack of worry about everyone around them.

"I never had the chance to tell you how happy you made me, or how your laughter was the highlight of my day, or that I saw the rest of my life with you. And that I accept the mistake I made in leaving. When I walked away from you, I walked away from Lauren too. She'd said some hurtful things, and I didn't know what else to do. I couldn't reason with myself when it mattered most."

"I sat on your bed almost a week ago and crumbled, Vanessa."

"I'm so sorry." Vanessa leaned in as she placed her hand over Emma's. "I thought I was doing the right thing."

"I thought the right thing was you and I together."

Vanessa smiled, tears falling. "It is. Or was. You and I were the only thing that ever felt right. Even when it wasn't supposed to."

"You really broke my heart." The pain in Emma's voice was almost too much for she, herself, to take.

Vanessa chanced a kiss, one hand gripping Emma's thigh when she realised Emma was reciprocating.

Vanessa's lips, her scent, those soft yet urgent hands…they *always* reminded Emma of a love she craved. A life, a home, someone who cherished and respected her. Vanessa, as unsure as Emma was, would always be the woman she wanted.

But then Vanessa pulled back ever so slightly, pressing her forehead to Emma's. "I'll never break your heart again. Please, give me one more chance to make this right."

Could she do that? Was the potential pain worth it? At times, Emma felt as though she was the one constantly being hurt, and it shouldn't be that way. She hadn't done a single thing wrong. Falling in love could *never* be wrong.

She studied Vanessa's eyes. The greatest memories came flooding back instantly. "Ask me to stay," Emma murmured against Vanessa's lips. "Forget about not standing in my way or holding me back. If you want me, *us*, ask me to stay. *Tell me* to stay."

"Please, stay." Fresh tears spilled from Vanessa's eyes, pained yet still so beautiful. "I need you by my side. I always did."

"God," Emma whispered. This was far too much to deal with. She wanted Vanessa, but was Emma one hundred percent sure Vanessa wanted her too? It felt as though she did, but could Emma put her heart on the line one final time? "I feel like I can't breathe when I'm not with you." Emma captured Vanessa's lips, that urgency ever present. "But Africa wants me…"

Vanessa replaced her lips with the pad of her thumb, feathering it across Emma's bottom lip. "Africa can't have you, baby. Because you're mine."

"But am I? Honestly?"

"Come home," Vanessa said, begging in her tone.

"I don't have a home."

Vanessa smiled into a kiss, holding Emma's face in her hands. "You do. With me. Just us."

"I miss you." Emma sobbed, wrapping her arms around Vanessa's neck and pulling their bodies together. "I miss you, and I don't think I can ever move on from you."

"I don't want you to move on," Vanessa whispered against the side of Emma's face. Her soft breath tickled Emma's ear, the warmth of Vanessa's body comforting. "I want you to come home so we can have the life I always dreamed about."

"Yeah?" Emma pulled back, wiping her tears with the back of her hand. She studied Vanessa for a moment, a slight smile curling on her lips, and nodded ever so slightly. "If you want that…okay."

"I want so much, Emma. But let's start here. Right now."

Emma relaxed against Vanessa, allowing the weight of everything to settle. Nobody knew what the future held, and perhaps things wouldn't always be perfect, but could Emma leave the country when Vanessa was sitting beside her, an emotional wreck? In all honesty, Emma wasn't sure she could physically board a plane when the time came, regardless of where their relationship was at. Vanessa would always take precedence in her life.

Vanessa rested her head on Emma's shoulder, sighing. "Get your things together. I've had enough of being without you."

CHAPTER TWENTY-SEVEN

Vanessa took the stairs slowly, fixing her robe around her as she stepped into the living room. Emma was lying on the couch, the TV playing low, wrapping her hair around her index finger. She always looked so good lounging around as though she didn't have a care in the world. And for the time being, she didn't. They were together, Lauren was...God, Vanessa had no words. Things around them were calm for once. She had no idea how she'd convinced Emma to come home with her three nights ago, but so far, so good. Lauren had visited with Rob, they'd both been invited to their new home again, and Emma seemed fully on board this time around.

Vanessa knew how incredibly lucky she was to be given a final opportunity. Life could now begin for them. She wasn't concerned about trying to make Emma happy—before she'd left, Vanessa knew they were both already there—but she'd taken it slow the last few nights. She'd given Emma whatever space she needed, only pushing the conversation of what they'd gone through recently when she thought Emma was willing to talk about it.

But last night, they'd discussed everything for the final time.

Emma had made it clear the past could be buried and remain there forever. She didn't want to go over everything again. She didn't want to waste time discussing something which was no longer an issue. Emma, in her own words, wanted to love Vanessa.

Vanessa cleared her throat. "I wondered if maybe you'd share a glass of champagne with me?"

Emma's eyes slowly shifted towards Vanessa, trailing down her body as they did. "I'd love to share a glass."

"And then I thought perhaps we could have an early night..." Vanessa stared down at Emma, aware the look she was giving her had sent a shiver down Emma's spine. "And I don't know, maybe you're not quite ready for more yet after everything that's happened—"

"I want to take you to bed." Emma climbed from the couch, landing in front of Vanessa in a split second. "I want to feel that connection with you." Emma took Vanessa in her arms, resting them around Vanessa's waist. "We are going to be so good together."

"Even now when I'm about to become a much less sexy version of myself?" Vanessa laughed. "I'll check back with you in a year or so."

"I don't follow." Emma's frown lines deepened. "Why would you be less sexy?"

"A grandmother? *Really?*"

"Ah. I did wonder how that title would make you feel." Emma backed Vanessa out into the hallway. "And to answer your question, how about we skip the champagne, and I'll take you upstairs and show you just how sexy you are?"

Vanessa dragged Emma up the stairs, pulling her into the bedroom and pressing her against the door. When Emma said things like that, Vanessa knew she didn't have a single thing to worry about. She *always* made Vanessa feel young and alive.

"You good, babe?"

Vanessa lifted her eyes, focusing on Emma's. Those eyes, the intensity of them, how they dragged her into a parallel universe… "Make love to me," Vanessa whispered, pressing her body to Emma's. "Until the end of time. Just make love to me."

Without another word, Emma pushed off the door, wrapping her hands around Vanessa's thighs and lifting her. Once she was secured around Emma's waist, the button on her jeans pressing against her clit, Vanessa dipped her head and captured Emma's lips.

"The thought of never kissing you again," Vanessa moaned as she gripped Emma's raven hair in her fists. "Never feeling you against me." Their lips met as Emma lowered Vanessa onto the bed. "Baby, I missed you."

Emma ground down against her, nipping at Vanessa's bottom lip as she hovered over her. "Are you sure this is what you want?"

"You're *all* I've ever wanted…" Vanessa whispered, her mind reeling from the sensation of Emma against her. "Only. Ever. You."

Emma pulled back, staring directly into Vanessa's eyes. "Then I'm right here with you. Always."

Vanessa's eyes pricked with tears. "I love you."

Emma brushed Vanessa's hair from her face. "I love you too." She sat back on her knees, tugging at the belt holding Vanessa's robe in place. "You're so beautiful. Every last inch of you is delectable."

Vanessa's robe fell open, her skin sticky as Emma peered down at her. Nobody had ever made Vanessa feel so much in mere seconds, but Emma…well, she had the capacity to undo Vanessa time and time again.

Emma's eyes travelled down Vanessa's naked body, her lip firmly between her teeth. "I never got one last night with you."

"And it's not what this is." Vanessa held Emma's face in her hands. "So, please, don't think that."

"But if it is…" Emma's bottom lip trembled. "If this is my last night with you, I have to make it count. If I wake up tomorrow, and you ask me to leave, I have to know I gave you exactly what you want."

"You being here is *exactly* what I want. Sex or no sex. And if you don't want this tonight, I'm happy lying beside you."

Emma pushed the silk away from Vanessa's skin, lowering her lips to her collar bone. And then she kissed a path to the other, her hands pressing into the mattress. Emma rolled her hips against Vanessa, lightly moaning as she lowered her mouth further, sucking a nipple into her mouth.

Vanessa gasped, bucking her hips. She needed more. She desperately craved Emma's naked body on top of her. Holding her in place. Controlling everything. Vanessa struggled to reach down and unbutton Emma's jeans, a frustrated groan rumbling in her throat. "Baby, I need you naked."

Emma pushed off the mattress, stripping everything from her body. And then she guided Vanessa further up the bed, opening her legs as she dragged her nails down the backs of Vanessa's thighs. When Emma lowered herself onto Vanessa, spreading her slick lips, Vanessa lost her mind. Emma brushed her clit against Vanessa's, a surge of electricity thrumming in her veins. "You feel fucking amazing," Emma whispered, capturing Vanessa's lips. "I can never get enough of you."

Vanessa held Emma's face, ghosting a thumb over her cheek. "Spend forever with me, Emma."

Emma, her eyes wet, simply nodded. Taking Vanessa's hands from her face, Emma held her down against the bed, their fingers laced together. "Tell me what you need from me."

"I need you to take control of this entire night," Vanessa whispered, her eyes switching from Emma's to her lips. "I need you to claim me and never let me go."

Emma sat back on her knees, pressing her thumb to Vanessa's clit. The moan she received for that simple action had a grin spreading on Emma's perfect, soft mouth. "Anything goes?"

Vanessa nodded. She had no words for the look in Emma's eyes tonight. It was far more than desire.

"Lie on your stomach." Emma ghosted a fingertip up Vanessa's belly, a shudder following.

Vanessa turned, discarding her robe as she relaxed on her belly. Emma rummaged around behind her. And then the sound of footsteps at the side of the bed had Vanessa turning her head. The bedside lamp flickered on, and then Vanessa lost her breath.

"O-oh." If Vanessa hadn't already been wet, she certainly was now. Because as Emma stood before her, a pair of black briefs covering her beautiful ass, Vanessa's eyes strayed to the toy fixed to them. Vanessa ground against the bedspread, her hands fisting in the material as Emma applied several pumps of lube to the length of the dildo. Just watching her hands, how they worked the silicone, Vanessa was dripping wet. "You'd better move yourself."

"Yeah?" Emma quirked an eyebrow, her hand slowly pumping the length, her eyes focused on Vanessa. "Getting a little excited?"

"Oh, you always excite me." Vanessa moaned, slipping a hand between her body and the bed. She touched herself lightly, a quiver running through her as she pressed a finger to her clit. "Mm, yes. Very excited."

Emma watched, her lips parting ever so slightly as Vanessa lifted her ass in the air. As she rounded the foot of the bed, Vanessa offering the perfect view, Emma groaned. "You know I could watch you fucking yourself for the rest of my life, don't you?"

"Oh, as much as I love how it makes you feel, I'd rather *you* were fucking me." Vanessa glanced over her shoulder, sinking two fingers inside herself. "Because nobody has ever fucked me quite like you do."

"S-shit," Emma whispered, kneeling on the bed behind Vanessa. "Keep doing that." Emma's hands smoothed over Vanessa's ass, spreading her open as the sound of her wetness floated around the room. "Yeah. Fuck. Just like that, babe." Emma sat back on her knees, the bed dipping slightly as she shifted painfully close to Vanessa. She palmed the back of Vanessa's thighs, only heightening her arousal as Vanessa sunk deeper. Knowing Emma was watching every move she made had Vanessa's thighs shaking.

"Baby, I'm not going to last much longer."

Emma pressed a kiss to the base of Vanessa's spine, smiling against her skin. "Let me take over, beautiful." Vanessa gasped, slipping out of herself. The head of the toy pressed against her already soaked lips, and as Emma slowly guided it back and forth, teasing, she reached forward and grabbed two pillows from the headboard. Propping them up under Vanessa's stomach, Emma placed a soothing hand on her lower back. "Relax, babe. Let me take care of you."

Sweet Jesus. While Emma was unbelievably sexy and more than enough in the bedroom, when she said those little things, it melted Vanessa's heart. It made her want to turn around and hold Emma against her, the silence of the room enveloping them. But then Emma dragged her nails up the back of Vanessa's thigh, pressing the head of the toy against her entrance.

Vanessa's shoulders instantly relaxed. Emma had always taken care of her. And as the toy slid inside Vanessa, an overwhelming sense of love crashed through her. Nothing and nobody could ever compare to Emma Bradley.

"Feeling okay?" Emma asked, stilling her movements while Vanessa adjusted to the size.

But Vanessa wanted more. She wanted Emma to take her to a place she'd never been. God, she needed to be pounded into the bed. "More than okay."

Emma pulled back slowly, only to sink deeper with the next thrust. "Fuck, you take it so well." She gripped Vanessa's hips, pushing all of the way in. "Shit." Emma ground against Vanessa's ass, moaning as she held her place momentarily. "Babe, I *really* want to fuck you…"

"Do it." Vanessa whimpered when Emma almost slipped right out of her. "Fuck me. *P-please.*"

Emma's hips moved in perfect rhythm as she pulled Vanessa back against her with each thrust. Her pace picked up, skin slapping against skin, wetness slipping from Vanessa and down her thighs.

Nobody had ever been so deep. Nobody had ever lit up Vanessa's world quite like this. "H-harder." Vanessa lifted her body, braced on her hands and knees. The bed creaked in protest, but Emma didn't let up. She pounded Vanessa harder, exactly as she'd asked. "Fuck, yes." But then the overwhelming urge to watch Emma's pretty face became too much. Vanessa wanted to see her, to connect on a deeper level, to come undone for Emma and *only* Emma. "I want to see you."

Emma pulled out suddenly, flipping Vanessa and pushing her hips up with her own. Vanessa's legs sat over Emma's shoulders, and then she pushed back inside, a guttural moan ripping from Vanessa's throat as she buried the toy to the hilt. Emma grinned as she stared down at Vanessa, pounding as sweat beaded on her chest. "Babe, you're too fucking much."

"Oh," Vanessa paused, her breath hitching as Emma thrust slow and sharp. "Y-you can handle me."

"Damn right I can." Vanessa's words only spurred Emma on, slamming repeatedly, but fuck, it felt incredible. "Fuck, I'm gonna come." Emma trembled, her strong arms straining as the muscles in her shoulders flexed. "Watching you, seeing how deep you take me…I'm so gonna come."

Vanessa's orgasm roared towards the peak with that admission. And then she craned her neck and brushed her lips against Emma's ear. "Fuck me harder," she whispered, grinning against the shell of Emma's ear. "Make me yours…"

Emma's arms collapsed from under her, those incredible hips

still thrusting deep. She shook against Vanessa, her hips losing their rhythm as she came, breathy moans filling their bedroom. "S-shit. Fuck." Emma bucked against Vanessa, the short sharp thrusts hitting that sweet spot. "O-oh, fuck." Emma moaned, gripping Vanessa's body.

Vanessa flipped Emma onto her back, the dildo slipping out of her. Emma's eyes remained closed, her chest heaving, but she only needed a moment; Vanessa was sure of it. She eased down onto the toy, placing her palms on Emma's stomach. "Baby?"

"I-I can't even look at you," Emma said, her forearm covering her eyes. "You're definitely too much."

Vanessa leaned forward, grinding against the silicone inside her, knowing what it was doing to Emma. The base was pushing against Emma's clit; Vanessa could tell by the way Emma gasped repeatedly it was *exactly* where she wanted it to be. "Kiss me." Vanessa's lips hovered above Emma's, her breath light as she lifted her body, only to sink back down to the hilt. "All I ever want is for you to be kissing me."

Emma's eyes opened, a shy smile playing on her mouth. "Do you have any idea what you do to me?"

"I could give it a good guess, yes."

Emma ran a hand over Vanessa's shoulder, curling it around the back of her neck. The kiss was soft, gentle, but filled with the desire Vanessa felt coursing through her.

As Emma continued with her languid kisses, Vanessa moved back and forth, delighting in the moment. Seeing Emma take over like this, giving Vanessa exactly what she needed, it was intense. More so than the night she was caught masturbating. This evening could be considered the greatest sex of her life.

Emma lifted Vanessa's hips, holding them above her as she pushed her own up. "Fuck, you're tight." Emma strengthened her thrusts, but Vanessa was about ready to come. Her walls squeezed the toy, hot white heat building in the pit of her stomach as Vanessa pressed her fingers to her clit.

"S-shit, Emma." Vanessa's mouth fell open, her fingers furiously lashing her clit, but it was the final penetration from the toy that had Vanessa crying out into the silence of the room. Her eyes slammed shut, one of Emma's hands dug into her hip, and Vanessa was coming harder than she ever had before. The tremble, the shaking body...Vanessa had *always* wanted to experience it. And now she had, there was no going back. Emma was a revelation. "O-oh, baby," she whispered, slowly rolling her hips back and forth. She was more than done, but she couldn't stop herself from needing an extra moment longer with Emma inside her. "Oh." Vanessa slumped against Emma, strong arms embracing her, not a single word spoken.

And then Emma turned her head, pressing her lips to Vanessa's forehead as she whispered, "The love of my life. Don't ever forget it."

CHAPTER TWENTY-EIGHT

Seated on the edge of the bed, Emma stared down at the box in her hand. She sat in the very same spot she had two months ago, but so much had changed since then. Emma wasn't sitting here because she was preparing to leave. No, she was sitting here while she listened to Vanessa humming in the shower. This evening seemed a million miles from recent events.

Lauren and Rob had moved into their new place, Vanessa was back on good terms with her daughter, and Emma was about ready to tackle her career head on as she prepared for her first week in her new teaching position. Africa had floated into her mind once or twice since she turned down the offer, but she knew in her heart where she wanted to be. In this very house, beside Vanessa...Hughes.

Emma hadn't quite gotten her head around the fact Vanessa had returned to her maiden name, but in time, it would stick. She was just glad they were together; the surname didn't matter.

The shower cut off, leaving Emma in a state of uncertainty. She'd wanted to give this to Vanessa a couple of weeks ago, but everything fell apart. Was the ring now a bad omen? Should she bury it in the back garden and hope the dog they may one day own together wouldn't dig it up? Anxiety swirled in Emma's belly. Would Vanessa assume it was a proposal?

"God, this is a bad idea," she muttered, startled when the en suite bathroom door opened.

"What's a bad idea?" Vanessa asked, towel drying her hair as her short silk robe clung to her damp skin. "Is something wrong? You're not still worried about starting work on Monday, are you?"

"N-no." Emma inconspicuously pushed the box between her thighs, closing her legs against it. If she was unsure about this, then now wasn't the right time to hand it over. "Just…thinking about stuff."

Vanessa narrowed her eyes as she leant against the frame of the door. "What stuff?"

"I don't know. Everything. Lauren and Rob have settled down, and you and I are working through things at our own pace." Emma lifted a shoulder. "Everything feels different."

"Different, but perfect." Vanessa pushed off the doorframe, dropping her damp towel to the floor.

As she opened her robe and slid it from her shoulders, Emma swallowed hard. She wouldn't ever not drool over the sight of this woman. Not now, and not in ten years' time. Vanessa reached for the oversized button-down shirt on the edge of the bed, covering herself with it. When she took a seat beside Emma, she had an unfamiliar look in her eyes. Emma couldn't quite put her finger on exactly what it represented.

"Babe, is everything okay?"

Vanessa took Emma's hands as she twisted her body, one leg curling beneath her. "For me, everything is exactly how it should be."

Emma frowned. Did Vanessa think she wasn't happy?

"And I know this is the first time we're truly finding ourselves, spending uninterrupted time with one another, but… you're happy, right?"

Emma grinned. "So happy."

"Promise me." Vanessa lifted one of Emma's hands, lingering as she kissed her knuckles. "I know Africa was in the cards for you, and if I have to let you go so you can do what you love, I will. And when you come home, I'll be here waiting for you."

"Africa isn't important to me."

Vanessa's eyes fluttered closed. "That's not true. I watched your eyes light up when you were leaving last time, and I saw how excited you were when you told us about your time there. I…I don't want to hold you back in any way at all, Emma. That's not what our relationship is about. I want you to be happy, and if it's in another country while we figure out a long-distance relationship…I'd do it for you. Only you."

"You think I could leave here knowing I wouldn't see you?"

Vanessa sighed, her shoulders curling. "It'd be hard, but I know how much I love you, and I know you'd come home to me one day."

Emma appreciated the concern Vanessa had for her future, but Emma wasn't single anymore. She wasn't—in her opinion—in a position to up and leave the country. This was where she was supposed to be, and if things had been different the first time around, Emma would have turned down Africa then, too.

"All I want is to see you smiling. To see you doing what you love. Because nothing is more important than your happiness."

"And what about your happiness?" Emma quirked an eyebrow. "We're in this together, Vanessa. You matter as much."

"I'd…manage." Vanessa's voice cracked; her eyes squeezed shut as a tear slid down her cheek. "I'd miss you terribly, but I'd manage."

Emma caught Vanessa's tear with the pad of her thumb, gently cradling her face. "Babe, I'm not going anywhere. Please don't be upset. This is a new chapter for us both, and I'm excited for what's to come."

"Bellfield Comp isn't Africa."

"But you're not in Africa. So, Africa doesn't matter to me. A lot has changed, and this, right here, is where I want to be."

"If you ever change your mind..."

Emma pressed her body to Vanessa as she leaned in to kiss her. "I won't. I love you."

"I love you, too."

Vanessa fell into Emma, her hands wandering over her chest, down her stomach, before caressing her thigh. There was an urgency to every move she made, yet Vanessa was as soft and tender as always. This shouldn't work, Emma knew it, but nothing else had ever felt so right. Nobody had ever touched her soul quite like Vanessa did.

And then courage suddenly built in her chest as she slowly and reluctantly pulled away from Vanessa's lips. "God, you have to stop kissing me like that."

"Now why would I want to?" Vanessa's voice, dripping in honey, sent Emma's blood south.

Emma reached between her legs, retrieving the box she'd hidden there. "I...I have something for you." Emma took a breath, placing the box gently into Vanessa's hand. "It's something I was supposed to give you a couple of months ago."

"Why didn't you?" Vanessa asked, peering down at the small square box.

"Well." Emma paused, smiling weakly. "Because you left me. And then I wasn't sure it was the right thing to do. You know, giving it to you. But I feel like now is the right time."

Vanessa's heavenly blue eyes stared back at Emma, the recognition of the pain she'd caused when she'd left that letter ever present. "I'm sorry."

"No, that's not what this is about. You asked why I didn't give it to you, and that's the reason why. We don't need to go over it all again, okay?"

Vanessa nodded.

"So, open it." Emma was aware Vanessa may not like the piece of jewellery she'd bought, but it wouldn't be the end of the world. "Go on."

Vanessa lifted the lid on the box, her breath catching in her throat. "Oh, Emma. I-I—"

"Babe, it's not a proposal. Don't worry." Emma grinned. The last thing on Vanessa's mind surely had to be the idea of getting married again. Emma wouldn't ever expect it. "I saw it, and I couldn't walk away from the store without it. And I know what this looks like, but I'm happy with what we have. I'm more than satisfied with you and I remaining like this. I wouldn't expect, you know..."

Vanessa's gaze lifted; her forehead creased. "No, I don't know."

"I wouldn't expect us to get married." Emma sighed, holding her upright posture. Of course, she'd thought about the potential, but Vanessa had spent enough time married. "I mean, don't think I wouldn't. But I know I'm not marriage material. And you...well, it'd have to be someone pretty special to put *that* kind of ring on your finger ever again."

"You're pretty special..."

Emma shrugged. "Maybe. But I don't want you to think I'm expecting anything further. This is more of a...promise ring. Perhaps an eternity ring. Something to remind you that I'm here by your side, and I'm never leaving."

"It's beautiful." Vanessa trailed her fingertip across the diamond sitting in the middle, smiling as she sniffled. "It's typical you. And I love it."

"Yeah?" Emma's heart rate slowed. *Thank God.* "You're sure?"

Vanessa encouraged Emma back onto the bed, crawling into her lap and settling against her. She lowered the box to the bed beside them, tangling her fingers into Emma's long dark locks as she kissed her hard. Her nails grazed Emma's scalp, eliciting a moan. This woman was her world. Emma's hands fell to Vanessa's backside, pulling her impossibly close.

"Wanna stay like this forever?" Emma looked into Vanessa's eyes, their foreheads pressed together, Vanessa's legs wrapped around Emma's waist. "Lock ourselves away and enjoy one another..."

"Oh, wouldn't that be divine?" Vanessa smirked against Emma's lips. "And for the record, you're the only person in this world I would *ever* consider wearing another ring for." Vanessa took Emma's bottom lip between her teeth, grinning when she released it slowly. Was Vanessa trying to tell her something? "Which finger do you want me to wear it on?"

Oh, Emma hadn't even considered the options. "I, uh...wherever you want."

Vanessa rested back on Emma's thighs, removing the ring from the box. She held it between her index finger and thumb between them, looking directly into Emma's eyes. "What does this mean to *you*?"

Emma chewed her lip before she exhaled a slow breath. If Vanessa wanted her to be completely honest, she would. "It means you're mine. Always and forever. It means I'm so in love with you, I find it hard to breathe when we're apart." Emma took a moment to admire Vanessa. Everything about her. "It means no other woman in this world will ever have my heart, and that one day, I *may* be lucky enough to call you my wife, but for the time being...I want this. Us. Love."

Vanessa's lips curled upward, her eyelids fluttering lazily. "I don't know what I ever did to deserve you."

"You and I..." Emma paused when Vanessa slid the ring onto her engagement finger. And then she grinned, her heart pounding with what she'd just witnessed. "You and I were meant to be."

"Well, you're stuck with me now." Vanessa winked, leaning into a kiss as she held her palm to Emma's chest. "You can't take back anything you've said."

Emma's entire body thrummed. Had Vanessa genuinely put

the ring on her engagement finger? Was Emma...engaged? And to Vanessa? Holy shit! "Babe?" Emma pulled back, wearing a slight frown. "D-did you...did we... I mean, what's going on here?"

Vanessa smirked against Emma's lips. "I just think it looks better on that finger."

"Right." Emma didn't want to sound disappointed, but she suddenly felt it. "Yeah. It's only a ring."

"No, it's not *only* a ring. But it is staying there until you decide if you ever want to make something more of this."

"You mean...you would?"

"Would what?"

Okay, Vanessa was going to force the words out of Emma's mouth, wasn't she?

"You'd consider marrying me one day? Being my wife?" Emma's gaze fell to Vanessa's exposed chest and stomach. Was it actually possible this masterpiece of a woman could be her wife someday? Surely not; Emma wasn't that lucky.

Vanessa shrugged the oversized shirt from her shoulders, her naked body begging to be touched. Emma sat forward, wrapping her arms around Vanessa's waist as she peered up at her.

"Well?"

Vanessa held Emma's chin in her hand, smiling into a kiss. "I'd make you my wife tomorrow, Emma Bradley."

EPILOGUE

The number of suitcases sat by the front door was excessive. Vanessa never travelled light, but this was far too much. If Emma had told Vanessa once, she'd told her a thousand times. Still, her girlfriend would do as she pleased. Who was Emma to change her mind?

"Babe?" Emma yelled, still eyeing the luggage.

Vanessa landed at the top of the stairs; her face red as she blew unruly strands of hair from her eyes. "Yes?"

"What the hell have you been doing?" Emma barked a laugh, shaking her head. Vanessa had been running around like a headless chicken for days now. She'd told her to pack sooner.

"I'm looking for those heels. The ones I love."

"Uh, you love all your heels. As do I." Emma simpered.

"No, the ones I had on when we went to dinner a couple of weeks ago with Lauren, Rob, and Daisy."

"Those? What do you want them for?"

"Because they're my favourite."

Emma frowned. "But you complained all night that your feet were killing you. Or was that just an excuse for a foot massage when we got home?"

Vanessa smirked. "You're very easy to convince."

"Huh. I'll remember that." Emma folded her arms across her chest, staring up at Vanessa.

"I also don't recall you complaining when I kept them on in bed."

Emma flushed. Vanessa saying and doing things like that would never not leave her flustered. "What kind of person would it make me if I refused a gorgeous woman in nothing but a pair of heels?"

Vanessa slowly took the stairs, stopping in front of Emma. She tugged the front of Emma's shirt, pulling them together. "What on earth do you see in me?" Vanessa's devastatingly blue eyes sparkled. "Of all the women in this city, why *the hell* did you choose me?"

Emma wrapped her arms around Vanessa, leaning into the slowest of kisses. When she pulled back, she pressed her forehead to Vanessa's. "What do I see in you?" Emma searched Vanessa's eyes. Truth be told, she didn't know where to begin. "You know how we show up on the drive the same time as one another every day after work?"

Vanessa nodded.

"Well, I time myself so I get home the same moment you do. Because I can't stand sitting around missing you." Emma stroked her thumb against Vanessa's hip. "Or how I get lunch ready for you every night even though you tell me I don't need to do it? I do it so I know you've eaten in work the next day." Emma could list every single thing if Vanessa needed her to. "Then there is the feeling I get when you snuggle me on the couch when it's my time of the month. You always bring me paracetamol, a hot water bottle for my back, and rub my belly for me."

"I don't like seeing you in pain."

"And then there's the nights we cook dinner together. Laughing, dancing around the kitchen to the radio, talking about our day with one another."

"All I ever wanted was someone to talk about my day with," Vanessa said, her voice breaking. "And that means nothing to a lot of people, but to me…it's everything."

"I hate seeing you stressed with work."

"You don't only sit and listen. You rub my shoulders, prepare a bath, or just be there to support me."

"And I always will do those things for you."

Vanessa smiled, lifting a hand and caressing Emma's cheek. "It's been a year, and I still can't believe you're mine."

"Well, I am. I always will be. And I'll *always* choose you."

"I know."

"So, when you ask me what I see in you, it's difficult to explain. But what I can say, is I don't imagine a life without you." Emma brought Vanessa's hand to her lips, kissing the ring which had sat on her engagement finger for a year. "Be my wife, Vanessa."

"W-what?"

"I know we kinda skimmed over it last year, but I want more. I always did, deep down. I want to spend my life with you, and I want to wake up every morning knowing you're my wife. And that I'm yours. Forever. I just…I'd love it if you would make me the happiest person on this earth and say yes."

"Yes. A million times over, yes."

Emma's entire body ignited with a sensation only Vanessa could provide. It was love, admiration, the support they gave to one another. Everything. "You mean that?"

"Oh, I mean it." Vanessa lifted Emma's chin, their lips brushing so tenderly that Emma had to grip Vanessa's body to remain standing. "We can't really discuss and plan right now, but when we get home, I'm so going to marry you."

Emma grinned as she shook her head. "I can't even believe you're coming away with me, but this? A wedding…"

"Hey, you asked." Vanessa held up her hands, laughing.

"And I'm going to ask you every day until it happens. Every morning, every night, you better believe it."

"And I will still give you the same answer."

A car horn sounded outside, reminding them both that they really needed to get a move on. The cab wouldn't wait, and neither would the plane they'd be boarding in a few hours. "Come on. Let's get ready to leave."

"I'm excited," Vanessa said, slowly backing up the stairs.

Emma shoved her hands in her pockets, staring up at Vanessa. And then she sighed, the most genuine smile she'd ever smiled curling on her mouth. "I always knew you'd see Africa with me."

SIGN UP TO WIN

Sign up to my mailing list to be the first to hear about new releases, and to be in with a chance of winning books!

www.melissaterezeauthor.com

REVIEWS

Thank you for purchasing Mrs Middleton.

I hope you enjoyed it. Please consider leaving a review on your preferred site. As an independent author, reviews help to promote our work. One line or two really does make the difference.

Thank you, truly.

Love,
Melissa x

ABOUT THE AUTHOR

Oh, hi! It's nice to see you!

I'm Melissa Tereze, author of The Arrangement, and other bestsellers. Born, raised, and living in Liverpool, UK, I spend my time writing angsty romance about complex, real-life, women who love women. My heart lies within the age-gap trope, but you'll also find a wide range of different characters and stories to sink your teeth into.

SOCIAL MEDIA

You can contact me through my social media or my website.
I'm mostly active on Twitter.

Twitter: @MelissaTereze
Facebook: www.facebook.com/Author.MelissaTereze
Instagram: @melissatereze_author
Find out more at: www.melissaterezeauthor.com
Contact: info@melissaterezeauthor.com

ALSO BY MELISSA TEREZE

Another Love Series

The Arrangement (Book One)

The Call (Book Two)

The Ashforth Series

Playing For Her Heart (Book One)

Holding Her Heart (Book Two)

Other Novels

Breaking Routine

In Her Arms

Before You Go

Forever Yours

The Heat of Summer

Forget Me Not

More Than A Feeling

Where We Belong: Love Returns

Naked

Co-writes

Teach Me

Titles under L.M Croft (Erotica)

Pieces of Me

Printed in Great Britain
by Amazon

56974857R00162